COLOR OUTSIDE

Stories About Love the

About Love

LINES

COLOR OUTSIDE

Stories About Love the

LINES

EDITED BY

Sangu Mandanna

SOHO
TEEN

Published in the United States by Soho Teen
an imprint of Soho Press, Inc.
227 W 17th Street
New York, NY 10011

Library of Congress Cataloging-in-Publication Data

Mandanna, Sangu, editor.
Color outside the lines : stories about love / edited by Sangu Mandanna

ISBN 978-1-64129-046-3
eISBN 978-1-64129-047-0

1. Love—Juvenile fiction. 2. Short stories, American. 3. Short stories. 4. Love—Fiction.
I. Title
PZ5 .C723 2019 [Fic]—dc23 2019017621

Interior design by Janine Agro, Soho Press, Inc.

Printed in the United States of America

10 9 8 7 6 5 4 3 2 1

COLOR OUTSIDE

Stories About Love the

LINES

Editor's Note

When people ask me why I wanted to put this anthology together, I'm often tempted to give them the simplest answer: because representation matters.

That's not the whole story.

I first started thinking about this project at a restaurant near my home in Norwich (which, for those of you who haven't heard of it, is a beautiful little city in the east of England). A waiter looked at my husband, at me, and at our three children, and asked, "Are you paying separately?"

It was a pebble in my shoe that I couldn't quite shake. Given the backdrop of the Brexit vote, especially, with countless families afraid they would be forced to separate, I found myself thinking about what it means to be in a relationship like mine.

Interracial. Multicultural.

Families like mine are just like families where everyone's the same color. We get excited about Christmas. We go to the beach. We fight over who forgot to post that letter last week (spoiler: it's never me). We're just like other families, *and* we're not. Interracial dynamics are different. My husband and I spent eight years together before someone asked us if we were paying separately, but someone did eventually. It was this small, unimportant thing that made me think about all the other small, unimportant things and big, important things about families like mine that can't be told in a single story.

So why not a whole collection of stories?

That was in April 2017. Many, *many* months later, here

we are. With the help of my endlessly enthusiastic agent, Eric Smith, and the incredible support of Daniel Ehrenhaft and the rest of the fantastic team at Soho Teen, we've found fifteen other incredible authors to contribute stories to this anthology, and I could not be prouder to have worked with them. From the bottom of my heart, thank you all.

When people ask me what this anthology is about, I'm often tempted to give them the complicated answer: it's about race, about being different from the person you love—how it can matter and also *not* matter—and it's about Chinese pirate ghosts, and black girl vigilantes, and colonial India, and a flower festival, and a garden of poisons, and so, so much else.

Honestly, though? I think the answer's much simpler than that.

Color outside the Lines is a collection of stories about young, fierce, brilliantly hopeful characters of all colors. And I hope you fall as in love with them as I have.

Love,
Sangu

Table of Contents

Turn the Sky to Petals

Anna-Marie McLemore

I guess I could start with the flowers, the hundreds of thousands of red dahlia petals gathered into baskets at the behest of a rich man. But that would make what happened more about the rich man than about you and me.

This is the way I would tell it, what happened between us. This is how I would piece it together from what I saw and the things you told me:

We did not grow up far apart. My school played yours in a handful of sports, so we might have met. You had that season on the soccer team before deciding that the practices took too much time away from the cimbalom.

Me, I never played school sports. I never even tried. There was never one I loved enough to spend my tendons on it.

You know what I'm talking about. You knew the first time I told you. Because the feeling I know in my ankles—the countless small tears, the sensation of muscle wringing itself out—is one you know in your wrists, your lower forearms, parts of you that you need for the instrument that has you by the heart.

Your gringo teacher often told you what immense promise she saw in you. She said that you would elevate the cimbalom to the level of great orchestra. You winced every time, shrugging away the insult, because while she thought of it as a carnival instrument, you always knew it to be the collection of wood and metal strings that gives music all its colors.

You learned to repair the steel and copper strings yourself, because there were so few who knew how to do it, and finding a repair shop in our constellation of rural towns was never easy. Or cheap. And there was no one you really wanted to trust with the instrument your grandfather had left you. Your grandfather, who performed in both city squares and grand halls, and who you thought of when your music teacher watched you, her stare so intense it burned into your back.

She is beautiful, your music teacher, but I think her beauty dimmed to you every time she pushed you to play the Liszt again, even when you were past the time the lesson was meant to end, even when your tendons felt like they were tearing apart in your wrists. Even when your forearms felt like they were turning to flames.

Your mother, you told me, worried as you iced your wrists at night. And you told her not to, that if musicians wanted to become great, sometimes it involved pain. She pressed her lips together and made you lay bags of frozen peppers under your forearms, because if you had to ice your wrists you might as well bring yourself a little luck at the same time. After a bag had half-thawed, she would throw it into a heated pan, add it to what she was cooking. You told me that, later, when your family ate together you couldn't decide if you were eating your own pain or your own luck.

Any bystander might not think the instrument you love so much would wear down the tendons in the wrists and forearms. They would simply marvel at how quickly your hands moved, how precisely you struck the beaters against the strings, the tips making the timbre sound different depending on whether the leather is hard or soft. But that is because your skill, your effort, the hours of practice on your grandfather's cimbalom and the one at your music teacher's house, made it look easy. Your hands flew, changing direction as quickly as hummingbirds, always finding the right place to land.

But any bystander would not feel the collecting effect of all those impacts. They would not know the wearing down caused by, hundreds of thousands of times, striking the beaters just where they needed to hit. They would not guess at the tension in your wrists, the taut muscle in your forearms, the tiny friction every time you bring a beater down.

Do that enough times, and the pain in your wrists will probably be enough to wake you up at night. Do that enough times, and it will startle you out of sleep, leaving you with the memory of dreams in which your arms are branches on fire.

Still, you took the brush-lined road to your music teacher's house, your feet as accustomed to the dampening pedal as to the long walk. You did as she told you, repeating the Stravinsky until she said yes, you were feeling the music, not just playing it. Running through the original score of *Les Noces* until you thought your veins were molten. Wincing as you held your wrists under cold water in her downstairs bathroom, because you did not want the pain showing on your face as you sounded each note of Bartók's Rhapsody No. 1.

But the pain did show on your face, and your music teacher said that such cringing, such hardening in your jaw, would never let you on the grandest stages. She said you could not take each wrist in the opposite hand between sections or movements, no more than a ballerina can stretch her calves onstage.

Your hands, and your wrists, and your forearms—they spoke, even when you told them, asked them, begged them to be quiet. And the more that pain took hold of you, the more your music teacher cast you aside like a frayed bow.

This is the part that took you the longest to tell me. This

is the part that, when you did, made my heart feel like it was cracking open. Because I could feel it. The cold water as you tried to put out the flames in your muscles. The feeling of your teacher losing both patience and the sparkling faith she once had in you. I know the look. I got it from my own dance teachers, when they saw me falter on ankles that were giving out under me, when they caught the wince under my stage smile.

I wish you hadn't known it too.

That look, I guess, is how you came to be in my great-grandmother's village, even though you are unrelated to anyone there. Even though you are a different kind of brown-skinned boy than I am a brown-skinned girl.

You came to be in my bisabuela's village because there is an old man who lives there.

El viejo moves so slowly that he seems to cross the street in rhythm with honey dripping from a spoon.

All of him, that is, except his hands.

He plays, knows, the cimbalom better than you, better than your music teacher. But he also knows what music takes from the body. So when a friend of a friend of my mother mentioned him to your mother, your mother and father thought this man might teach you to save both your hands and the part of your heart that has turned to wood and metal strings.

You would not pay him for his lessons, the man said. Nor would you pay him for the bed at the back of his house where you would sleep, the bed his own son sleeps in whenever he visits. Your payment, he said, would be to help with the flower harvest. You would not do anything that would stress your wrists, he said. No picking plumeria or cosmos. No twisting poinsettias off their stems. But you would help carry the baskets of flowers, las canastas de palma that would be light with their cargo but awkward with their size.

You wondered if this flower harvest happened every year. You wondered this out loud the first time you ever spoke to me. We were standing, waiting for the señoras to tell us what to do.

I told you no, this does not happen every year. I told you what my bisabuela told me. That a man getting married a village away said his bride was so beautiful, he wanted the clouds to rain flowers in her honor. For their wedding day, he wanted to turn the sky to petals.

Another man, one who had grown up here, who had gone to school and then to more school and become a lawyer, told the rich man that he could make this happen. The sky could rain flowers for his bride.

But he would have to pay.

The rich man had owned shares in the maquiladora, whose runoff had poisoned the creeks, whose trucks had torn up the roads. Then, having found a place they could operate for even less money, they left, taking the jobs and the youngest families, with them, leaving the shell of the factory crumbling by the side of the road.

The village, the lawyer said, would only give his bride her sky full of petals in exchange for these things: Clean water (at the time everyone had to buy gallons from a far-off store, relying on the kindness of friends with trucks). Repaired roads. Replaced electrical lines. A building for the school so it did not have to meet in the back of Señora Delgado-Cruz's house anymore.

The village would sell him the color off its trees and vines and bushes, if he would pay for these things. And the man was so in love that he agreed.

This is how you came to be in my great-grandmother's village during the flower harvest, those feverish, bright-colored days of picking and carrying cream yucca petals, the pink satin ribbons of brush trees, the blue lilac of jacarandas.

I came to be there because my parents were sick of me moping on their living room sofa during the hours each day I used to be in dance class.

What was happening in your wrists and forearms had been happening in my ankles for months. Maybe longer. But it was in those past months that the wild rush of dancing was no longer enough to mask the pain lighting up my tendons.

I did what you did. Well, almost. I smiled harder to keep myself from wincing, while you held your jaw to keep the stoic face of a concert musician. I lifted my body to pretend there was no weight on my ankles, while you bent lower to the cimbalom, trying to make any pain seem like a fierce intensity.

It ended anyway.

My parents tolerated me burying my face in the sofa for only the first two weeks of summer. Then they told me I would help with the flower harvest. A petal at a time, I would help bring the village my bisabuela loved closer to clean water, and electricity that flickered out less often, and roads that wouldn't take out a transmission with their ruts and potholes.

So they brought me to my bisabuela's small but tidy house, with that aluminum roof. (You asked once what it sounds like when it rains, and you know when you used to play "Flight of the Bumblebee" on the cimbalom with hard leather beaters? Like that, only louder.)

My bisabuela knew you and I had something in common, an echo of familiar pain in our bodies. She knew that each evening, you were working at the cimbalom in frustratingly slow movements, the old man teaching you to keep something you love without letting it take everything from you. She knew that every sunrise the curanderas rubbed chili powder and turmeric into your forearms; when we gathered for the harvest, I could see it tinting the brown of your wrists red and gold.

And my great-grandmother knew I could not dance, not like I had been dancing, or in a few years I might not walk. I could dance for the joy of it, the doctors told me, and that was as little comfort as being told I could breathe, but only on weekends.

It was into las canastas de palma you carried that I collected marigolds and cuetlaxochitl, petals the color of the fire we felt in our tendons. It was into those baskets that I set passion flowers, green-and-red and yellow-and-purple, that curled up from dry roadsides. You were chivalrous enough to look away when I cried while plucking morning glories, because as a child I learned that la campanilla morada was a symbol of unrequited love, and the only unrequited love I had known up to then was dancing. It took my heart. It told me I was beautiful.

And then it ravaged the body it had so completely possessed.

The sun beat down on our backs as we filled the baskets, fluffing the petals to let them air.

We did not give the rich man and his bride all our flowers. There were mariposas and hummingbirds to think of. So we left the Mexican sage; the purple velvet of the petals was too heavy anyway, and they were a favorite of the violet sabrewings and fork-tailed emeralds. Same with the honeysuckle, and the pineapple and tangerine sage, which would not survive the flight anyway. We left the opuntia flowers; the weight of their closed buds would make them too difficult to send airborne. We gave him our yellow and rust-red and purple marigolds, but kept the orange and brown to ourselves, because no village should ever give up all they have of cempasúchil.

I volunteered to be among the women picking the plumeria, those tiny white and yellow flowers whose perfume grows stronger at night, and the delicate pink and green pouches of the lady's slippers. These are the flowers that sting and redden the skin if you handle them for too long, and I wanted pain on my fingers to distract me from the pain in my chest and my ankles.

I did not wear gloves, the ones the lawyer had demanded be provided. I wanted to keep that pain that only went as deep as my skin, that might fade with a little ungüento and a few days' time. It let me pretend my ankles might heal so quickly, that I might dance again, so furiously that any pain would escape my notice.

But when you saw the backs of my hands bleeding from the flower petals' sting, you must have asked my bisabuela about me. Because that night, with the soap smell of yucca flowers in the air, you happened to be taking a walk that passed down my great-grandmother's street.

You must have known I would be where I always was that time of night, leaning against the front of the house, breathing the flower-laced air while my great-grandmother watched her static-y TV. (My father had bought her a new one, which she instantly sold, not trusting it, as though it were a wild horse.)

You took a deep breath, either of the plumeria or simply of the night air.

"I can still play," you said, "but only very, very slowly."

And before I thought much about what I would say back, I was sighing a resigned sigh, matching your deep breath, mirroring your words.

"I can still dance," I said, "but only very, very carefully."

Then my bisabuela heard you outside and insisted you come in, because to her mind you were worryingly thin and sad, and needed chilaquiles to fatten you up and chiles to brighten your spirit.

You stayed. You told us both about your grandfather, who loved music but whose fear was even deeper than his love. Your grandfather had seen so many men in his family look for work, their spirits thinning out as they were told a hundred times, by a hundred different gadje, that they did not hire their kind.

You told us this with the resigned, good-natured look of knowing anything you told my bisabuela would be gossip on the señoras' tongues by morning. *Pobrecito*, they would say. *No wonder he must play. It is in his heart, his blood. It is a family trade.*

It was the next day that we all went up into the hills. We carried our baskets of wine-deep cosmos, and red dahlias, and yellow poppies to the highest peaks we could bring such bulky canastas. We went so high that the air cooled, and we could see far enough to spot the rich man's wedding, the bride a point of black hair and white lace on a walled lawn.

And when the right wind came, we tipped the baskets and shook them into the currents of air. The pink and green and red petals of cuetlaxochitl. The gladiolus in every shade from peach to deep blue. The sunflower petals the old women so carefully plucked from their centers, saving the seeds for toasted semillas de girasol. The black-brown thimble flowers edged in gold, like my cousins wearing necklaces in their hair.

I plunged my arms into those baskets of lady's slippers and plumeria, the petals reddening my skin up to the elbows.

And when there were no more flowers to throw, when we all stood watching as the sky turned to petals, you reached for my hand. Even with the oil of those vicious flowers on my palm, you reached for my hand. You brushed your fingers against mine, and I moved my hand, without thinking, into yours.

You did not look at me, either out of shyness or awkwardness. Your hand held on to mine as all the color we had stripped from my great-grandmother's village streamed through the air. We watched a river of cosmos and la flor de nochebuena cross the sky and then rain down over the rich man and his new wife.

Between our hands was the slight sting of those flowers I had handled. You shared it with me, a pain we would speak of later when, laughing, we put pomada on each other's reddened palms. Laughing, as the few petals the wind was still tossing around fell down on us like dyed rain.

You looked at me, pausing in the middle of your own laugh, your mouth half-open like you were thinking of saying something.

Maybe I'm wrong. Maybe you weren't. Maybe the way you would tell it would be very different. Maybe after the sky rained flowers, after we both went home, you began to forget me.

I don't have your number. So I won't know unless I follow the return address on your letters (because you still write paper letters, even though your own mother calls you a hundred years old for it). Letters I have not answered, because to look at you, to look at the pain in your hands, to remember the things it will take you years to have again, is to be reminded of the pain in my ankles, the wearing-down of my own tendons, and all the things I will probably never have again.

But I have kept every piece of your life those letters have given me. Your low opinion of the required summer reading list. Your sister's rescue dog, who acts as distant and aloof as a cat. How the tree in the back of your house is heavy with lemons, how your father salts, slices, and eats them as though they're oranges.

I won't know unless I ask.

I won't know unless I get out of this car.

My mother is already looking at me in a way that says, without her speaking, *We came all this way y eres una gallina?* I know she's talked to your mother, warned her, though probably not you, that I'm coming, which makes me want to sink into the front seat of my mother's four-door and vanish.

Maybe those letters mean nothing, except what you always said, *Someone has to keep paper letters alive.*

I won't know unless I walk the steps to your front door, and ask you.

Prom

Danielle Paige

We were eight when we met. You offered to trade half your peanut butter sandwich for half of my turkey sandwich on the first day of school. I was all legs and curls, and you were shaggy blond bangs that hung over too big glasses.

We were twelve when we dressed up as our favorite wizards and stood in line for hours to get the last book in that series. Every new book marked a new year of our friendship.

We were thirteen when I wondered for the first time what it would be like to kiss you.

We were sixteen when you asked me to prom.

In an hour you will kiss me in front of all our friends and not-friends and teachers on the dance floor. And I will kiss you back. And it will be all the things I imagined, sweet and breathless and heart quickening.

But when the kiss is done, I will look around to see if our friends and not-friends and teachers are looking. And you won't.

Because I know you.

I know that you like the Stones better than The Beatles. I know what your face looked like when your dad moved out. I know how it looks when he picks you up for weekends. Maybe I know you better than anyone else.

And you know me, too.

You know how I like my coffee, and you know not to talk to me in the morning until I've made it a third of the way through the cup. You know how scared I was when my dad got sick, and how relieved I was when he got better.

But you don't know what it means to be us.

There will always be looking. There will always be those who stare too long or look away too quickly.

"What it is?" you ask, looking down at me as the music slows. You put your arms around my waist.

"Nothing."

You say my name in the way you do when you call me on my shit.

"Everyone is looking at us. Everyone will always be looking at us."

"Because you're so beautiful. And I'm so lucky."

I say your name like I do when I call you on your shit.

"I only see you," you tell me with urgency.

"But I need you to see *them*, too."

And then you nod.

That's when I kiss you. It is all the things I imagined, sweet and breathless and heart quickening, all the things that I'd never known. It's the beginning of us. And when the kiss is done, you look around to see if our friends and not-friends and teachers are looking—

And I don't.

What We Love

Lauren Gibaldi

"What do you think *purgatory* means? Viv?"

I look up from my tattered library copy of Dante's *Inferno* and answer, "It's an in-between place. Like, between heaven and hell and they're debating where you're going."

"Good," Ms. Rizzoli says, turning back to the whiteboard. "Now in the book . . ."

"Poor you," a voice whispers, and I brace myself for the insult. "You may know about purgatory, but you're definitely not going there."

"Sure," I say with a roll of my eyes at Jessica Prichard, sitting next to me with her perfect posture, perfect straight blonde hair, and perfect manicure. She maintains a look of perfection to make up for the awfulness deep down inside her.

"Because you're going to hell," she says. I would have been surprised, insulted, had she not been telling me this all year, since she "discovered Jesus." Really she just discovered a hot guy who wears a cross.

"Cool," I say and go back to my book, flipping the soft pages with my thumb. I feel someone looking at me and turn back to see Nikhil. He does that embarrassed head nod thing when our eyes meet, then looks down. Great, he heard.

A million years later, the bell finally rings and I get up as quickly as possible.

"Hey, Viv?"

I pull on my shoulder bag and glance up at Nik. "Hey, what's up?"

He looks past me and I follow his gaze as Jessica floats by, bumping into me. She keeps walking, her cronies following behind her and obviously giggling—the type of giggling they want you to hear. "Oh my God, it's going to be the *best* party ever!" one screeches, and I assume it's yet another party I'm not invited to, and whatever.

"I heard what she said."

I look back at him and ask, "About the party?"

"No, about you."

My face heats up and I look down, to the side, anywhere but at him. Yeah, I can handle this, but that doesn't mean I want the whole school knowing about what she says. "It's nothing." I start walking away, knowing he's following me.

"She does it to me too."

I look back at him, taking in his tan skin and dark eyes, and ask, "You're Jewish?"

"No, no," he says, catching up to me at the door. He ducks his head a little and we walk toward the cafeteria. "She calls me a terrorist."

"Wait, what?" I ask, stopping now. "Why?"

"Because I'm brown?"

"Yeah, I know that, but why would she say you're a terrorist?"

"Because clearly all Indians are. Didn't you know?"

I thought he was meek before, looking away whenever her icy eyes looked at him. But he's not; he's just irritated and hurt. Like me. "She says I'm going to hell, even though

Jewish people don't, you know, believe in hell. She's an awful human being."

"Pretty much. I'm just, and I know this sounds weird, but I'm glad it's not just me."

I look at him. "You're glad other people are being insulted by her?" As he shakes his head and starts to explain, I interrupt. "I get what you're saying. It's nice knowing she's not *just* against you. You're not her one and only target."

"Yeah, exactly," he says. "She makes the Apu voice at me."

"And let me guess, she assumes your parents own a gas station."

He looks away and dodges when two members of the football team run down the hall shouting. They're allowed to do that, of course. "Okay, so they do, but it's not the worst?"

I smile because, aw, and say, "It's cool. My grandparents regularly sneak food out from buffets. That whole 'Jewish people are cheap' thing? Not true about everyone, but totally true about them."

He looks at me, and a moment of camaraderie passes between us. Like, I get him, and he gets me, and it's weird having this understanding with someone I barely know.

The hallway chatter is lower, and I know what that means. "Bell's about to ring," I say. "I should get to lunch."

"Yeah, me too," he says. "See you tomorrow?"

"Yeah," I say, smiling. "I look forward to it."

When I get home from school, my mom is in the kitchen with her I LOVE YOU A LATKE apron on, and okay, we are stereotypes sometimes. But the thing is, we're not very Jewish. I've been to temple only a handful of times. I can't tell you any religious stories. But I know how to make some mean hamantaschen, which is, incidentally, what Mom is doing right now.

"We need pastries," she says, rolling out the dough with Bubbe's rolling pin, which she gave us when she left for the nursing home. She loves it there. She's become a champion Wii bowler and leader of the mahjong club.

"Fruit or chocolate?" I ask, already walking to the Nutella.

"What do you think?" Mom asks, holding her hand out. I give her the container and we scoop small amounts of chocolate onto the pastries, then fold them up to look like triangles. Some people make the dough from scratch, but Mom uses ready-made croissants. Bubbe called this meshuggeneh, we call it quicker.

As my mom puts them in the oven, I look at her and am reminded how much I look like her. Same dark, curly hair. Same bumpy nose. Same tanned skin. Teenage pictures of my mom are essentially me. It's weird how that happens—poor Dad isn't represented at all.

As we wait, Mom asks about school, about classes, and I answer, but I'm not really thinking of that. I'm thinking of Nik, of Jessica, of how unfair it is that she can go about with no one mocking her. That she's the default—beautiful, blonde, white, Christian—and the rest of us are merely "others" to her. To society, I guess. I see the news. I see the anti-Semitic movements. I see the travel bans.

It's easier to ignore than embrace. But is it worth it?

So when Mom asks, "Any plans for the rest of the week?"

I answer, "Yeah, I think so."

After class the next day, I walk up to Nik, grab his arm, and pull him outside. He comes willingly.

"Okay, hi," he says with a confused smile.

"Hey, so I've been thinking." As I brace myself to tell him

my idea, none other than Jessica walks out, followed by her posse. She glances at us quickly, rolls her eyes, and says, "Figures you're friends. You're both losers anyway." Then she walks away, an air of superiority surrounding her.

"You were saying?" Nik says with a groan, turning back to me.

"We need revenge."

"Revenge . . ." he says.

"We need to do something that'll show her we're humans, we have feelings, and she can't, like, keep talking to us the way she does. She can't keep bullying us."

He nods, then asks, "What do you have in mind?"

"I don't . . . I don't know, really. But I want to do something," I say as we start walking toward the cafeteria.

"Okay, I'm in. Let's just think of something good, you know?"

"Obviously," I say, both relief and fear filling me. Glad he's on board, but also—this means it's happening. That it can't be just words anymore. And, okay, we're doing this. We swap numbers and plan to text later.

I leave him for the cafeteria but double back quickly to get my chemistry textbook. I get to the stairwell and hear someone under the stairs. Kind of movement, kind of humming. I look down and my jaw drops. Jessica is making out with a guy who is most definitely not her boyfriend, Brett. I do the first thing that comes to mind—I take a picture and run away as fast as I can.

Important development, I text Nik.

What's up?

I send him the picture, and a minute later he responds.

Ohhhhhhhhhhhh.

Meet after school?

Yeah, ok

I'm practically jumping, waiting for Nik in front of the library.

"So why am I not surprised by this?" he asks when he sees me.

"'Cause she's the worst?" I answer, raising an eyebrow.

"Does Brett know?" he asks.

"Can't imagine," I say.

"So . . . is this the revenge? We show him?"

"I don't know. I mean, and then he'll dump her, and that'll suck, but she'll have another guy to fall back on. It's mean, yeah, but she'll be fine," I say. I don't want to scar her for life or anything, but she clearly has her options with guys, and embarrassing her can only do so much. Knowing her, she'll make it all about her and somehow become the victim.

"Yeah," he agrees. "That makes sense."

I think back to her comments earlier and something stands out. Something important. "Or wait. We can show him this Saturday."

"Why this Saturday?" Nik asks.

"It's her Sweet Sixteen."

"Oh. Wow. How do you know?"

"She mentioned it around me earlier and then said, 'Sorry, only good people come to my party. I don't need any demons by me.'"

"Wow, she is awful."

"Yeah. So that could, like, embarrass her in front of her friends. He can dump her there, ruining her big party."

"That could work," he says softly, and a flush of realness washes over me.

We discuss logistics a bit longer, then head out, the future ahead of us. A future that may not involve snide remarks every time we enter a room.

When we exit the school, I look at Nik.

"I take the bus?" he says, a bit embarrassed. "So, uh, I have to wait for my mom to pick me up. She'll be here in about an hour."

I look at him and smile. "I live right down there." I point down the street, to the right. "I walk to school. Tell your mom to pick you up at my house."

"Really?" he asks, seemingly happy.

"Totally."

We walk to my house, not really chatting, but getting in step with each other. I wonder if it's a good idea bringing him home—I barely know him—but at the same time, I've known him my entire high school career. He's always been in my classes; we just never hung out.

"What's that?" he asks as we approach our very red front door. My mom wanted something bright. This is definitely bright.

I look at the small metal decoration on the doorpost and say, "A mezuzah? It's a Jewish thing. It has a piece of the Torah inside. It's just something we have."

"For luck?"

"Um, sort of." Truth is I kind of know the story behind it, but also don't? I know we've always had it. I know all the Jews have one. I unlock the door and walk in.

"When we moved into our new place, my mom hit a coconut on the door."

"That's weird. Why?"

"Same—good luck for us."

"Oh," I say, feeling bad for the "weird" comment. "Cool. Sorry. I didn't know." He shrugs and follows me inside. "Um, my mom should be home soon. I texted her to say you were coming."

"She's okay with it?"

"Totally. Honestly, I think she's happy I have a guy coming over." He raises his eyebrows, and I explain, "Every dude is like a possible husband. Don't be alarmed; I'm not marrying you. You're not Jewish."

"Okay. I was worried there might be some big surprise ceremony and I'd be, like, trapped for life."

"That's what you think of me?" I joke. "That if we ended up together, you'd be trapped?"

"Well, if we were married within two days of hanging out, yeah. If you wait a third day, I may feel more comfortable." I laugh, then lead him into the living room, at ease with our banter. "My mom's kind of the same," he continues. "Only with Hindu girls. Too bad there aren't many around."

"Does she expect you to marry one?"

"Not expect—hopes, I think."

"Do you hope you will too?" I ask curiously. My mom *is* interested in my nonexistent dating life, and she jokes about my eventual marriage to a Jewish doctor, but I also know she isn't serious. I know she won't mind, since my dad isn't Jewish.

"I don't know, it's weird. Like, I don't want to plan my life like that," he says, sitting on the couch with me. "And I don't even want to *think* about that stuff right now. 'Cause, you know, sixteen and all. But I guess part of me wants to . . . just make my mom happy. Since she came here for me and all. But the other part knows she'll be okay if I don't? Like, she won't be thrilled at first, but she loves me. Which makes me feel guilty. And, yeah, complex."

"She came here for you?" I ask.

"Well, not *me* me. After my parents got married, they moved to the States so their kids could grow up with more opportunities. I wasn't born yet, so the idea of me, I guess. They remind me of this sometimes when I, like, play too many video games or whatever. And I know they sacrificed a lot, leaving family and all. So I feel . . . guilty?"

"Believe me, I understand guilt. Have you heard of Jewish guilt? It's in our DNA. My grandma . . ." I never say "Bubbe" in front of people, mostly because I don't want to stop and define it. I mean, it's the same thing. "She gives us the Holocaust spiel a lot. She came from Germany, so . . ."

"Oh wow, did she—"

"No, no, not like that. She's German but was already living here during the war. So she was okay physically. Mentally, not so much, as you'd imagine."

"Your dad Jewish too?"

"No . . . he's Catholic. So I'm a Cashew."

"Cashew?"

"Catholic . . . Jew."

"Oh." He laughs. "Oh, that's bad."

"I know!"

"How was your grandma about that?"

"She wasn't the *happiest* at first, but she was okay from what I hear. Mom got a lot of guilt—like I said, it's passed down—but there wasn't any disowning or anything."

"My parents' marriage was arranged."

"Seriously?" I ask, sitting up straighter. "I've heard of that before, but didn't know it still happened. You know, like 'Matchmaker, Matchmaker.'"

"Huh?"

"*Fiddler on the Roof*? Never mind. Continue."

"Okay, yeah, so they were by my grandparents. They were family friends, so it wasn't too weird, I guess. My mom said it was more casual—they were allowed to say no if they wanted to. But they didn't want to, and they didn't say no. So here we are."

"Does that still happen in India?"

"Oh yeah. My cousin has a biodata. It's like . . . a profile? A résumé, kind of? With a photo that goes to 'prospective husbands,'" he says, making quotation marks with his fingers.

"That's crazy! What if she finds someone she likes outside of the biodata?"

"Uh, it depends. There's still a class system, so, like, if he's within her class or above, it's cool. But if he's below, it's a THING. I don't know."

"How old is she?"

"Twenty-five."

"Wow."

"Yeah, things are different over there. Not in a bad way—like, I've visited and it's super awesome—but in a . . . different way."

The door opens and my mom walks in, all businesslike in her lawyer suit.

"Hello!" she says, then stops and looks at me, then at Nik. "I'm Aviva's mom. You must be Nik?" I look at Mom and wonder why she's being so formal. It's Viv.

"Hi!" he says, standing up. "Nik, yes, Nikhil. Family name."

"I'm going to go put my bag down. Do you kids want any snacks?"

"We're good," I say, then realize we should leave before she says anything embarrassing. "Hey, I'm going to show him BB."

"Okay!"

I nod to him and get up. He follows me into my room. I keep the door open because . . . I don't want to deal with a curious mother right now.

"BB?" Nik asks, looking around my, uh, slightly dorky room. "Oh. BB-8?"

"Yeah," I say slowly, seeing my very *Star Wars*–themed

room through his eyes. Posters, toys on the bookshelves, books on the bedside table. Okay, I'm a bit obsessed. "He's my hamster." I point to the little spinning hamster, and Nik smiles and waves to him.

"Nice to meet you, BB!"

"He says hello." I smile, then sit on my bed.

"So I take it you like . . . *Star Trek*?" I glare at him. "I'm kidding. Which movie is your favorite?"

"Seven because of Rey. I had Leia and Padmé before, but Rey is just like . . . she's badass, right?"

"Totally. In eight she has that awesome lightsaber scene in the red room."

"Yeah! I was actually watching eight last night . . ."

"I haven't seen it since theaters." I look at him with complete surprise on my face. "What?"

"You're a disgrace."

He smiles and says, "Well, put it on then."

"Let's start where I left off."

As I'm opening my laptop, he says, "So, question."

"If it's who shot first, I have an answer for you."

"What?"

"Oh God, you're so not a fan. What's up?"

"Do you . . . do you think what we're doing to Jessica is right? Revenge and all that?"

I start up the DVD, but press pause and look at him. "I don't know. Do you think what she's doing to us is right?"

"Not at all."

"Yeah, so why not do it back to her?"

"Because we're better than her?"

I nod. Yeah, it's true. We are. But does that matter? "There's so much crap going on in the world that I just . . . I feel helpless sometimes, you know? Like I can't stop all the bad. My JCC got a bomb threat last year. I can't stop that from happening. But can I stop one girl from being such a shitty person? Maybe. I want to try, I guess."

"Point taken." He nods and sits on my bed next to me. I look at him, then back at the laptop, hoping he doesn't see my face flush. I haven't had a guy sit on my bed with me before.

I press play and let the movie fill in our conversation. I feel his arm next to mine, and think about how I barely knew him a few days ago, and now we're sharing this. How I know so much more about him, his family. How cute he looks during the lightsaber scene, all excited and stuff.

It gets to the end, when Finn is flying toward the laser, and Nik whispers, "Are you . . . are you reciting the lines along with it?"

"No," I whisper back, not having realized I was even doing it. Then, a second later, I whisper, "This is my favorite line," just as Rose says how they'll win the war. Not with hate, but by saving what they love.

Saturday arrives, and with it a bunch of nerves. We're actually doing this. Jessica practically announced when and where the party would be. This made planning easy. It's in the ballroom of a hotel. We agree to meet across the street from the hotel, at the lake, at five-thirty.

At five I get a text from Nik.

Hey

IF YOU DITCH ME I WILL HUNT YOU DOWN. Maybe I overreact a little.

That was intense.

I AM A BIT ANXIOUS RIGHT NOW.

Not ditching. Just saying I'm leaving now. Mom's dropping me off at the mall. Want to meet there?

K. That works.

You need a vacation
I'm gonna lightsaber you.
☺
Oh boy.

At five-thirty, Mom drops me off at the mall too. The mall is
on the lake, so it's a quick walk to the hotel from there. I find
Nik in the bookstore.

"Hey," I say, tapping him on the shoulder. He's looking at
a manga book.

"Oh, hey," he says, putting it back. He looks at me, blinks,
then says, "You, uh, you look nice."

I look down at the light blue spring dress I put on. If
we're going to a Sweet Sixteen, I figured I'd look the part.
It's soft and flowy like a cupcake. "Thanks. You too." He
also dressed up, in a black button-down shirt and dark
jeans.

"Hey, uh, I have something for you?" he says, as if it's a
question, as if he's asking permission to give me something. I
tilt my head, and he takes out a braided bracelet. A friendship
bracelet? "So, it's Rakhi right now, which is, like, a Hindu
holiday where sisters give their brothers this kind of bracelet. Anyway, my sister was making a ton of them today and
wanted me to give you one. You don't have to wear it or
anything, but she'd kill me if I didn't pass it along. She's six
and terrifies me."

I smile at him and take the woven bracelet. It has tiny blue
beads on it and red string, and it kind of matches my dress.
"Of course I'll wear it. I'm terrified of six-year-olds. Thank
you. And, you know, her."

He looks away, and I see a similar bracelet on his wrist.
He starts playing with his, twisting his finger around it, and
says, "I didn't know your favorite color, so I went with red,

because of that *Star Wars* scene. And then Rey's lightsaber color for the beads. Because she's your favorite."

I'm struck by this. How he put so much thought into something so small. How he's sharing his culture with me. How he's here with me, right now. I don't know what to say, so I just kind of look at the bracelet, then him, then the bracelet, then him, until I look away and laugh. Good going, Viv.

"Uh, we should get going . . ." Nik says, and I nod and follow him out of the mall.

We walk along the lake, on this running track, and it's still light out, so everything has a pinkish glow, reflecting off the water. Jazz music is playing over a speaker, and I turn as a duck splashes into the water.

"May the Force be with you," he says, and grabs my hand and squeezes it. He lets go before I can react, but I know one thing: the simple gesture made me smile.

The party has already started; I can tell just by walking in because there's a row of rose petals leading to the ballroom, which has a shut door and music blasting out of it. Great, dancing is happening. No one notices if you sneak in when the lights are low and there's dancing.

I hold my phone tight. Go time.

Just as we approach the door, it opens and two waiters holding trays walk out, looking exhausted. I hold the door open for them and look in. Just as I expected—it's dark and everyone is occupied. I grab Nik by the arm and sneak in. We make ourselves invisible in the back.

"You good?" I ask Nik, and he nods. It's loud, but we can hear each other.

"I'm glad the lights are dimmed," he says into my ear. "I'm definitely the only nonwhite person here. I kind of stand out."

"No, you're not," I say, shaking my head. "There's . . ."

Then I realize that, yeah, he's probably right. Our school is pretty white. I never thought about being the only one before. "Okay, well, good thing we're only going to be here a second."

We start walking to the dance floor, and the song changes and it's a slow song. I can see Jessica—oh man, she's wearing the pinkest, shortest, tightest dress with her long hair waving down her back—practically grinding on Brett.

A hand grabs mine and spins me around. Nik puts us in a slow-dancing position, and I look at him curiously. "Blend in," he says into my ear. "Just walking around while everyone is dancing doesn't really work, you know?"

"You've got a point," I say, and I give in, letting him lead me in a circle. "You can dance."

"Not really. I can walk in a circle and say it's dancing."

"I like it," I say, looking into his eyes. We're in this weird, awkward middle school dance position where we've kind of got a circle between us, so I close the gap, wrapping my arms around his neck. He embraces my back and I catch my head resting on his chest. This is nice. This is comfortable.

"This is weird, but"—I feel his chest move as he talks—"I'm glad we're here."

"Planning sabotage?"

"No. Dancing."

"Me too," I say, and I squeeze him a little and think of how this week has been. How have we gone from classmates to this? What is this, anyway? Are we going to keep hanging out after tonight? Are we going to keep talking and watching movies and dancing?

I think of when he came over and we watched *The Last Jedi* on my bed and how, even though we barely knew each other, I wanted him to kiss me. Just a little. Maybe.

Out of our hate for Jessica came this. I feel my bracelet with my other hand and suddenly I realize that we can't fight her, we can't do this.

"This isn't right . . ." I start.

"Oh, okay," Nik says, pulling away a little.

"No, no," I say, grabbing him. "Not us dancing—what we're about to do."

"It's a little late to have second thoughts . . ."

"No, it's not. We haven't done anything yet. We can leave. We can . . ." I look up into his eyes.

"What's wrong?"

"We shouldn't fight what we hate. We need to save what we love."

"Huh?"

"If we do this and get caught, that's it. We're in trouble. She hates us. Why risk that? As awful as she is, she brought us together. I'm happier . . . knowing that."

"So we're going to let the bad guy win?"

"We're just going to protect each other instead of fighting."

A smile spreads on his face and he hugs me. "Come on."

My heart soars as he holds my hand and we quickly walk to the back of the ballroom and out the door. We start walking down the hall until we hear, "What. The. Hell."

I turn and, of course, see Jessica glaring at us, pure death in her eyes.

"WHAT are you doing here? Were you *crashing* my party? Are you really that stupid?"

"Jessica, we're leaving, it's nothing," I try to explain while still backing up.

"No way. I can, like, get you arrested," she says, a smug look on her face.

"Why are you so awful?" Nik asks.

"EXCUSE me?"

"You say stuff like that, but you're the bad one. You know that, right?"

"Oh no. No, you do not say that."

I take a cue from Nik and pull out my phone. "Listen, we weren't just crashing your party."

"Yes, you were. You were so sad you weren't invited, so you decided to come. What, were you hoping one of the guys would feel bad and dance with you? Doubt it. They all have taste, unlike terrorist over here."

That's it. I show her the picture. Her mouth drops.

"We were going to show Brett, but we didn't. We're choosing not to because we're not as bad as you."

"Give me that." I put the phone back in my pocket. "Give it to me."

"Nope, we're leaving now."

"How do I know you won't share it later?"

"You just have to trust me," I say, and I turn around, grab Nik's hand, and run. I don't look back.

We run out of the hotel, hearing voices and music behind us. We run back to the lake. We keep running until we get to a little grassy patch, falling down and breathing heavy.

"That was savage." He laughs.

"I don't know where that came from," I say.

He smiles and squeezes my hand, which I realize he's still holding.

Nik leans his forehead against mine, our noses touching. We smile. He kisses me.

We won tonight because we saved what we love.

Giving Up the Ghost

Tarun Shanker and Kelly Zekas

Fourteen hours . . .

"Talk to her. That's an order," Ching declared from her perch, floating cross-legged in the air above the library table. "You know what I did to anyone who disobeyed my ord—"

"Yeah, yeah, beheadings, you've told me," Sanjiv said, slumping over his tablet. He had ten minutes before his first calc test and he was going to fail. The equations swam before his eyes, wiggling and curling into nonsensical patterns. All Ching's fault.

She didn't look particularly concerned, mainly because she wasn't. Sanjiv regularly wondered how he had ended up with Ching, who had to be one of the worst possible Ghost Mentors a mortal could be related to. His mom had this really sweet Buddhist monk dude, and she turned out cool and even-keeled. His dad had a humble cobbler from Mumbai, and didn't his shoes always look great? What did Sanjiv have? Oh, just the one murderous nineteenth-century pirate ancestor in his family tree. Very practical for modern life.

Ching looked at him like she knew what he was thinking,

even though the latest theory on Ghost–Mortal relationships said ghosts could *not* tell.

I hate you. Sanjiv beamed it at Ching, who just smiled more beatifically.

"Talk. To. Her."

"No. Shut. Up. Shut up, shut up."

Ching rolled her eyes and spun herself around in the air super dramatically, 'cause what else was new?

"It's been a month since school started!"

"Oh wow, did you know I actually knew that? Because I have this little calc thing today? Have I mentioned that?" Panic was crawling up Sanjiv's back. He'd fucked up. The goddamn test was goddamn now and goddamn Ching had done nothing but distract him.

"Look. She's *right there*. Just be like, 'Hi, do you remember me? I'm Sanji and we used to try and glue our hands together in preschool so we wouldn't be separated at the end of the day—wanna bang?'"

Sanjiv whipped his head around to see that Ching was right.

Not about telling Addy he wanted to bang her.

(He did???)

Sitting in a beanbag chair, curled over her laptop, Addy was at the other end of the library. If she could hear his ghost talk, Sanjiv would have walked directly out of school, found the closest ocean, and kept walking.

Thankfully, she and everyone else could see and hear only their own ghost. Addy seemed to be talking to someone in midair, nodding thoughtfully and typing quickly. So. Her ghost was helpful. Imagine. What would that even be like?

Behind him, Ching made a weird growl/cough sound as she eyed Addy.

"What?"

"Nothing. Go talk to her."

"Stop it! I'm not gonna say anything! She doesn't remember me and it's super weird if I do anything now!"

Sanjiv had gotten really good at whisper-fighting with Ching so he wouldn't stick out in school. Most kids seemed to be so in sync with their ghosts that they only ever needed to say, "Oh hey, thank you, good to know," and just not talk to them the rest of the time. He was the only one who had to ask that please, for the love of God, she *not* scream at his world history teacher throughout the entire class.

Ching really hated Ms. Phelps.

"Dude, dude, dude, she totally just looked at you." Ching started batting at his shoulder, which she knew he couldn't feel and didn't like but constantly did anyway. Sanjiv focused on not moving a single muscle as he battled with the desire to turn around and check.

"No, she didn't."

"Yes, she did!" she argued. "Just talk to her and I'll tell you where my treasure is buried and you can take her out to a romantic dinner—"

The treasure shit again. "You're lying."

"Most of the time, yes!" Ching stuck her tongue out at him and flipped her short hair back so it curled rakishly around her ears. "But not about treasure. Pirates don't lie about treasure."

"That's easily the number one thing they lie about," Sanjiv said. "There are so many unresolved disputes online—"

"She's honestly super adorable," Ching interrupted, studying Addy. "And I'm sure she was when you guys were six or whatever, yet you somehow managed to talk to her then. Six-year-old Sanjiv was much braver. And you didn't even have me as a mentor."

"Maybe that's the problem," Sanjiv muttered, his eyes

scanning the cheesy pro-ghost posters along the library wall. They all featured absurdly happy humans and their benevolent ghosts reading or laughing or riding tandem bicycles together with messages like LEARN FROM THE PAST! and WISER TOGETHER!

Sanjiv couldn't see himself with Ching in any of those scenes, no matter how hard he tried. And he'd been trying for years, ever since she'd manifested on his ninth birthday. But he kept wondering if he'd be happier without her. A lot of the ghostless people he saw seemed so much more confident and unburdened without a voice constantly berating them. There was this really popular radio show about how it was actually a sign of self-sufficiency and dominance to give up your ghost. And yeah, the hosts sounded like pompous jerks who would be insufferable to meet in person, but they also seemed totally at ease with their awful selves. Sanjiv was sort of jealous of that. Maybe they *were* onto something.

"I can't believe you've wasted a whole month of her being back and didn't say anything," Ching chastised, staring again in Addy's direction.

"We haven't had any classes together." Wow, if only Sanjiv's test was on "Talking about Addy with Ching." He would get an A. He knew exactly how this would go. They'd done this thirty-six billion times.

"I gave you so many ideas for a meet-cute. Knocking into her in the hall and dropping your books."

"I don't . . . no one carries books, that isn't a thing."

"Walking into her diner and asking if 'a date with her' is on the menu."

"Please tell me that wasn't a serious one."

Predictably, Ching continued, ignoring him. "Telling her you died in a freak accident two years ago but got resurrected into a human-ghost hybrid by the power of your love for her and the only way you can remain is if she lov—"

"That was a terrible movie, you're terrible, everything is terrible, we have to go."

Sanjiv pushed back from the table, and the horrible combination of cheap metal chair screeching on old tiled floor broke the perfect silence of the library. Fantastic! Awesome. Now everyone was looking at him while Ching just cackled, like she was watching an enemy's ship sink to the ocean floor.

Even Addy. Who he tried valiantly not to notice as he stalked out of the library, the bell ringing just as the door swung shut behind him.

"Talk to her! Talk. To. Her. Talk! To! Her!" Ching floated along by his shoulder, throwing her fist with each word, as though she was going to get a whole crowd to join in.

"What did I do to deserve you, honestly?"

"Sanji! You got lucky." Ching grinned and waggled her eyebrows. "Now let's go; you have a calc test to fail!"

Nine hours . . .

He didn't fail. Hopefully. He had kinda paid attention during class, which was probably enough to get a C. Everyone was allowed to use their ghosts on tests, which was really great if your ghost was highly educated or, say, the inventor of calculus, but most people had ghosts who were experts only in some highly specialized and probably outdated trade. Ching couldn't help him in much, except for fencing. And navigation. And, despite the fact that he tried desperately to block out her detailed stories, he knew way, way too much about running a brothel in the 1800s.

Way. Too. Much.

Life with Ching was basically a nightmare.

"What's for lunch? Is it the little dinosaur nugget things

again?" She was looking lustily at the cafeteria, eyes wide with anticipation. Sanjiv often thought that she never looked more like a pirate than when thinking about food. She couldn't eat, but she liked to watch him eat, which was rather uncomfortable three times a day. "Do they really taste like chicken?"

"No, not really."

"What then?"

"Like soggy cardboard."

"I don't believe you."

"Fine." Sanjiv didn't care. He wasn't hungry and he had only English left after lunch. He wouldn't have to do much except make a few points about the poetry homework, which was simple enough. He just wanted to go to the lake and think. He was turning seventeen tomorrow. He could legally have his ghost removed forever with a simple procedure. If he wanted.

His heartbeat sped a little just imagining it.

"Let's find Addy and ask if she wants to share the cardboard with you!" Ching was wiggling her eyebrows.

"Why are you pushing this?" he grumbled in a low whisper as they entered the bustling cafeteria. A cacophony of sound assaulted him as he grabbed a tray and chopsticks.

"'Cause she's cute and you need to get laid."

"Please . . . never talk again."

"Sanji, you asked a question. Besides, by the time I was your age—"

"No, no, no." Sanjiv pulled on his huge, ghost-canceling headphones to block her out, which he resorted to only when she was at her worst. The distorted guitars of his favorite band, Beethoven's Ghost, filled his ears.

Ching gave a dramatic heave of her shoulders and rolled her eyes. He rolled his eyes back and grabbed a tray of cardboard.

None of his friends had the terrible, late lunch period he had. It sucked and he usually just finished reading or whatever. He pulled out the collection of Elizabethan sonnets and went over the iambic pentameter, tapping lightly on the table.

And then there was an uncomfortable, cold sensation in the same rhythm on his shoulder. Cold COLD. Cold COLD.

Ching was swatting at him and saying something, but Sanjiv had bought these headphones specifically so he wouldn't have to hear whatever awful thing she wanted to tell him. He gave her an innocent stare, which always drove her nuts.

She glared at him and made several obscene gestures. He restrained himself from sticking his tongue out at her. He'd managed to get through half of high school without people noticing how weird he and his ghost were; he could get through the last day of being sixteen.

But out of the corner of his eye, he could still see Ching working herself up into a furious tirade, so he gave in and pulled one ear of the headphones off.

"—GOD FORBID SANJI TALK TO A GIRL HE LIKES. YEAH, I'M THE BAD GUY!"

"You are an actual, literal, murderous pirate."

"THAT WAS CENTURIES AGO!"

"Jesus Christ." Sanjiv finished the last chicken nugget thing (they were pretty okay, actually), set his chopsticks down, and got up.

"Just talk to her! You're going to regret this!" He couldn't tell if that was, like, a suggestion of how he would feel if he missed out or a threat that Ching would *make* him regret it. "For once, just do something you actually want to do! What is the worst that could happen?"

The worst possible thing? He had the answer to that

question because it had already happened, and like everything, it was Ching's fault. In sixth grade he'd asked Ching
to find out from Sarah Harper's ghost if she liked him, and
by the end of the day, every kid and ghost in the school knew
Sarah's answer.

Her answer was no.

"For once in *your* life—death—whatever, Ching, just fucking drop it!"

"Dude, I'm just trying to get you laid—"

"Well, I don't want to! So just . . . *stop*!"

She did stop and hesitated, looking like there was something more, something different she wanted to say. But she
changed her mind and changed tactics.

"Sanji, you're being ridiculous—"

"Why are you so insistent on this? Do you have some stupid plan that's going humiliate me or get me expelled? I don't
fucking want the yogurt incident again!"

"No, I just—"

"Come on, C, look at me and tell me this is simply that
you want me to be happy. Come on, tell me." Sanjiv stared
hard at her, blood boiling. He knew it. Knew there had to
be something terrible behind this. She'd been annoying him
about Addy for weeks, ramping it up the closer they got to
his birthday.

Ching wasn't really meeting his eye. She may have ruled
a fleet of thirty pirate ships, but she didn't like lying about
things that matter.

Which meant she was, for sure, planning something stupid
or cruel or ridiculous. And that meant Sanjiv was done, done
for good with her antics and setting him up for failure.

"You know what? I only have one mandated day left with
you. Let's spend it not talking. Maybe that'll be easier for
both of us."

If ghosts could go pale, if blood could drain from their faces, then Ching did that. Her lashes swept down, covering the confusion that had sprung to her eyes.

"Sanji . . ."

The hurt in her voice was so unfamiliar, so surprising, that he barely registered it for what it was. He'd actually upset her this time.

Well, she'd been upsetting him for years.

"I'm done, Ching. It's over."

She didn't follow when he picked up his bag and went to English.

Seven hours . . .

Two hours later and Sanjiv was *finally* at the lake. It was getting colder going into October, but the sun was out, the summer refusing to give ground to fall. The club was dead, so his boss, Trish, let him take a boat out without too much hassle. Sanjiv had worked there the whole summer, handling two jobs' worth of responsibilities. She knew he wouldn't screw anything up.

Ching had disappeared after their fight in the cafeteria, vanishing into her mysterious ghost dimension—a refuge for whenever Sanjiv was sleeping or doing something equally uneventful. She didn't return for the rest of the school day, leaving him to a rather boring last period and a strangely quiet car ride. But he was certain this ride would call her back.

As he pushed off the dock and the boat slid across the water, picking up speed, he could swear his blood pressure began to drop. And sure enough, a few moments later, he could sense another presence joining him. Ching was on the bow, her face tipped up to the sky, as though she could almost feel the sun, the breeze.

She'd taught him this, of course. Barked orders for years, until she trusted that Sanjiv could sail even if he was hungover and puking.

That had happened exactly one time, when she convinced him that peach schnapps wasn't alcoholic.

But now it was as intuitive as walking. Maybe more so. And it was the best thing Ching has ever done for him, sharing her love of this. He couldn't stay mad at her here, even if sailing was the whitest, richest possible hobby he could possibly have.

He joined her at the front of the small skiff, letting the wind take them gently toward the far end of the lake.

"Sorry for yelling at you . . . and saying all that stuff." Even as Sanjiv said it, he knew he wasn't really sorry. But he also knew Ching never apologized first.

Ching shrugged. "Whatever."

"And maybe you . . . are . . . also something . . . ?" Sanjiv started, like a fill-in-the-blank test.

"I am . . . something," she said, stubbornly staring ahead.

"You are sorry . . . for doing something . . . to someone?" Sanjiv prodded.

"Fine," Ching growled. "I definitely did have an ulterior motive. You were right."

"Of course you did." Sanjiv sighed. He hadn't been sure about that at all. He'd just wanted an apology for the constant harassment.

"I, uh." She paused and seemed almost ashamed for a second, which was so spectacularly unlikely that all Sanjiv could do was stare at her, a little worried.

"I know her ghost."

"Addy's?"

"Yep."

"Okay . . ."

Ching nodded once, like this was a perfectly normal and complete explanation.

"And who is her ghost?"

"A fucking asshole."

"So . . . you want me to get with Addy 'cause her ghost is an asshole. This makes perfect sense."

Ching groaned and leaned back. "Her ghost is a bounty hunter I met in the summer of 1808. He pretended to be a . . . an ally. But then he fucking betrayed me and was going to turn me in for the biggest bounty the world had ever seen."

Sanjiv raised an eyebrow. "I thought you never got captured."

"I didn't. I fought his crew off and managed to escape. But while I was recovering from my injuries, my stupid, utterly incapable first mate lost at the goddamn Battle of the Tiger's Mouth and surrendered our fleet."

That last part, Sanjiv had heard before. He'd heard all of Ching's rants about Cheung Po Tsai and Tiger's Mouth and the Portuguese, and till now, he would have said Cheung was Ching's least favorite person ever.

But it seemed this bounty hunter guy was somehow even worse. Ching was still yelling something about Addy's ghost when Sanjiv interrupted.

"So you hate this guy because he injured you—"

"His crew did," Ching said. "He was too cowardly to even face me."

"But why would you want me to talk to Addy, then, if you hate this guy so much?"

"Revenge." And she did look pretty vengeful then, standing tall at the prow of the ship, staring into the middle distance, her mouth set firmly.

Sanjiv nodded slowly. "So what was your plan? For me to ask Addy out and just . . . ?"

She cut her eyes at Sanjiv. "I had a very long list of possibilities. Get her to fall in love with you and then you disappear with all her money. Get her to fall in love with you and then you break her heart into sixty-seven thousand pieces. Get her to fall in love with you and then you throw a burrito at her—"

"All right, all right, I got it," Sanjiv interrupted.

"Hurts more if they love you first," Ching said, which was her usual recommendation for getting back at enemies.

"The pattern's pretty clear."

Ching deigned to give him a half smile at that.

Sanjiv didn't return it. "So . . . revenge. Using my childhood crush. New low."

"Oh, whatever." The smile turned into a scowl. "You're never any fun."

"Well. Maybe you'll manifest for someone more fun next time." The anger that had been simmering down bubbled back over. Freaking vengeful Ching, who couldn't just be on his side and help him out. Always had to be something else going on.

She turned to face him, arms crossed, a curl of dark hair covering one of her eyes. "So you're really still thinking about it?"

"I don't even know why you want to stick around. You've made it pretty clear you think I'm a loser."

Ching snorted. "And I'm trying to give you ways to not be a loser."

"And I always think they are terrible ideas," Sanjiv said. "We're too different."

"Superficial differences." Ching waved him away. "It was the same with my ghost. We fought all the time. He'd always be like, 'Stop pillaging' and 'Please, truly, stop pillaging.'"

"That . . . is not superficial."

"Having a ghost that's similar to you isn't the most important thing."

"Then what is?"

Ching frowned at him, but then just sighed. "So you're fine never learning where the treasure is?"

"Just stop with this treasure bullshit," he said. "I'm not ten anymore. I know you don't have any."

"I have my secrets."

Sanjiv steered the boat through the wind. "Well, even if you did have buried treasure, I'm sure you would have given it to one of your previous humans who were so much cooler and anti-authority. Like that motorcycle gang guy."

"Ah yes, Chen Wentong," Ching said, looking out at the sunset. "You burned too bright."

Sanjiv rolled his eyes and maneuvered the sail around. "How are we even related?"

"I don't know. But I'm just trying to make sure you don't end the line."

He sighed as he turned the boat, sending them back toward the dock. "I just think we should have gotten paired up with other people."

She drifted to the deck and hovered in a sitting position, knees hugged in. She looked really young. "Well, it sounds like you've already made your decision."

Happy birthday . . .

Sanjiv couldn't sleep.

He rolled over. He threw his blanket off. He pulled the blanket half on. He rolled over again. He checked his phone.

Three "happy bday!" notifications from random acquaintances lit up the screen.

12:35 A.M.

It was officially his birthday.

The bedroom was dark, quiet, and cozy, but he knew that wasn't going to be enough to put him to sleep. Not with this weight hanging over him. He slipped out of bed, put on a hoodie and jeans, and crept downstairs. He took care not to wake his parents, even though he didn't really have an official curfew. He'd never given them reason to assign one.

He eased his car out onto the empty street and headed north. He didn't need to look up directions. He'd passed the ghost removal clinic hundreds of times on the way to school, wondering what it would be like the day he finally stopped there. At some point during the drive, Ching silently appeared by his side, floating in the passenger seat. She didn't ask him where they were going. She didn't ask him to turn around. Maybe she was too proud or stubborn. Or maybe she agreed with him that the removal was the best idea.

They had always been a weird pair—there was no arguing that. Different cultures, different values. Sanjiv was sick of being pulled in different directions. He was sick of having to explain his ghost, or feeling self-conscious about her. He wanted to be comfortable in his own skin. He wanted everything to be simpler.

As he neared the clinic, his palms grew sweaty and his breath shortened. This was the right decision. He was sure of it. After all, she had just tried to use him for revenge.

But there was something about Ching's explanation that didn't make sense to him. It was strange that she was so fixated on Addy's ghost, who wasn't even the one who had injured her, when there were so many others she could hold responsible. Or maybe it was the way she talked about the bounty hunter. She didn't just look angry. She looked *sad*. And almost . . . Sanjiv didn't know what heartbreak would look like on Ching's terrifying face, but he kinda thought it might look like thinned lips, shadowed eyes, and a dark stare. Ching was definitely hiding something. And since he'd spent more time with her than anyone else, alive or dead, he had a pretty good idea of what it was.

Hurts more if they love you first.

He jerked the steering wheel to the right, taking a sudden turn off the main road. The wheels screeched in protest.

Ching spun around to look out the window. "Where are you going?"

He pulled into the twenty-four-hour diner parking lot, the hot spot for truckers and kids without fake IDs. "I'm going to talk to Addy."

"But . . . oh." Ching looked at him carefully. "I thought you were mad at me about that."

"Oh, for sure," he said, getting out of the car. "But now I have the perfect excuse to talk to her."

"What excuse?" Her voice sounded hollow.

"Your true feelings about her ghost." He took a moment to appreciate how his door slamming was an excellent punctuation mark.

Ching froze. She was looking almost green now.

"Sanjiv Kumar Reddy, don't do it," Ching ordered with all the captain authority she could muster. "Don't you dare."

He slid past her attempt to stand in his path. "And don't think you can hide in your ghost dimension. If you do, I'll go straight to the de-ghosting center." This was kinda fun. Had he never issued an ultimatum to Ching before?

"*You* . . . are blackmailing *me*?"

"You'll thank me later."

"No, I'm going to haunt you later," she threatened, eyes a little wild and voice too high. "Even if you de-ghost me, I will find a way to haunt you for the rest of your life."

"And that will be different from the last eight years?" Sanjiv asked.

The diner was lit up, glowing a little at the edges, the only bright thing in the darkness.

Until Addy stepped out.

She was waving goodbye to a coworker, her jacket over her uniform. Her hair was curlier than his, which was almost impossible, and kinda short. She wore this purple-y lipstick color and had this way of looking like she was just about to laugh most of the time. She was still Addy from the house three doors down. But she was also Addy from halfway across the country. And he just really wanted to ask her about everything he'd missed in between.

"Hi."

She looked up from her phone, her brown eyes round with surprise. "Oh, uh, hi."

"I don't know if you remember me from when you lived here ten years ago, but I'm Sanjiv. And I think my ghost was in love with your ghost."

"You are the fucking scourge of the earth."

Thankfully this came from Ching, not Addy, though Sanjiv wasn't 100 percent sure if she was talking to him or Addy's ghost.

Addy's eyes went even rounder as she turned to her side, where her ghost presumably floated, and raised her eyebrows. Then she looked back at Sanjiv. Then she finally burst out laughing.

"I knew it," she gasped.

"You did?" Sanjiv asked.

"Well, I knew there was something," she said, then looked to her ghost again. "He was really weird about wanting me not to talk to you. He said we didn't know each other . . ."

"But we do."

"That's what I said when I first saw you." Addy smiled, and Sanjiv was suddenly aware of being *very* sweaty. "But he convinced me that I was combining childhood memories and I was confusing you with someone else."

Sanjiv frowned. "This is complicated."

Addy nodded, glaring at her ghost. "I think we've uncovered a massive ghost conspiracy."

"So you just planned on avoiding me?" Ching shouted at the air, vibrating with fury.

"How do they know each other?" Addy asked, oblivious to Sanjiv's raging ghost. "Who was your relative?"

"Ching Shih. She's a pirate captain from the early nineteenth century. Then after a defeat by the Portuguese—"

"I didn't get defeated!" Ching yelled, and again it was unclear whether this was directed at Sanjiv or not.

"After, uh, her fleet was defeated, she struck a deal and retired and opened a brothel."

"Ooh," Addy said. "That makes sense."

"That is an insulting description of my life!" Ching rounded on Sanjiv.

Sanjiv ignored that. "What makes sense?"

"My ghost was a bounty hunter during the same time period," Addy answered, then winced as her ghost presumably yelled something at Ching.

"You lost me my entire fucking fleet!" Ching screeched.

Sanjiv nodded and diplomatically translated. "My ghost said your ghost's men injured her when they tried to capture her, and her fleet lost an important battle because she hadn't recovered in time to take command."

Addy nodded as her ghost seemed to respond to Ching. "My ghost is saying your ghost invited him onto her ship for a peaceful meeting and left him to die on an island."

"He was planning to betray me!" Ching argued. "I saw the letters!"

"Apparently he was going to betray her," Sanjiv said. "There are letters?"

"Those were from his partner," Addy said, coming to stand next to him so they could both look at the screaming ghosts. "Who thought she was manipulating him."

"Oh yes, of course! I was seducing you for nefarious reasons!" Ching shouted. Sanjiv shivered as Addy shifted nearer to him.

"Well, how was I supposed to know that?" Ching argued after a pause.

Addy leaned her head closer to him, a curl tickling his shoulder as she whispered, "Yeah, they definitely want to bang."

Sanjiv choked on a laugh. "How do ghosts even do that?"

Addy snorted. "I don't know. I'm glad I can't see your ghost, though. I don't want to be picturing that."

"That is a very good point," Sanjiv said, pointedly turning away. Addy did too.

There was a very, very painful pause as they tried to ignore the fighting behind them.

"So." *Oh cool, Sanjiv, good start! Excellently done.*

Sometimes the critical voice in his head sounded *a lot* like Ching.

"Yeah. So how have the past ten years been?" Addy asked.

"You know. School, ghost, the usual." Sanjiv really was trying to think of something interesting to say.

"Yeah. I guess we didn't really get the ghosts we imagined, huh?"

Sanjiv immediately recalled Addy thinking she might get to have her grandmother as a ghost, the one who died when they were five. Addy had really missed her. He hadn't been sure who would be his, but he hadn't ever guessed he had a great-great-great-great-great-great grandmother from China. Who was also a pirate.

"I like Sven, though," Addy quickly added. "He usually isn't as, uh, shouty. He's kinda strict and stuff, but I think he really wants me to be happy."

"Yeah." Sanjiv didn't really know how to respond. Did Ching want him to be happy? Most of the time he would have emphatically said no. But that wasn't quite right. She did try to make him happy, just in the most miserable ways.

"I don't know how people de-ghost. It'd be so strange to not have him around, you know?"

"Mmm." Sanjiv really needed to learn how to talk in full sentences with Addy.

"Hey, so this is weird . . ." Addy wasn't looking at him.

Oh God, this was going even worse than he thought.

"Isn't today your birthday?"

Wait, what? Sanjiv looked up. Addy was pink in the cheeks.

"Uh, yeah, it is." Was this the best feeling anyone had ever had? Sanjiv was pretty sure it was.

"I just remembered we had to move from our house, like, the day before your birthday party. I know it's really weird—"

"No, no, I get it. I remember the party." Which was a lie because he hadn't even attended his own party. He'd refused under the misguided belief that boycotting would somehow get his parents to bring Addy back.

"Oh! Hey!" Addy flicked her eyes back to the diner. "Pie. We have really, really good pumpkin pie. I'm going to get you birthday pie."

"Oh, you don't have to, really—"

She was so pink now. "No, no, I want to. Also, our ghosts are making out, so I feel incredibly uncomfortable and want to go inside and get you pie."

As the door chimed behind her, Sanjiv made the mistake

of turning around. He found Ching contorted into some kind of weird shape, embracing the air, her tongue licking at nothing.

Oh.

God.

Car.

Now.

He slammed the door behind him and turned the radio on. Static. Loud static was good. The best.

After a minute, a throat cleared next to him. "Is everything okay?" Ching asked. "Where did Addy go?"

Sanjiv turned the static down. "She went to get me pumpkin pie. For my birthday."

Ching's eyes lit up. "Mmm, pumpkin, your favorite."

"I hope you aren't going to stare at me while I eat that too."

"No, I'll have to miss this one," Ching said, smiling a little forlornly. "I should get back to Sven. I don't know when I'll talk to him again."

Sanjiv shrugged. "The next time I see Addy, I assume."

Ching stared at him, speechless. But speech wasn't really necessary. He knew her well enough to know what her silence meant.

"If I could, I'd buy you a lot of booze right now," Ching finally said.

"That's fine," Sanjiv replied. "Though if you really want to do something for me, you could tell me where your mysterious treasure is."

The diner door chimed as Addy made her way out and toward the car.

Ching leaned in closer to Sanjiv. "She really likes you; I wasn't lying about that. You know why? Because you're the treasure."

He stared at her.

She stared back at him.

"I hate you."

Ching gave him a wink as she floated out of the car. "I hate you too."

Your Life Matters

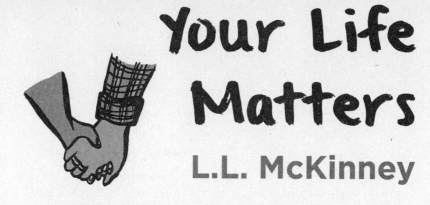

L.L. McKinney

Candace wasn't in the mood to have this fight again. She kept her attention on the television while the weatherman warned about thunderstorms tonight leading into tomorrow, trying to ignore Ari as the other girl wore a path into the carpet.

"And you couldn't just leave it alone, could you?" Ari tugged at her blonde ponytail as she paced back and forth. Her pale cheeks were flushed red, making the freckles along her nose stand out. Candace liked to kiss those freckles so that Ari's face scrunched adorably. Instead, right now, Ari's face was all fire and fury. Still cute, though.

"I didn't even say anything." Candace turned up the volume as some Black man started talking about sports.

"The shirt said it for you!" Ari snatched the remote and hit mute, then flung it at the other end of the couch. It bounced off a throw pillow and thudded against the floor.

Irritation started to buzz between Candace's ears. "And what's wrong with what it says?" She folded her arms across her chest, right beneath where the white letters spelled #BlackLivesMatter along the blue material.

"Nothing!" Ari flung her hands into the air, then pressed them to her face. "Nothing is wrong with it."

"But?" Candace coaxed.

"But . . ." Ari sighed and peeked through her fingers. "I've told you how my dad is."

And she had. Ari had lamented several times about dealing with her very white, very conservative cop father who "wasn't racist" but always wanted to hear both sides of "these things," thought all lives mattered, and wished athletes would leave politics out of sports.

"That's the definition of *racist*, you realize," Candace had said one night while they studied for some test. She and Ari had been talking for a minute, and the topic of telling their families had come up. Better to say something before someone walked in while hands were up shirts, skirts, or wherever else instead of flipping through textbooks.

"Yeah, *I* know." Ari had puffed out her cheeks and shaken her head. "But trying to tell him is like talking to a brick wall. A brick wall that lives in my house and pays the bills and makes the rules."

Candace smirked. "It's cool. I'm dating you, not your pops." She had pulled Ari into her arms and nestled into the couch with her.

Ari had woven their fingers together, white skin against dark brown. "Lucky me."

They'd fallen asleep on that couch. The same couch Candace now slouched against almost two years after that night. Two years of love, laughter, and arguments, usually about Mr. White.

"Tonight was supposed to be perfect." Ari went back to pacing. "I made his favorite dinner. I made your favorite dessert. We were going to talk and get along and he'd like you and we'd ride off to college together this fall with his blessing."

"Uh-huh." Candace gently smoothed a hand over her braids, still very sensitive and somewhat slick from where her stylist had finished just in time for her to make it to Ari's for dinner. "That's why I wore it. I wanted him to know the real me, to like the real me." Even if she thought that last part would be a bit of a stretch. "What, you want me to sanitize parts of myself for him?"

Ari whirled around. Her green eyes sparkled with anger. Her lips pursed. "Of course not!"

"Want me to act like I don't give a damn about what's happening in the world? That his COPS ARE PEOPLE TOO bumper sticker doesn't piss me off every time I see it?" Heat filled Candace's face.

"No."

"That I don't notice the way he acts when he knows you're with me, or coming over here?" They spent a lot of time at Candace's house because her parents were just fine with their relationship. Mr. White . . . had to warm up to it. "That he tells you to be careful on 'that side of town'?"

"Candy—"

"Want me to put on a show?" Candace forced a jovial lilt into her tone. "Why, I'll do whatever ya wan'! I'll dance for ya paw, I sure will, yessuh!" Her head bobbed.

"Stop!" Tears sprang to Ari's eyes. "I don't want you to do that, I just . . ." She shook her head, swiping at her cheeks. "You don't get what it's like. Listening to some of the things he says. Trying to talk to him about how messed up it is. *Knowing* he's not a bad person, but . . ." Ari trailed off, sniffling.

Something tugged at the center of Candace's chest, tightening and twisting. She hated seeing Ari cry, mostly because she knew it was due to anger and not sadness. But she also knew this situation wasn't her fault. She wasn't the one who had turned the conversation toward the latest police shooting and how dangerous it was to walk the streets with a badge these days. She wasn't the one who had talked about how "certain people" needed to learn how to protest peacefully or their message would just go on being ignored.

That was when Candace had asked who he'd voted for. And Ari had dropped the salad bowl.

". . . he wasn't like this before the divorce." Ari sniffed.

Candace sighed. "He probably just didn't show i—" Something on the TV caught her attention. "Wait a sec." She dove for the other end of the couch, snatched up the remote, and turned the volume back up.

Still sniffling, Ari faced the TV. "What is it?"

"I don't know." Candace hit rewind, stopping at the point where BREAKING NEWS swept across the screen.

A white woman looked into the camera. "A story is developing in Central Square, where a third night of protests have begun to escalate. The protests are in response to the officer-involved shooting that resulted in the death of an African American man Wednesday of last week. We now go live to Mark Ruiz, who is on the ground. Mark, what's it look like out there?"

The screen shifted to a somewhat jostled vantage of Central Square at dusk. Cloudy skies bloated with the last rays of sunlight could be glimpsed between the buildings. At the center of the screen, a man with sandy skin and wide brown eyes addressed the camera. "Sara, what started as a peaceful protest against the latest shooting of an unarmed Black man has escalated in a few pocket areas of the square. Three storefront windows have been shattered, no looting has been reported, and police are on the scene with riot gear and orders for the crowd to disperse."

Candace didn't hear what he said after that. She didn't have to in order to know what came next. She pushed to her feet, reaching for her hoodie. "I gotta go."

"I know." Ari sounded defeated. She wiped at her nose, her face still red.

Candace paused in gathering her things and leaned in to

press a kiss to those freckles. She smirked as Ari scrunched her face. "Cover for me?"

"Of course." Ari leaned in and pressed their lips together. The kiss was soft and warm, and sent a hot, fluttery feeling dancing through Candace. It settled in her stomach by the time they broke apart. "One life?" Candace murmured.

"One love," Ari replied.

Candace stole a brief second kiss before moving over to the window. She shoved it open and slipped out onto the slightly slanted overhang below. Thankfully a big tree, she didn't know what kind, hid her bedroom window from view.

With a deep breath, she pushed into a leap. Gravity took hold of her but didn't pull her down. Instead she shot toward the sky, a blur to anyone standing below. When she was certain she was high enough that no one would be able to tell who she was, she turned and headed for the square.

Wind licked her face and tugged at her clothes and braids. It clapped at her ears in a low whoosh. Man, she loved flying. Up here, it was like nothing could touch her. None of the problems on the ground were tall enough to reach her. Sometimes she just picked a direction and went for hours. It was the best feeling in the world, but she couldn't get lost in that now; she had a job to do.

She tugged a bud from her pocket and pressed it into her right ear. A few taps from her phone, and she was dialed into a local news station.

"Police in riot gear have arrived on the scene and are ordering protesters to disperse," Sara the newslady drawled. "After last night's riots, and with the curfew looming, there's no telling which way things could go."

Oh yes, there was. These things always went one way when Black people were trying to get justice: bad. And after last night, they were bound to get worse.

"With tensions rising, locals are hoping to catch a glimpse of the latest sensation to hit our fair city: Freefall, the super-powered hero who's been spotted several times over the past year, but has made an almost nightly appearance during the worst of the riots."

That's my cue. Candace dove toward a low building, push-ing her speed and pulling up to a stop just before slamming into the roof. She lowered herself to stand, then hurried to pull out a backpack hidden in a nearby vent. A quick outfit change, and she stood in the suit she and Ari had come up with together last year. Black with gray accents, formfitting, made from a wet suit and other materials. It was completed with combat boots and a hood with white patches for the eyes and a shock of white "hair" at the crown. Her mouth was the only visible part of her face, concealing her identity. Ari was half of the genius behind the design. Turns out there were benefits to being students at one of the country's fanci-est tech schools.

Shoving her phone into a zipper pocket on her thigh, Candace took off once more, pushing into the air. She shot toward the square, the lights of the city dancing below. The distant flash of red and blue and the boom of a voice over a loudspeaker were like a beacon in the night, calling out the coming troubles.

There was a sudden rise in shouting and the blast of gas canisters being fired. A hazy gray billow rose into the air, fol-lowed by panicked and pained screams.

Candace drew in a deep breath and went into a dive. She hit the ground in a crouch, the wind rushing outward. Sur-prised shouts went up from the advancing officers, followed by orders to get on the ground. She ignored them, throw-ing her arms out as she began to spin. Faster and faster she went, the roar of the wind loud in her ears. The material of her costume protected her from the worst of the effects, and soon the cloud began to rise. So did she, still spinning, aiming it up and away, to be carried off and diluted by the slipstream.

Somewhat dizzy and a little achy, she slowed, panting as she finally took a breath.

"It's her!" someone shouted from below.

"Freefall!" another person cried.

A smattering of cheers rose around her.

"You, in . . . in the air," someone on a loudspeaker started. They didn't sound at all confident. "Come . . . come down? Come down with your hands up!"

Candace couldn't help but snicker when what sounded like a small scuffle broke out as someone fought to take over. She turned to go just as there was a screech and a different voice rumbled.

"Descend or we will open fire."

She froze. She knew that voice. Whirling, she stared down at the gathering of officers, her gaze homing in on the one with the megaphone. She knew those green eyes; she stared into them often. Those were Ari's eyes. Or, at least where she'd gotten them.

Mr. White stood amidst the cops, his jaw set, his expression thunderous.

"You have until the count of three. One." He lifted a hand. The officers lifted their guns.

Fear fluttered to life in Candace's chest. She could fly away, but would she be fast enough? And why the hell did they want to shoot her? She hadn't done anything to them, just kept 'em from hurting the people.

"Two." His voice echoed in the night. Around them people had stopped and started shouting, pointing, calling out for them to leave her alone.

"Th—"

BOOM!

The front of one of the nearby buildings erupted. A cloud of fire and glass burst into the air. Shards rained down on screaming pedestrians, concrete chunks pelted bystanders. Everyone who hadn't dropped to the ground ran. Candace, who'd been sent tumbling through the air, righted herself. Her ears rang, and her whole body felt like she'd hit a brick wall. Shaking off the feeling of someone holding her head under water, she searched the newborn chaos for signs of Mr. White. Nothing. She couldn't see him. "Shit . . ." A shrill beep sounded in her ear.

"There you are!" Candace called.

"Sorry, sorry!" Ari panted over the device in Candace's ear. "Had to run interference with your folks. How're things out there?"

"Wild," Candace murmured as she hovered as close as she dared to the building for a better look. "First National on Elm just exploded."

"Exploded?" Ari sounded as disbelieving as Candace felt, even as she faced the inferno.

"Kaboom. Yeah. Oh, that was after your pops tried to kill me." She looked at the officers, who seemed to have forgotten all about her as they rushed to get injured bystanders to safety. Still no sign of Mr. White.

"W-what?" Ari tripped over the word. "Is . . . are you both okay?!"

"Fine," Candace grumbled. "I'll explain later. I got a situation." She dropped to the ground, where she spied a few people trying to lift a stone slab off an old white woman. Waving them aside, she gripped the edge of the concrete, and lifted. Her muscles strained but held, burning slightly as she hauled the slab up high enough for the others to help pull the woman out. With a grunt, she let the slab drop once everyone was clear.

"Take her to get medical attention!" Candace called above the roar of flames and the scream of approaching sirens.

The woman sobbed a thank-you as she was carried off.

Candace whirled to face the building. "Are there people inside?" She searched the giant panes for any signs of life.

The sound of Ari's fingers flying over keys with swift clacks filled Candace's ears. Not only did her girlfriend help design her suit, after finding out she was, y'know, "different," Ari was often the one thing that stood between Candace getting caught or killed, feeding her information pulled from various sources and information hubs. Ari's methods weren't exactly legal, but she knew what she was doing to cover her ass. She was the Guy in the chair. Well, Gal.

"No residences. It's all event spaces the owner rents out for fancy affairs. Usually just the bank is occupied, and that's during business hours."

"Good." Relief pulsed through Candace. She didn't see anyone in trouble. What she did notice was how the third, fourth, and fifth stories were ablaze, but not the first. "I don't think this was an accident."

"Me neither," Ari murmured. "There've been other explosions like this one across the country. All banks."

"What can you tell me?"

"Give me two seconds."

Candace approached the building, mindful of the blaze above. She narrowed her eyes, trying to see into the dark lobby.

"Apparently a few instances where there have been riots over the past handful of years, from protests to rowdy sports fans, some banks were seemingly caught in the destruction. It's not until after everything has calmed down that authorities realize it was a job. They don't have anything to go on, what with most of the evidence being burned to a crisp."

Candace froze when something shifted farther into the darkness of the building. Someone was definitely in there—a burglar or someone working late who might be about to walk into some serious shit.

"Someone's inside. They might be in trouble."

"Can you wait for backup?" Ari asked.

Candace threw a glance over her shoulder. The street was still chaos, officers now trying to get the barriers they'd erected to corral protesters out of the way for approaching emergency response.

"If they need help, I'm it." Taking a slow breath, Candace slipped into the building, quick and quiet. She moved with her hands out, feeling along the tables and dividers meant to guide lines of customers. The deeper she went, the darker things grew, even with the blaze of the fire outside.

"I can't see," she whispered. *This damn hood.* She and Ari were in the process of designing a new one, that would let her see in low visibility situations exactly like this one, but it was still a prototype. Candace pushed the hood from her head, taking a slow breath as the world broke fresh against her senses. It was a risk—someone might see her face—but better than walking into an ambush or the barrel of a gun.

"Be careful, babe." Ari's voice drifted into her ear. "Emergency response is trying to get through, but it's a mess out there."

"Copy." Candace crept deeper into the building. She moved as fast as she dared, keeping an ear out for groans or cracks or other signs of structural stress as an inferno blazed not two stories above her head. The air was hot and thick. A faint haze of smoke crawled along the ceiling. Parts of the building creaked and moaned, no doubt ready to cave in.

She froze when someone yelped in pain just ahead, in a

side area where the vault was likely located. With a slow breath, she slipped closer. Voices filtered through the air.

"We can't just shoot a cop, man."

"We can't just leave him, either."

"He knows too much."

There was a bang and a crash in another room.

"Whatever we do, better do it before this place comes down on top of us."

"P-please," a familiar voice begged. Ari's dad.

"Shit," Candace whispered.

"What?" Ari asked.

She hesitated. "It's the thieves. They got a hostage. Sounds like your pop."

Ari squeaked and Candace winced.

"You have to do something!" Ari shouted.

"I know!"

"Please, Candy, he's n—"

Candace tugged the bud from her ear. She couldn't focus with Ari freaking out in her head.

It sounded like three perps. Maybe four. She could take four assholes. But they had guns . . . Bulletproof she was not. But this was Ari's dad. She had to try! Even if his headass didn't think the best of her. She tugged her hood back on, her vision having adjusted to the gloom.

"I-I was just searching for anyone who might be hurt! I haven't seen your faces," Mr. White went on.

Candace pressed the bud back in her ear to the sound of Ari demanding to know what was going on, her voice thick with tears.

"Babe, I need you—*he* needs you—to focus."

Ari went silent except for a few sniffles. She was probably nodding even though Candace couldn't see her. "Can you help him?" Her words escaped in a whimper.

"They got guns. I don't think I can do anything."

"Oh God . . ."

"Let the cops know what's going on in here. One of theirs is in tr—"

"Just shoot him," one of the thieves finally grunted.

Candace shifted to dart forward.

"Wait!" a second thug hissed.

Candace nearly toppled over as she went still.

"Don't be stupid, man. Bad enough we're leaving a body, but a bullet will mean an investigation. Knock him out and let the fire handle things."

"No, no!"

There was a scuffle, along with groans as blows landed.

"Backup is on the way. What's happening?" Ari asked. "Candy? Candy!"

"Break his leg so he can't get out."

She had to act now, while they were busy. Candace took a quick breath, then pushed forward. She came around the wall and crashed into the first upright body she saw. She felt bone break under the force of her blow. The guy went flying as he cried out, crashed into a wall, and fell still.

His buddies spun with shouts of surprise. She whirled and drove her knee into the nearest guy's gut. He made a huffing sound like a wounded dog and dropped to his knees, as she twisted into a kick. Her boot hit the side of his head, and he hit the ground.

The last guy standing backpedaled, gun lifted. "Y-you!"

"Me." Candace eyed the weapon, her body tense, her muscles singing, her nerves jumping. This was it.

The guy backed away. His hand shook hard enough for Candace to notice in the darkness. He aimed the gun at Mr. White, then at her, back and forth.

"You don't wanna do this," she cautioned.

Above them the ceiling groaned. Something smashed into it from above.

Sweat rolled down the back of Candace's neck. It soaked into the fabric stretched across her face. *Damn, it's hot in here.*

"Your boys are down, the building could collapse, backup is on the way."

"What's happening?" Ari asked.

Candace ignored her. "If you want out, you better go now."

The thief gripped the gun with both hands. Movement shifted in Candace's peripheral vision. Mr. White groaned. The thug aimed at him.

"No!" Candace dove.

POW.

The ceiling gave with a sharp snap and a howling crackle. Pain danced up Candace's arm, white hot. Flame rained down on her. Bits of stone and twisted metal battered her body. She shifted to shield Mr. White while Ari screamed.

"Candace! CANDACE!"

Heat and light washed over everything.

Then it all went black.

Beep . . . beep . . . beep . . . beep . . .

Candace stared at the monitor on the wall across from where she sat in what had to be one of the most uncomfortable chairs ever conceived. She stretched carefully, minding her injured shoulder—she could scratch "bullet wound" off her Official Hero list—now that she had a little room, with Ari having made a run to the vending machine.

Mr. White lay against the bed, hooked to machines that kept an eye on his vitals and pumped him full of medications and fluids. The explosion had been three days ago, and the doctors said if he didn't wake up soon, he may not wake up at all. That didn't sound right, but Candace wasn't in the mood to argue with "professionals." Ari did enough of that for the both of them.

Poor Ari. She'd barely slept, ate only when Candace was around to make her—like now—and probably wouldn't have showered if Candace's folks hadn't been nice enough to get her a room at the hotel across the street.

Candace pulled out her phone to check on updates. Those two dudes she'd knocked out had been arrested and were snitching like it was going out of style. Soon the third guy would be in custody, but he was on the run.

Good. Hope they bust his ass for shooting me.

"Ari?" a voice rasped.

Candace lowered her phone and spotted Mr. White glancing around all glassy-eyed.

She sent a quick text—He's up—to Ari and set her phone aside. "She's getting food."

He snapped his attention to her and stared.

For several seconds, nothing happened, save the faint beeping of the monitor as Candace held his gaze.

"Why'd you do it?" he finally asked.

"Do what?"

He pursed his lips, looked to the door, then back to her. His attention went to her shoulder and the sling.

She arched an eyebrow. "Fell down some stairs."

He snorted a laugh that ended in a cough. She shifted forward to hold out a glass of water. He drank the whole thing in slow pulls, then settled against the pillows.

"It was you," he mumbled. "In the bank."

"I don't know what you're talkin' 'bout."

"You saved my life. After I almost ordered my officers to fire on you."

Candace went quiet. There was no point in denying it, but she wasn't going to admit to anything just yet.

"Those men were going to shoot me or beat me and leave me to burn." He stared at the ceiling, his eyes misty, his lips trembling.

"Sounds like you had a rough night."

"You stopped them." His eyes found her again.

"Daddy!" Ari burst through the door and rushed over to the side of her father's bed. A nurse came in behind her and started checking the machines.

Mr. White hugged his daughter as they exchanged a tearful greeting, with all the "I love yous," and "I was worried," and "thank goodness," and so on.

Ari drew back to let the nurse work and flashed a wide smile, which Candace returned. When the nurse finished she left Mr. White with orders to try and get some more water down, then they'd move to broth. She'd be back with some medications and to check on him shortly.

He watched the nurse go before looking back at Candace. She watched him watching her. Her thumb played across Ari's fingers where she held her hand.

Ari glanced between them, chewing at her lower lip. "Daddy, it—"

"Thank you," he murmured, dropping his gaze.

The look of surprise that moved across Ari's face mirrored the shock that jolted through Candace.

"You didn't have to do what you did." He swallowed thickly. "You had every right not to, but . . ."

Candace felt a swell of sympathy for the man. Not a big one—he was still a racist asshole—but it was there. He seemed to be having some sort of enlightening experience at the moment, plus, he was her boo's dad. Her racist asshole dad.

"Well, Mr. White, your life matters."

His head snapped up. He and Ari stared at Candace with those wide, matching green eyes. He went white. Ari went red.

Candace pushed to her feet. "I know that. I knew it when I jumped in front of you."

Mr. White's jaw tightened.

"I knew it, even though I also knew how you felt about Black lives mattering."

"Candy," Ari started, but her dad gestured for her to be quiet.

"Even though you told your boys to shoot me like some big-ass bird. Your life has always mattered. I just want mine, and the lives of people like me, to matter too."

Clearing his throat, Mr. White nodded tightly. "I'm s-sorry it took you . . . jumping in front of a bullet for me to realize what should've been clear. You're a hero."

"Yeah. But there are plenty of normal Black folk out there. Their lives matter too. What I did doesn't make me special or better than them, if that's what you think."

He was clearly uncomfortable with the current conversation. "Ari has been talking about it for some time, being a good alline."

"Ally, Dad."

"Yes. And I . . . I'm an old fool. And I . . . hope you can accept this old fool's apology."

Ari smiled then, wiping at her face and sniffling. Girl was such a crybaby.

"I accept. *If* you do more than say you're sorry. If you start acting like my life matters. Like Black lives matter. *If* you listen to Ari when she talks about this stuff. I mean really listen. *If* you show me you *mean* you're sorry."

He nodded again, his jaw tight. Probably didn't like the ifs, but Candace didn't give two good goddamns. "And if you promise not to tell anyone what happened."

His brow furrowed. "What did happen?"

"As far as anyone is aware," Ari said, "Candace was at the

protest. Turns out she was close to the bank and caught the thief's stray shot."

"Some bystanders saw Freefall pull you and a couple other guys out of the building." Candace smirked. "I missed the whole thing since I was being hauled away to get help."

"Huh . . ." Mr. White rubbed the side of his head. "It's best if my recollection of the events faded. From a bump on the head."

"It's best." Ari kissed her dad's forehead. "Besides, even if you told anyone, they probably wouldn't believe you anyway. Candace was with me at the protest. I brought her to the hospital, so it'd be your word against ours, and I'd gladly say you were lying."

Candace felt a swell of something warm and fuzzy as Ari talked. Damn, her bae was good. And if anything, this let her know Ari was fully on her side.

Mr. White nodded, swallowing again. "Your secret is safe with me, Candace."

"Glad to hear it. Ari says you're a good guy, Mr. White. I'd like to believe that." Her phone buzzed, and she glanced at the screen. A message from her mom said she was out front. "My ride's here. I need to get going."

Ari walked her to the door and pulled her in gently for a soft, slow kiss. "Call me?"

"Soon as I'm home." Candace turned to go but drew up short when Mr. White called her name. She glanced over her shoulder, eyebrow arched.

"I look forward to working with you. If you get my meaning."

Candace chuckled and shook her head. She hadn't planned on being anyone's Batman, but if Freefall was going to do this superhero thing for serious? She'd need someone on the inside looking out for her.

"You got my back now, Mr. White?"

"I owe you, and I aim to repay."

"You wanna repay me? Help my people. Listen to your daughter. Listen to *us*."

A look crossed his face, but he set his jaw and nodded curtly.

"See you on the protest line, Mr. White." She winked at Ari and let the door fall shut behind her. Her phone buzzed again as she reached the elevator. A text from Ari.

Thank you.

Candace tapped out a reply: He's still got some work to do.

Ari responded: We both do. ♥

Out in the car, Candace's mom kissed her cheek in greeting. "Any change?"

"Maybe." Candace couldn't help the smile that broke over her face. "We'll see."

Starlight and Moondust

Lori M. Lee

According to the locals of Little Nova, a witch lived in their woods. They said she brewed potions, cursed trespassers, and grew her garden on the bones of sacrifices.

Hlee Khue knew better, though. Niam Tais wasn't a witch; she was a shaman.

Every Wednesday and Friday, Hlee took the trail that wound through the woods north of town. The trail eventually led to a small house guarded by lawn sculptures and a brood of chickens, where Hlee delivered a hearty dinner prepared by her mom, with plenty left over for the next day's lunch. It was the duty of the tiny Hmong community in Little Nova to look out for Niam Tais, as the woman lived alone with no children to care for her.

Niam Tais had lost her father and brother in the war and then her mother to sickness in the jungles of Southeast Asia. The history of tragedy and frantic escape was the shared story of all refugees. But how Niam Tais came to be here, in Little Nova, was a different kind of story entirely.

When Niam Tais was a young woman, she'd woken from her bed, driven from the sweat-damp sheets by the humidity and the bright face of the moon through the window of her family's hut. She'd wandered down to the riverbank and fallen asleep at its shore to the gentle shushing of the water.

The next morning, she brushed moondust from the creases of her clothes as her thoughts grasped for the vestiges of a dream about a man in shining robes and a string of white stones against his brow.

It was a sign, the village elder decided, that she'd been called by the spirits to the revered duties of a shaman.

Some years later, after the war had displaced her halfway around the world, she fell asleep with the moonlight full against the backs of her eyelids and dreamed again of the Moon Emperor. In the dream, he shot an arrow across the night sky, a streak of brilliant silver, and beckoned her to retrieve it. As in her childhood, she'd obeyed the calling and ended up in the sleepy town of Little Nova.

What Niam Tais did after that wasn't clear, and Hlee had never been satisfied by the open ending. Instead, she couldn't help but wonder if the story hadn't yet found its conclusion.

She shifted her backpack, the Tupperware inside clacking together, and kicked at a pine cone lying in her path. On any given day, Little Nova was a quiet town, the stillness broken only by the grinding roar of old cars. In the woods, though, the silence took on a presence all its own, a companion that Hlee always welcomed.

As she jumped over a narrow brook nearly dried out from the summer heat, laughter flitted through the trees. She paused, her skin prickling as the wind slid warm fingers against her neck. The laughter came again, closer this time, along with the snap of twigs beneath heavy feet. Hunching her shoulders, she lowered her head and continued walking more quickly.

"Hlee?"

She winced and glanced toward the voice. Emilia Hart stood some distance away, her blonde hair slightly mussed.

Her boyfriend—Hlee thought his name might be Sam—stood behind her, arm draped over her bare shoulders, his fingers playing with the strap of her pink tank top.

"Were you *spying* on us?" she asked, glossy lips curling, her words sharp with laughter.

Hlee's face went hot. She stared hard at her worn gray sneakers, wishing Emilia would stop talking so Hlee wouldn't feel like she was fleeing. "No," she mumbled. "I'm just . . ." She gestured to the trail.

"Oh, *her*," Emilia said. "Hey, Sam, you remember when Rina lost her dog?"

Hlee walked faster, fingers clutched tight around her backpack straps. But the silence that had only moments ago been her friend carried the snide words straight to her ears.

"She found bones washed up down the brook a couple months ago, and *she* thinks the witch probably kidnapped it for one of her sacrifices."

That's a lie, Hlee thought, teeth clenched tight.

"You're not hiding someone's pet in your backpack, are you, Hlee?" she called. "Are you her delivery service?"

Their laughter rang through her thoughts long after she'd left them behind. Her hands balled into fists as her heart raced, nostrils flaring with every furious breath.

Hlee had begged her parents to move for years, but they liked Little Nova. They liked the size and the distance from larger cities. The trees, crowned by the peaks of distant mountains, reminded them a little of the country they'd left behind. So Hlee said nothing, simmering in her resentment.

Anything she said in defense of Niam Tais would be turned against her, and the last thing she wanted was to call more attention to herself. It was better to try to be invisible than to invite ridicule for things she couldn't control.

Ahead, Niam Tais's house materialized from behind the

trees. It was small and leaned a bit to one side. The paint had long since peeled from the door and window frames, exposing old wood that curled away from the walls. Chickens roamed the yard, their coop visible behind a vibrant garden that sat to the right of the house.

Above the door hung a chipped sign that said NYOB ZOO. *Welcome.* The sight of it made Hlee's arms vibrate with renewed anger. Niam Tais embraced what and who she was and made no apologies for it, but Hlee didn't have the same confidence. Sometimes she wished Niam Tais would be less flagrantly different, given the way she reflected on the rest of the Hmong community and on Hlee.

She stalked past the garden, scattering the chickens, who squawked at her intrusion. The pungent aroma of cilantro, green onions, and lemongrass assaulted her nostrils. Once the house was out of sight, she pressed her back against a tree and tossed her backpack into the dirt.

She sank to the soft earth, her hair snagging against rivets of bark that tugged sharply at her scalp. Although the sun had only just begun to set, the moon was already visible through the branches. It was nearly full, milky and stark against the purpling sky.

Because she was looking up, she saw the exact moment when a shock of silver streaked through the sky, brief and brilliant. Her eyes widened. Before she'd even consciously decided, she made a wish.

Please . . . please let me find where I belong. There has to be more than this.

She felt instantly like an idiot. *Kids* made wishes on falling stars, not a sixteen-year-old who knew better. Her mom had once told her that falling stars were the tears of the Moon Emperor, whose daughter had been taken beneath the sea as a bride for the Serpent God. Every night, the Moon Emperor sat on the water's surface and peered down in the hopes of glimpsing his lost daughter.

That was why you couldn't point at the moon. The Moon Emperor regarded it as an accusation. In retribution, he descended from his obsidian throne astride his rainbow-scaled dragon and slashed at your ear as you slept.

Hlee knew, of course, that the story wasn't the least bit true. Hmong folktales were passed down orally from parent to child, sibling to sibling, embellished or altered depending on who told it. But the warning was so ingrained that she still couldn't bring herself to point at the stupid thing. She'd made the mistake of telling a classmate that once. He'd mocked her for months by shouting her name as he clutched his ear and pointed at the sky.

It was infuriating, really. What made wishing on a falling star any less ridiculous than not pointing at the moon? They were equally unlikely, equally childish. The only difference was the culture each belief came from, which, she supposed, made all the difference to some people.

She sighed and bent to retrieve her backpack. The Tupperware inside clanked dully. She swore, guilt chasing away the last of her anger. It wasn't Niam Tais's fault that people like Emilia were ignorant and hateful, and the only thing her brooding had accomplished was to keep Niam Tais waiting for her dinner.

The next day, Hlee's mother spent the entire morning on the phone with Niam Tais. Hlee waited anxiously to see if she'd be scolded for the night before. But when her mother at last came into her bedroom, it was only to say she'd volunteered Hlee to keep Niam Tais's new guest company.

Hlee still felt guilty enough not to argue. When she'd at last shown up on Niam Tais's doorstep with the food gone cold in the Tupperware, Niam Tais had been so relieved. She'd worried that something had happened to Hlee in the woods, which made Hlee feel like a complete heel.

When she reached Niam Tais's house again, she spotted the guest immediately. He sat out front, pale hair gleaming beneath the midday sun.

It wasn't unusual for Niam Tais to have guests. Towns-folk showed up regularly to purchase fresh vegetables and her various herbal remedies. Distant relatives sometimes visited for the weekend.

But the boy sitting on Niam Tais's favorite wicker stool was a white teenager. Hlee had been expecting an older Hmong woman, like the aunt who'd stayed with Niam Tais a few months ago. The boy was sawing at a wooden sculpture with a small knife. Splinters of wood lay scattered around his shoes.

As she approached, his gaze lifted. For the briefest of moments, his eyes flashed silver, like the sudden flare of a fall-ing star. Then she was looking into bright gray eyes framed by lashes so pale that they could have been frosted in white.

"Hi," he said, mouth stretching into a broad smile. He brushed flecks of dirt and wood off his jeans. "You must be Hlee."

"Yeaaah," she replied, uncertain. She gave him an awk-ward hip-level wave and then hurried past him into the house.

Aside from the bathroom and the altar room, the house was mostly one large space. A bed took up the corner, piled with blankets. Hlee recognized her mom's embroidery among the pillows. A large paj ntaub hung on one wall, the story cloth depicting figures with black hair and traditional Hmong clothing in careful, skilled stitches. Beneath it sat an enormous cube of a television that was probably several decades old.

Niam Tais stood at the kitchen counter, bent over a heavy stone mortar and wielding a pestle the size of a small baseball bat. Crumpled sheets of old newspapers crowded the countertop, nestling bunches of dried herbs.

"Tuaj los?" the woman said in greeting, a smile splitting her brown face. Niam Tais was a tiny woman, barely five feet, with dark hair that had just begun to gray pulled back into a messy bun.

Her diminutive size was deceiving, though. A huge cleaver rested in a butcher block at the far side of the counter, and Hlee had seen her take apart a pig carcass with terrifying efficiency. Hlee didn't doubt the woman could take care of herself, despite the way the Hmong elders clucked in disapproval at Niam Tais's choice to remain unmarried.

Although Hlee understood Hmong well enough, she couldn't really speak it herself. Niam Tais was the same, except with English. So Hlee stood awkwardly inside the door as she struggled to find the right words to ask about the boy outside. Frustration pressed at her temples as the language eluded her.

Giving up, she asked in English instead, and they managed to piece together enough of a conversation for Hlee to gather that the boy was the son of a friend.

"Can I help?" Hlee gestured to the countertop and the array of herbs.

Niam Tais shook her head, instead pointing to the table where a tray of football-shaped sweet buns waited, steaming faintly. "Koj puas tshaib plab? Los noj. Saib seb nws puas xav noj ib qho."

With a polite nod, Hlee wrapped a warm bun with a napkin and grabbed a second for the boy outside. He was cutting ineffectually at the sculpture again, the slight curve of his mouth indicating he wasn't worried about his lack of skill.

The sculpture in question was supposed to be a crane, its slender neck extended.

"Um, Niam Tais was wondering if you wanted one," she said as he looked up again. The genuine *joy* in his face as he took the proffered sweet bun made her insides squirm.

"Thanks." He took an enormous bite. His eyes fluttered shut, the pleasure in his expression so acute that it was almost indecent.

Her face went hot, and she looked away. Nearby, a chicken perched on the stone cap of a large mushroom sculpture. She shooed the bird away and took its place on the mushroom.

"I'm Argus," he said between bites.

Making small talk wasn't a talent she possessed, so she said nothing. Instead, she watched the chickens putter about the yard as she ate through the middle of the sweet bun, where it was stuffed with vibrant green pandan jelly.

Argus shoved the last of the bread into his mouth, swallowed thickly, and asked, "So what's your story?"

Brushing crumbs off her fingertips, Hlee raised one eyebrow and repeated, "My story? Like . . . where'd I come from?"

She hated that question. *Where are you from?* It immediately set her apart, made her something *other*. Her parents had lived in Boston when they had her, and then moved to Little Nova when she was two. Hlee was Hmong, but that didn't mean she wasn't also completely American.

"Not necessarily," he said. "Where you're from and what your story is can be two completely separate things."

She didn't know what he meant, so she shrugged one shoulder. He seemed not to mind, because he retrieved the knife from the dirt and held it out, handle first.

She shook her head. "I'll ruin it."

"Not any more than I already have." He grinned. "If it

makes you feel better, she said I could resculpt it however I wanted."

Niam Tais rarely let anyone touch her mismatched lawn sculptures. Hlee supposed that if the woman had welcomed this boy into her home, he couldn't be anywhere near as bad as the kids in Little Nova. She rose from the mushroom cap, and they swapped seats.

"Niam Tais has been chipping away at this thing for years," she said, running her fingers along the jagged inden-tations left by Argus.

"Yeah, I think she just wanted to keep me from doing any more damage in there," he said. His ears turned pink as he grimaced. "I threw out a bunch of the bark shavings she'd left on her counter."

Hlee's eyes went wide. "Those are her medicines. She sells those."

He winced, his smile self-deprecating. "I didn't know! I thought I was helping to clean up. She put me outside with the chickens."

To her complete surprise, Hlee dropped her head back and laughed.

For the next few days, Hlee and Argus took turns hacking at the sculpture in between feeding the chickens, weeding the garden, and sweeping the house. Once Niam Tais finished grinding all the herbs into a fine powder, she set Argus and Hlee to helping her partition, bag, and label them for sale. The general store set out Niam Tais's home remedies in a cute wicker basket beside the cash register, in between the lip balms and lighters.

For the better part of her life, Hlee had done everything with her cousin. After her aunt's family moved away, they texted and called each other on weekends, but it wasn't the same. She hated to admit it, but having someone to hang out with again wasn't terrible.

It helped that Argus was easy to talk to, partly because he took genuine delight in everything, even the most menial of chores, but mostly because he wasn't one of the townsfolk. Nothing she said or did with him mattered. She could let her guard down. Plus, after that first time, he didn't ask again for her "story" or whatever that meant. Instead, he asked for other stories.

Since topics of conversation were somewhat limited in Little Nova, she humored him. She began with the folktales her mom used to tell, like the one about the trickster god who used cunning and wit to get out of obeying the emperor's commands, and the one about the rooster who won a crimson crown for its ability to sing back the sun every morning.

The next week, Niam Tais sent them into the woods with a pail to gather pine cones for wreaths. They hadn't gone far before Hlee stumbled into a clearing and stopped breathing.

Silver dust blanketed the entire space, coating every inch of earth and every tree facing inward. Patches of grass glowed like mounds of jewels in the sunlight. The air *shimmered*.

"What . . . happened?" Hlee breathed. She brushed a fingertip against a leaf. It left a luminous sheen.

Setting down the pail, she stepped gingerly into the shining clearing. When she rubbed the silver from her finger, it disintegrated into a halo around her skin.

"Who would have done this?" she asked. "And *why*?"

Argus moved past her, turning in a slow circle to take it all in. Flashing a grin, he sank down and sprawled onto his back. When he spoke, his voice was hushed with awe. "It's like being caught inside a moonbeam."

She knelt beside him, gazing upward so that her vision

became nothing but silver and light. Directly overhead, several smaller branches had snapped, dangling limply. It looked as though something had smashed into them.

It isn't like a moonbeam, she thought. With the sunlight amplifying every shimmering surface, she would have said it felt more like the heart of a star. The thought should have been embarrassing, but in this moment, wishing on stars didn't seem quite so silly.

"Do you believe in fairy tales?" she asked abruptly.

His gaze shifted to her. There were slight shadows beneath his eyes, as if he hadn't slept well. "Fairy tales are stories."

"Yeah, but like the stories about falling stars. Would you make a wish?"

Brows furrowing in a rare instance of gravity, Argus seemed to seriously consider the question. He looked so natural lying there in the silver haze, the lines of his body fuzzy and indistinct a creature of starlight and moondust. She realized she was staring when his mouth curved into a slow smile. Heat crawled up her neck.

"Well," he said, before the awkwardness could fully take hold, "if I were a star hurtling billions of miles per second through the atmosphere, I should think I'd be the last thing anyone would want to entrust with a wish."

Hlee laughed, unable to look him in the eye again. "That might be the first time anyone's considered the feelings of the star."

He crossed his ankles and stacked his hands behind his head, looking pleased with himself. "Stories belong to everyone, not just the ones telling them."

Hlee began to look forward to days spent with Niam Tais and Argus. On other days, she went to Little Nova's tiny library to read, tucking away more stories to share with Argus and looking up medicinal herbs to better help Niam Tais.

Every weekend, customers appeared at Niam Tais's doorstep, not just from Little Nova but from all across the state, to purchase curatives for their aching joints and sore backs, bitter teas to chase away bad dreams or increase blood circulation.

They came for other things too. On those days, when Niam Tais hung fresh silver and gold joss paper and lit incense, chanting to the spirits as gray smoke curled through the altar room like a ghost, Hlee and Argus knew to make themselves scarce.

They usually went to the clearing. The shine faded a little with each day, the natural greens and browns of the woods beginning to break through. With the earth still soaked from a recent downpour and the branches dripping rainwater into their hair and clothing, Argus stretched out again at the center of the clearing, unmindful of the dampness.

Hlee folded her jacket before sitting on it to keep her jeans dry. She pointed at the translucent streak of a rainbow arching overhead. "My mom used to say that rainbows are dragons, ridden by the gods through the heavens."

Argus's face lit with interest, although his smiles seemed less exuberant lately. The shadows beneath his eyes had darkened, and his pale skin held a slight gray pallor. "And lunar rainbows?" he asked.

"I didn't know that was a thing."

"Oh, it's a thing," he said, grinning. "Rare, though." He rolled to face her, eyes closed as he scooted across the earth until he was all but curled around her folded legs, his elbow pillowed beneath his head. "Will you tell me about these rainbow dragons?"

Despite the cool drip of rainwater down her neck, she felt suddenly warm and flushed. Argus opened his eyes at her silence. When their gazes locked, something jolted through her, a white-hot flash of awareness. The air grew charged, heat gathering around them as if instead of starlight and moondust, he held all the brilliance of a dying star, engulfing her with the pull of his gravity.

He rose from his recline. She looked away, but his fingers caught her chin. "I like how you look at me. There's a story in your eyes that I would give anything to hear."

Pulse racing, she couldn't meet his gaze, too uncertain even as every part of her became acutely aware of every part of him.

"Can I kiss you?" he whispered.

Hlee's breath rushed from her lungs in a shaky exhale as his lips pressed to hers. His mouth was hot, and it burned through her with the devastation of a supernova.

The days passed in a blur. They touched hands beneath Niam Tais's table as they bagged herbs. They stole kisses behind the chicken coop between filling buckets with plump yellow cucumbers and red Thai chili peppers from the garden. And every moment they could spare, they fled to their clearing.

It would have been idyllic if not for the way Argus's skin continued to lose its color. His eyes looked sunken, his hands frail. His once exuberant smile came more fleeting, brightest only when he held her tucked against him in their clearing, with the last remnants of silver dust glittering against their skin.

Hlee worried about him but didn't know how to ask what was wrong. So instead, she held him tighter, pouring all her questions into the urgency of their kisses and the stories she continued to tell whenever he asked.

One night in mid-August, two months after Argus's arrival, after they'd had dinner with Niam Tais and helped clean the dishes afterward, Hlee took Argus's hand and led him through the woods to the edge of town. There they hid in the shadows of the trees and waited for Little Nova's End-of-Summer Festival fireworks to begin. Niam Tais had set up a tent to sell medicines, herbal teas, charms, and incense.

The lantern they'd brought cast a yellow pall on Argus's already wan face. As the first firework shot into the sky with a high whine and exploded into brilliant color, Hlee opened her mouth to ask what was happening to him.

"Hey!"

Her mouth snapped shut. Three figures emerged from the darkness, the harsh halo of a flashlight swinging over their feet. Emilia Hart stepped into the small circle of their lantern light, her friends flanking her.

"Argus," Emilia said. "I'm so glad you came to see the fireworks!"

Hlee was glad no one was looking at her, because her mouth fell open with the revelation that Emilia knew Argus's name. She shrank against the tree at her back, growing small to escape notice. It was like shoving herself back into an old skin, the desire to disappear almost unfamiliar after so many weeks of being *seen*.

Argus's gaze passed from Emilia to her friends, his smile an echo of what it'd been.

"Emilia, remember?" she said, and she leaned over to pick up the lantern, setting it aside so she could sit. The shift instantly bathed Hlee in darkness. "Is it true that you're actually *living* with the witch in the woods? What's that like?" The question came out in a hush, as if they were friends, as if this wasn't the first time they'd spoken.

If Argus replied, Hlee didn't hear it. Instead, the explosion of fireworks seemed to reverberate in her skull. She didn't care that Argus knew who Emilia was, but the way she and her friends gathered around him as if they'd already claimed him as their own, the way they laughed like they were all in on a joke that Hlee would always be excluded from . . .

Hlee shoved to her feet and stumbled into the woods. Argus called her name, but she didn't stop running until she'd left them all far behind.

Hlee hid away at the library for days to avoid his phone calls and attempts to visit. Her mother clucked her tongue in disapproval when she skipped out on helping Niam Tais with her garden, but Hlee would rather listen to her mom lecture her on respecting her elders than see Argus again.

The longer she dodged contact, though, the worse she felt. Argus had never made her want to feel invisible, and not because what she did with him didn't matter—rather the opposite. She missed Niam Tais, too, who made her want to be more comfortable in her own skin, to take pride in everything that made her different.

In a year, Hlee would leave Little Nova for college. She couldn't wait to embrace the adventure, to discover who she would become away from this tiny town. People like Emilia didn't care about anything outside of themselves, and even if they did, Hlee didn't want anything to do with it. She wasn't a sidekick in their story. It wasn't her job to take on the burden of their character development.

She had her own story to tell. To *live*, and wherever that took her . . . she hoped Argus would be a part of it.

The following day, Hlee helped her mom prepare Niam Tais's dinner before setting out, backpack stuffed with warm Tupperware. The door to Niam Tais's house was always unlocked except at night, so she let herself in. She could hear the rhythmic sounds of chanting from the altar room, so she unloaded her backpack as quietly as she could.

When she peeked into the altar room, to her surprise Argus sat behind Niam Tais on a low stool. Beside him was a table set with a bowl of uncooked rice, incense tucked into the grains, and a simple meal offering to the spirits.

She sucked in her breath at the sight of him, gray and dull, with hollows forming beneath his cheekbones. At the sound, his eyes flew open. His gaze found hers immediately.

She offered him a weak smile before fleeing outside. The chickens gathered around her as she sat on the stone mushroom cap and tossed feed into the dirt. Her chest ached, every breath thick with fear. It wasn't long before Argus joined her, looking awkward as he tucked his long fingers into his back pockets.

"Niam Tais is trying to heal you," she said.

Argus hesitated, and frustration pinched at her temples. Despite spending nearly every day together for the last two months, she barely knew anything about his life outside of Little Nova. She knew only that Niam Tais and Argus's father had been friends, and that Argus would leave when his father came for him.

"Yeah," he said quietly. He didn't offer anything else.

The frustration bloomed into anger. "I'm not stupid, Argus. I can see that you're sick. You need to be in a hospital."

"Niam Tais is very skilled," he said in that way he had of never really directly answering anything. It was infuriating.

"I know she is," she snapped. "But she's not a licensed doctor. You need medical care."

He sighed, his mouth stretching into a smile that made her heart stutter. Sinking onto the stool beside the wooden sculpture, he ran his fingers along the rough lines they'd left with their clumsy carving. "Once my dad comes for me, I'll be fine."

"And when will that be?"

"I don't know. Soon, hopefully."

Despite that she'd tried to prepare for the inevitability of his leaving from the moment he'd kissed her, his words still struck her like a physical blow. She felt winded and aching.

Soon, hopefully. And then what? "Argus, tell me a story."

His eyes widened a little, sparking with surprise and delight. She'd never asked him for a story. She'd always been the one telling them.

"Tell me *your* story," she amended.

The joy immediately bled from his expression, and he looked down at his feet. Hlee clenched her jaw. Somehow, she'd known he wouldn't. He still refused despite that he'd asked for *her* story the first time they'd met. Despite the time they'd spent together, despite that she now knew the feel of his bare shoulder beneath her palm, the press of his body along hers, the way he tasted with rainwater sliding between their mouths.

What was she to him? A summer fling? A way to pass the time until his dad came back to whisk him away to his real life somewhere? She'd told him so many stories, giving a bit of herself every time, but had they ever been real? Make-believe words for make-believe friends.

She rose, steeling herself against the way his eyes followed her, hungry for the sight of her. "There's dinner inside." She gestured to the house. "Guess I'll see you around."

"Hlee, wait," he began, before Niam Tais's voice rang from the house, calling his name.

She shook her head and hurried away, the weight of Argus's gaze on her back. Even though she knew it was stupid, she willed him to come after her, to call her name again, to do *something* other than what he did—which was to watch her leave and then turn away to answer Niam Tais.

Hlee spent the next week doing everything she could to distract herself from the certainty that with the start of term looming, Argus would be leaving soon. She cleaned her room, painted the fence with her dad, and helped her mom weed the yard.

It rained on the last Friday evening of summer break as the sun was setting. The downpour was brief, the clouds dispersing quickly. When Hlee glanced out her window, the faint impression of a rainbow arched across the dusky night sky. Its colors were barely discernible—it looked more silvery than anything—but still, it took her breath away.

Before she'd thought it through, she had her shoes on and was flying out her front door. She had to make sure Argus was seeing this. If nothing else, they'd have this memory of their summer together—like the lunar rainbow, rare and brief, but beautiful.

Warm squares of light from the windows illuminated the yard as she approached Niam Tais's house. When she burst inside, though, neither Niam Tais nor Argus appeared to be home. If they'd gone into town, it was possible she'd blown right past them on her bike.

Why would they leave all the lights on, though? Her skin prickled with unease as she left the empty house. The lunar rainbow shone overhead, startlingly close, silver rippling in the moonlight, almost like . . . scales?

Shaking her head, she wandered past the house, instinct guiding her feet. The glow of the lunar rainbow cast the trees in silver, as if all the woods had been dusted in the strange luminous shine as their clearing. Ahead, a familiar voice filtered through the night.

She rushed forward, scraping her palm against a sharp branch as she emerged into the clearing. At its center, Niam Tais sat hunched over Argus, who was sprawled on his back, his chest so still that she couldn't be sure he was breathing. His eyes glowed white-hot, not a trick of the light this time. Her stomach made an alarmed lurch.

"Hlee." Argus exhaled her name like a long-held breath.

Niam Tais looked up, her cheeks streaked with tears, as Hlee dropped down beside her. With a tremulous smile so unlike her usual confidence, she squeezed Hlee's shoulder and backed away to give them space.

"What's happening?" Hlee asked, her voice high with fear. Her hands flitted from his cheeks to his shoulders, uncertain how to comfort him.

"I was hoping you'd come," he gasped, as if each word fought to pass his lips. "Niam Tais wanted me to leave the second we saw the emperor's dragon, but I waited."

"Argus, what are you talking about?" She bent low, finally settling her fingers in his hair so that his shallow breaths brushed her cheek.

"I chose to fall," he said, hand sliding up to grip her wrist. He turned his face, pressing bloodless lips to the frantic flutter of her pulse. "To meet my mother, without any promise of returning home."

At this, Hlee reared back a little, glancing over at Niam Tais. Niam Tais was staring up at the lunar rainbow, face bathed in silver. She chanted softly under her breath. When Hlee followed her gaze, the lunar rainbow had transformed into a massive sinuous thing, its slick body glimmering.

"But after meeting you, I thought it'd be okay to stay." His voice faded into a hoarse whisper.

She swallowed thickly, her breaths coming fast and thin. She understood with sudden clarity that this was his only chance. If Argus didn't leave now, then he would die well before the next lunar rainbow.

"You can't stay," she said, the words breaking inside her.

Beside her, Niam Tais fell silent just as a violent gust of wind howled through the woods. The trees trembled, leaves ripped from their branches, as an enormous serpentine dragon descended into the clearing. Hlee yelped, clutching at Argus as the creature curled its long body into the small space, its scales shivering between silver and every hue of the rainbow.

Niam Tais rushed to Argus's other side, jolting Hlee back to her senses. Together, they hauled him onto the creature's back. She didn't let go right away, though, instead burying her face in his shoulder.

"Hlee," he whispered against her hair. "Come with me."

She drew back, eyes wide, thoughts tumbling through the infinite space of a possibility she never could have imagined. When she looked to Niam Tais, the woman only nodded, hands clasped over her heart.

She couldn't possibly. Could she? Moonlight began to pierce through the dragon's form. She was out of time.

She leaped onto its back and wrapped her arms around Argus's waist. His hands found hers, pulling her even tighter against him. To Niam Tais, she said, "My parents—"

"Kuv mam saib xyuas nkawv," Niam Tais assured her. "Tell the emperor I want to see you both again."

Hlee grinned, a wild energy roaring through her as the dragon rose into the night sky. As Niam Tais and Little Nova and all the earth fell away, she thought perhaps this was how Niam Tais's story had been meant to end.

And how her own began.

Five Times Shiva Met Harry

Sangu Mandanna

The first time Shiva met Harry, they reached for the same book about the Russian Revolution on the library shelf. They did the awkward laugh thing people do, and Shiva had time to notice that he had very, very nice green eyes, and then he said, "You go ahead; there's another one down here," and that should have been the end of it.

The second time she saw him, he was walking out of the library. She could see him from across the small cobblestone square between them and was about to look away when he spotted her and waved. She waved back and he crossed the square toward her. His shirt was untucked and he had his school sweater on this time, rumpled from the day, and the jade green did fairy-tale things to his eyes.

She tried to picture what he must be seeing. A girl sitting on the ground of the park on the other side of the square, legs outstretched, school shirt and skirt stained with damp grass, schoolbag next to her, and a bottle of cider in one hand. With not much left in it.

"This isn't as sad as it looks," she said.

He laughed. "So you're not drinking alone in the park?"

"My friends just left."

On impulse, she held the bottle out to him. He shrugged, sat down on the grass beside her, and took it. "I'm Harry."

"I'm Shiva."

"That's a cool name."

"Thanks." Some girls were called Juno, or Athena, or Freyja. She got Shiva. She liked it.

He handed the cider back to her, and she took another swig. He squinted at her. "There's a beetle in your hair."

"It's the latest in hair fashion. Didn't you know that?"

His eyes lit up with laughter. "Okay, I'll just leave it where it is, then."

"I suppose you can take it out if you *must*."

He was still laughing as he coaxed the bug onto his hand. His fingers brushed against her cheek, and she had to remind herself to breathe. *Be still, my wayward heart.* She watched him deposit the beetle carefully onto the grass.

The intense concentration with which he did it made her think that he was either very passionate about insect welfare, or he had also felt whatever it was she had felt when he had touched her.

The third time, she spotted him at a desk in the library, biting on the end of his pen as he stared at the page in front of him, and she went over to say hi.

They had barely swapped two sentences before a familiar figure appeared. "There you are!" It was her father, his hair a mess and his glasses more taped together than Harry Potter's. It was anyone's guess how his patients trusted him. "Shall we pop to the library café for a few minutes before we go home? You're welcome to come too," he said cheerfully to Harry.

"I like judging my kids' boyfriends' characters based on the coffee they drink."

"Well, I—"

"Dad, he's not my—"

"They'd better not sell out of fruit scones before we get there," Dad went on, as if neither of them had started speaking. "Come on, kids, shift a bit!"

And he was off, leaving them behind. "Sorry," Shiva said to Harry. "He's always like that. You don't have to come."

"And disappoint him? I would never."

And so they went to find her father in the library café, a small hole in the wall that had the best fruit scones in the city. Dad was already at the counter. "What'll it be?"

"Coconut frappé with extra whipped cream, please," Shiva said to the girl behind the counter. "And a scone if Dad hasn't ordered them all already."

"Um." Harry paused, obviously aware of how loaded this choice was. "Just a black coffee, please."

Dad tutted. "Unimaginative," he informed Harry, and then said to Shiva in a tone of wistful affection, "Jamie never drinks plain black coffee."

Shiva rolled her eyes. Her brother's boyfriend, Jamie, was the ideal against which her parents measured all their children's prospective love interests. And he was admittedly pretty bloody perfect, which made that ideal all the more impossible to live up to.

"So, Harry," Dad said, once they'd found a free table and he'd extracted Harry's name out of him, "I realize it's not my business, but it would be remiss of me not to mention at least once that I hope you're using condoms."

"*Dad*."

Harry choked on his unimaginative black coffee. "We're not—we haven't—"

"Oh, you haven't?" Dad had the nerve to look surprised, damn him. "Well, if I know Shiva, I'm sure you will sooner or later, so just remember to use them—"

"*Dad.*"

Harry's ears had gone red and he tried to hide his face behind his cup, but Shiva could still see something that looked suspiciously like a grin on his face.

"Dad," Shiva tried again, "he's not my—"

Dad had already moved on. "I see by your uniform that you're still in school," he said to Harry.

"We're in the same year, Dad. Not the same school, but the same year."

"We're both doing history," Harry added.

Shiva winced. *Here it comes.*

Dad peered at Harry over the top of his glasses. "Let me ask you this, Harry. In all the time you've studied history in some form or another, over the course of your entire school life, how much time have you spent on the British Empire?"

"I think we may have done a little bit in junior school, but I can't remember much." There was a pause, and then, apparently feeling that more was expected of him, Harry added, "I know we studied Gandhi and I think there was also a lesson about how Christian missionaries would teach English to people in the former colonies."

"Was that a good thing, do you think?"

"Sure. I mean, it opened a lot of doors."

Shiva winced again.

Later, after Harry had left, Dad cocked his head at her. "You're probably annoyed with me, but you know I believe that a boy who can't pass the British Empire test is not worthy of you."

"He's seventeen," Shiva said. "He has time to figure shit out."

"What if he doesn't want to figure shit out? I know you

think I make a big deal out of this, but it matters. And," he added, because he never could resist, "if you recall, Jamie was sixteen when he passed the test."

"Jamie's black. His grandparents moved here from Zimbabwe. He gets it in a way Harry can't possibly get it."

Dad considered her. "Exactly."

Shiva sighed. "Dad, it doesn't matter anyway. Harry's not actually my boyfriend. I barely know him."

"What?" Her father looked astonished. "Why didn't you say so?"

The fourth time they met, they found a nook in the corner of the library, ignored their homework, and talked about books, movies, and whether or not the other Harry should have ended up with Hermione (obviously, that was a decided *yes*).

"Oh hey," Harry said after a minute, and Shiva noticed his ears had gone red again. "I was wondering if, um, if you wanted to go get a takeaway. There's the Chinese place around the corner? Not today, I mean, not unless you want to. Just . . . sometime."

"You're afraid of going out for coffee again, aren't you?" she teased him, because she didn't know how to say yes without squealing.

He grinned. "Guilty. Your dad's a little intense."

"I think it's because he's a doctor. He takes sexual health very seriously."

"I didn't mean that."

Shiva tensed immediately. "Oh."

"I don't mean it like it's a bad thing," Harry said hastily. "Just that it felt like he wanted a certain answer from me and wasn't happy that he didn't get it?"

Shiva considered brushing it off like she so often did, but

she was tired of dancing around it and she wanted more from Harry. "He wanted to see whether or not you're capable of recognizing and undoing a lifetime of programming," she said bluntly.

"What?" He was startled.

"You know there's more than one side to every story, so why haven't you ever paid attention to the other side of this one? Why haven't you ever wondered what they're *not* telling us at school? I learned very early that I was not being told the truth. My parents made sure I got my information from more than one place. You told my dad it was a good thing that people in the former colonies were taught English because it opened doors and that's probably true, but you haven't considered why it was necessary to open those doors in the first place."

"Shiva," he said quietly, "it was one conversation. It doesn't mean I've been *programmed*."

What if he doesn't want to figure shit out?

"Of course you have. We all have. You just don't notice because the program has been meticulously designed to benefit you."

He opened his mouth, then closed it again.

Shiva stood up and started packing up her books. "I didn't want to have this conversation. I wanted to drink cider and not do our homework and go get Chinese food. But I'm not going to *not* say things either." She zipped up her schoolbag. "I have to go."

He didn't come after her.

The fifth time Shiva met Harry, she almost missed him altogether. He wasn't in any of his usual places in the library. She told herself she wasn't disappointed.

Then, as she looked for a free table somewhere near the

geography section, she bumped into him. He was coming out of the international studies aisle and he had a pile of books in his arms. He flushed pink at the ears when he saw her and clutched the books tighter, like he hoped they'd disappear, but she could see some of their titles. *India in the Twentieth Century. A True History of Colonial India. The Real Legacy of the British Empire.*

"I thought about what you said," he said in a rush, ears even redder now. "And you were right. I don't know as much as I think I do. So I wanted to learn."

"Guh?" she said intelligently.

"Sorry, what?"

"Just clearing my throat," she said.

"Um. Okay." He gave her a crooked smile. "I'll see you around."

She watched him go, a smile edging its way across her face. *He's seventeen*, she'd said to her dad that day after coffee. *He has time to figure shit out.* And he wanted to. So she smiled. This time, she had homework. So did he. But next time, maybe, just maybe, they could go get that Chinese takeaway.

The Agony of a Heart's Wish

Samira Ahmed

The time has not come true,
the words have not been rightly set;
only there is the agony
of wishing in my heart . . .

—Rabindranath Tagore

Gray smoke billowed ahead of the gleaming black beauty as it chuffed to a halt on the wide-gauge track. Tara peered down the platform, keeping one arm linked through her nanni's as she watched men jump from the train steps before it fully stopped. The cascade of sweaty, jostling bodies made her wonder why anyone would hurry in this kind of heat. Her nanni was commanding a coolie to be careful with their trunks, seemingly immune to the effects of weather or frenzied travelers. Tara wanted to be in Shimla already. Twelve stifling hours stood between her and the breezes of her family's summer home in the foothills of the Himalayas. At least most of the ride would pass through the night.

"I'm worried this coolie will scratch the leather on your nana's steamer trunk," Nanni muttered. "It went with us on our honeymoon to Kashmir, you know. It's borne the journey of a lifetime—of many lifetimes."

For as long as Tara could remember, her nanni had worn a widow's simple white sari—its end wrapped loosely around her head and across her shoulder—though Tara's nana had died nearly twenty years earlier, before she was born. The modest dress belied both her ferocity and her wealth, the way she preferred it. Tara towered over her, and sometimes she liked to play the part of the helpless grandmother. But she was not shy about using her mahogany cane to make a point when it was necessary.

Tara looked at the sinewy porter in his dirty white dhoti, sweat gleaming off his bare chest. A red-faced Britisher wearing a completely impractical shirt and tie stepped up to him and began animatedly pointing at his luggage as he removed some silver paisee from his pocket. The coolie looked down at the coins in the man's hands and simply shook his head no. The man pulled at his too-tight collar and pointed a meaty finger in the coolie's face and began screaming at him. "You filthy ingrate! You think you're worth more than this?" He shoved his open palm in the coolie's face. Tara strained her neck to peek at the money—anyone would be insulted at such a paltry sum.

Tara knew the coolie wasn't going to budge because he had already been paid to watch their trunks, but she appreciated his stony expression and stalwart refusal. The man looked like he was going to spit on the coolie, but rather hurried away to the next porter, who also refused him. Tara caught the coolie's eye and gave him a little nod. She made a note to give him an extra-large tip.

She glanced at her nanni, who had taken in the entire scene as well and was smiling. There was little her nanni detested more than British superiority. She turned her smile now on Tara. "You are quite wise for someone so young. You're certainly much smarter than that older brother of yours."

Tara laughed as she retied the ribbon at the end of her long braid. "Nanni! You're not supposed to play favorites."

"Nonsense, child. *Parents* are not supposed to play favorites. Grandparents, on the other hand, can do as they please. It is the privilege of old age. Now I'm going to check on our through tickets to Shimla. You stay here and make sure they put the luggage in the right berth."

Tara nodded to her nanni as she shuffled off to a ticket window. The coolie handling their trunks had stepped away for a moment, so Tara took a seat on the wooden bench behind her, pulled her book from the red cotton satchel she'd sewn from an old, worn sari, and began reading.

"What are you reading?"

Tara looked up at a ruddy-faced young soldier rudely blocking her sun and raised an eyebrow. She pulled her book to her chest. When she didn't respond, he tried again.

"Thum kya par-rahen hein?" When the soldier spoke Urdu his vowels were too soft and he seemed to lose his *r*s in the back of his mouth somewhere.

Tara grimaced. "Aap."

The soldier looked at Tara and shrugged.

"You don't know me, so you need to say 'aap,'" she explained in her perfect English. "The formal, not the familiar."

The soldier looked properly chastised, so Tara relaxed her clenched jaw.

"Sorry. I guess your English is much better than my Urdu," he said.

"Decidedly." Tara allowed herself a slight grin as she took in the soldier's charming, toothy smile that reached his twinkly green eyes. "Then again, that's the fate of every country subjected to British colonialism, isn't it? We learn your language and you're a disaster at learning ours."

The soldier nodded. And to Tara's alarm, he took a seat next to her on the bench. Tara looked around, but no one on the busy platform was paying much attention to their little corner. She inched over to put more space between them.

"That's certainly the truth. And it's what happened in Ireland, too. The Church uses English but me mam insists on Irish in the house."

"Never lose your language," Tara said, her dark brown eyes softening at the young man. She felt her cheeks warm as he gazed at her, a little longer than she was used to. He was a little peculiar, this soldier, who wore a khaki uniform but did not appear to be with any other troops or regiment.

"Memsahib?" The coolie drew Tara's attention away and pointed toward the train. Time to board.

Tara stood up to meet her nanni, who was walking back toward her.

"Where are you traveling to?" the soldier asked.

Tara turned her head. She hesitated for a moment, but there was something about this boy with his kind green eyes that made her feel . . . comfortable. "Shimla. Our family summers there."

"Perhaps we shall meet again, then?"

Tara laughed and shook her head. "Unlikely. Safe travels."

"Tá tú go h-álainn," the soldier said as Tara walked away, an impish grin spreading across his face.

Tara didn't have time to ask him to translate, but the lilt of the words sounded lovely.

The steady click and clack and the sway of the train on the tracks had lulled Nanni to sleep within an hour of their leaving the station. But Tara was listless and the air in their first-class berth was stifling. Tara twirled the small pankha in her hand, sweaty palm wrapped around the bamboo rod that she spun with a delicate twist of her wrist, attempting to stir the still air in her private compartment. She always thought this hand fan looked a bit like a battle-axe, if axes were made of a burnt orange raw silk and detailed with vermilion embroidery and tiny mirrors. Tara stared at her nanni, lying across the narrow aisle between bunks. She had made sure to put the handrail up so her nanni wouldn't roll off when there were sudden jolts, but her nanni was the heaviest sleeper she knew.

Tara turned her attention to the window. They'd left the city behind and Tara stared at the barren landscape as the flat-topped hills of Manmad passed by, the occasional bullock cart loaded up with tall grasses or hay coming into view, always driven by men in white dhotis and turbans wrapped around their heads to shield them from the red-brown dust and the heat. Shortly, more trees came into view, their green tops clearly drawing what water they could from the land, and then, soon, a round lake with children splashing in a small waterfall, mothers washing clothes along the banks. Farther on, a village and a stone well and women filling earthenware jugs with water. Tara loved traveling by train so she could see the countryside and the stark contrast to Hyderabad's booming population. Her papa said that by next year's 1920 census, he expected Hyderabadi residents to number over half a million, an almost inconceivable number to Tara, who preferred the green mountains and relative quiet of Shimla. Though her nanni complained that since the British had made Shimla their summer capital in 1864, there was no longer any true peace—only debauchery and the loud voices of drunken British hooligans polluting the quiet night air in the foothills.

Tara's mind drifted to the brown-haired soldier on the platform with the kind eyes. She smiled, almost sheepishly, despite herself. But the grin quickly faded from her lips when she thought of her book.

"Oh no," she muttered out loud to herself. "My Rumi poems." She quickly but quietly searched her red satchel for the book. No luck. She clenched her fists and squeezed her eyes shut, trying not to cry. The book was from her late nana's personal collection of books. What would her nanni say? How could she be so careless and lose something so dear? Hadn't her mother warned her to be careful with it? Her grandfather, like her, had been a great lover of poetry, and Rumi had been his favorite. Tara fell back against the bunk with a soft thud.

Why had she allowed herself to be distracted by a soldier? Why had this boy been so distracting?

. . . the boy, who, at that very moment, she spied through the small rectangular window on the door to her coupe as he walked by.

Without thinking, Tara rose and quietly stepped toward the door. She placed her fingers on the handle, then glanced back at her nanni, who snorted lightly—she could easily sleep for hours. Tara then took a deep breath and slid the door open, crossed through to the interior hallway, and gently slid the door closed.

"Pardon," she whispered. But the soldier did not hear. She cleared her throat and said, louder this time, "Pardon?"

He turned around. A smile spread across his face the moment their eyes met.

"I've been walking these halls, hoping to find you," he said.

"Oh?" Tara responded, arching her left eyebrow. "You mean you've been skulking about the first-class berths and no one has stopped to question you?"

The soldier shrugged and smiled. His smile was charming. Tara allowed herself the fleeting thought, but quickly shook her head as if to dislodge the idea from her brain. "If you were Indian, you would've been stopped. Colonizer privilege, I suppose," she responded, a sarcastic smile slowly spreading across her face.

"I'm no colonizer," he said, his lips drawn into a tight line.

"Oh no? You just wear the unif—" Tara's eyes widened as the soldier slightly shifted his body and his right hand came fully into view. "Well, you certainly colonized my book!" she said, pointing an accusatory finger at him.

"Wha—oh, this. Yes. I mean, no. I'm sorry. The reason I was skulking about, as you so generously assumed, was to return your book. You left it on the bench. I didn't notice until my view of you had already been blocked by passengers hurrying to the train and coolies running after them." He held out her prized volume.

Tara raised her hand to wrap her fingers around her grandfather's book of Rumi's poetry. For a brief moment, the pads of their fingertips occupied nearly the same space. She felt the heat of their proximity and blushed. She noticed his nails were neatly trimmed and unusually clean. "Thank you . . . uh . . . soldier?" she whispered.

He cleared his throat. "Jimmy," he said as Tara took the book firmly in her left hand. "Pleased to meet you . . ."

"Tara," she replied.

Jimmy held his hand out, palm facing up. Tara hesitated for a moment. This was certainly not the expected nor accepted greeting between strangers. Especially between strangers of the opposite sex. Especially when they were alone. Especially when one of them was a British soldier. An angreyz. A gora.

Tara took a breath. She was not sure what it was about this young man that made her lose some basic common sense— perhaps his warm smile or his guileless eyes? For a moment she felt feverish. Her heart raced. Tara remembered a phrase of English poetry from a volume she'd found in her nana's vast library, "Gather ye rosebuds while ye may." But the poem's title made her blush even deeper, "To the Virgins to Make Much of Time." What a scandalous title for the seventeenth century . . . or for this century, for that matter. She grinned and slipped her cool fingers into his hand. She held her breath as he lowered his face toward her knuckles and, gently, barely grazed them with his lips. Their warmth sent a shock through her. She felt a bead of sweat trickle down the back of her peacock-colored cotton kurta. Tara's eyes followed Jimmy's as he raised his head and smiled. He was still holding her hand.

Tara carefully withdrew her hand, their eyes still locked. "It's poetry," she blurted. "I mean . . . what you asked me on the platform. What I was reading. Poetry. Rumi. Do you know his work? Persian poet. Thirteenth century." She searched his eyes for any hint of recognition, but she found them full of sparks that she believed were meant for her.

Jimmy shook his head. "Sorry, I'm a bit of a literary heathen. But I do love the poetry of my fellow Irishmen. Do you know Yeats?"

Tara's eyes widened. "Yes, of course! He wrote the English introduction to Tagore's *Gitanjali* poems."

Jimmy stared at her blankly, so she continued. "Rabindranath Tagore? He won the Nobel Prize a few years back.

The first Indian—the first non-Westerner to ever do so." Tara did not try to hide the incredulity in her voice. "You *are* a heathen."

At that, Jimmy laughed so loudly Tara feared he might wake her grandmother. But the door to her berth stayed firmly shut.

"I'm terribly sorry to disappoint you, madame," Jimmy said, bowing slightly. "In my defense, I have committed many Yeats poems to memory."

"It speaks in your favor." Tara grinned. "But only a little. Yeats's writing is brilliant. My tutor gave me a book of his recent poems—*The Wild Swans at Coole*."

"I have that very volume with me," Jimmy said. Tara noticed his face light up, just as hers did when she talked about Rumi. "He—Yeats—went to school with my father. For a couple years, at least. They still exchange the occasional letter or two. Does that lend me some civility points, at least?"

Tara's mouth dropped. Imagine being so nonchalant about having a family connection to your nation's greatest living poet. "Have you . . . ever met him?"

"No. My father hasn't seen him in years," Jimmy said. Tara's wide smile eased as she nodded. "But he did send my father a poem recently before I shipped off for India. It's not been published yet. Yeats said that he hoped every Irish soldier would be able to make sense of it."

"That's . . . that's astonishing. My tutor says Yeats is one of the most magnificent writers in the English language. And you—you—have one of his unpublished poems."

"It's in my berth. Would you like to see it? You can join me for tea."

Tara's heart leaped at the chance. But she caught herself. How could she possibly go to a man's berth, alone? Her shoulders drooped. "You have a first-class berth? To yourself?" He must have at least some family money, Tara thought.

"My father treated me for this holiday before I rejoin my regiment—the Connaught Rangers—around Solon. It was a sort of gift for my eighteenth birthday."

"A handsome gift, indeed." Tara paused. "I don't think it would be seemly for me to join you in your cabin. Alone." They were the same age, she noted. How funny the vast differences in their lives. Differences due to their gender and nationality and race. Demography is destiny, she thought, and sighed.

"What if we kept the door open?"

Tara laughed. "Even more scandalous! What if someone saw me in there with you?"

Jimmy rubbed his chin. "I have an idea. I will leave you alone in my berth while I fetch tea from the train canteen. You can look at the poem while I'm on my tea errand and leave at any time. What do you think? Perfectly innocent and civilized."

Tara smiled. What would be the harm? Her nanni would be asleep for hours as would most people on the train. She wouldn't have to pass through any of the other cars. It would all be quite discreet. She nodded. Jimmy grinned and led her down the hall to the last door before the end of the car. He slid it open. Tara stepped inside.

Jimmy had been gone at least fifteen, perhaps twenty, minutes. Perhaps he meant not to return until I've left, she thought. She'd read the poem over and over again. Relatively short. Lyrical. Tragic. *We know their dream; enough / To know they dreamed and are dead.* The lines lodged in her throat like a dry bone and brought tears to her eyes. She thought of her grandfather rising up to help in the Indian freedom struggle of the 1850s when he was her age, younger even. Tara cried for all the Indians who dreamed of a free India. Who dreamed and died. Hindu. Muslim. Sikh. Young and old. Poets and warriors. She wondered if she would live to see Indians govern themselves. She wondered if the day would come when Indians would not be grossly taxed by the British for the salt of their own land—from the summer-dried marshes along the Rann of Kutch that had produced salt for five thousand years and Orissa with her miles of coastline along the Bay of Bengal, her ancient towers and temples rising into blue skies. Jai Hind.

The door swooshed open before Tara could wipe her tears away. Upon seeing her, Jimmy nearly spilled the small metal teapot and two stacked metal cups in his hands. He quickly put them down on the tiny table that was attached to the wall just below the rectangular window. An inky night had settled onto the landscape.

"Are you okay? What happened?" Jimmy asked as he took a seat next to Tara. He was so close they were almost touching. Tara didn't move away.

"Sorry," she said, embarrassed, raising her fingertips to wipe away the wetness on her cheeks. "This poem. Did you read it? Don't you see? Yeats doesn't want you to fight here. Not *for* them—the British. He told your dad to give you this poem so you would know who the enemy actually is."

Jimmy took the paper from Tara's shaky hands. He read out loud, his brogue curling perfectly around the consonants. "'MacDonagh and MacBride / And Connolly and Pearse.' They were just some of the Irish the British executed for their supposed role in the Easter Rising. Some of them didn't even do anything. All executed at Kilmainham Gaol. Connolly was tied to a chair when they shot him. On account of not being able to stand up. Bloody bastards."

Jimmy brought his hand to his mouth, then turned to Tara. "Forgive my language."

The air grew quiet and heavy between them. Tara could hear their individual breaths, rising, falling, out of tune. Hers, deep and deliberate, like she was trying to ground herself, keep herself in this space and time. His, shakier, shallow, until at last he slowed himself down to match her.

He looked up from the floor to meet her eyes. Slowly, she reached toward him, and he took her hand in his. A flame leaped from her chest and threatened to set the entire berth on fire. But Tara sat still. And close, so close, to this boy. This soldier. She looked down at their hands—fingers interlaced. This was all impossible.

"'Freedom from fear is the freedom / I claim for you, my Motherland.'" Tara's voice was a whisper.

"Who said that?"

"Tagore. That's from the book that Yeats wrote the introduction to."

"Yeats might have written similar sentiments himself—he may still."

"That's because Tagore and Yeats wanted the same thing. Freedom to rule themselves. Yeats wants freedom for Ireland. He wants you to want it, too."

"I do want it."

"Then how can you wear their uniform, knowing that your brothers died for Ireland to be free? Just like Indians are dying for India to be free. You must see that, Jimmy. It's such a simple and humble thing, isn't it? To want to live free. To make mistakes. To fail sometimes, perhaps, but even for those failures to be your own."

Jimmy nodded and looked down at his scuffed boots. Tara let out a small, tinkly laugh when she noticed a tiny sheen of bright orange syrup along his jawline. She raised her thumb to wipe it away. "Were you eating jalebis in the canteen? Is that why it took you so long to return?"

Jimmy turned his head and gave her a sheepish grin. "I wasn't sure if you would be here when I returned. I was drowning my sorrows in Indian sweets."

"I wasn't sure I would be here when you returned, either."

"Why did you stay?"

They leaned a bit closer to each other, their shoulders almost touching. Tara bit her lower lip. "I'm not sure. I—I guess I didn't want to say goodbye. Yet."

"Neither did I."

They heard heavy footsteps outside. Tara caught her breath. If she were found here, alone, with him—she could only imagine her grandmother's anger. And if anyone on the train were to recognize her . . . God forbid. Her marriage prospects would be ruined forever. The humiliation her family would suffer. She pulled her hand away from Jimmy's and stood up. Jimmy crossed the length of the berth to the door and listened. The footsteps faded away. Jimmy locked the door and walked back toward her.

Tara's heart pounded in her ears. From the nearness of him. From the foolishness of this choice. What was she *thinking*? Jimmy leaned toward her and whispered in her ear, "I'll keep you safe." It was a nice sentiment, but it didn't assuage her panic.

"This tea should still be . . . well, warm, at least." Jimmy poured two cups of milky chai and took a seat again on the bottom bunk. He took a swig and then motioned for Tara to join him. "Mam's shortbread would be excellent right now."

"Nothing tastes like home. But I'm sure you can find some delights here as well."

"I have no doubt." Jimmy grinned at her, a dimple appearing in his left cheek.

Tara opened her mouth but clamped it shut and simply shook her head. She sat next to Jimmy and took the offered tea. While they drank, Tara told him about her grandfather and how he had barely escaped with his life when the British cruelly crushed the mutiny among the sepoys and those who helped them. How he had to go into hiding and even change his name. Tara told Jimmy about her nanni's stories about how she and her nana had met at an anti-British protest and then had to reverse-engineer a marriage setup because a love-marriage would have been an utter scandal.

"So anti-colonial activities run deep in your family, I see," Jimmy said, then added, "and a penchant to live life on the edge."

"Yes, I suppose," said Tara. "My nanni would be horrified to see me talking to you like this, but I'm sure a part of her would be glad I was breaking some rules."

Jimmy took the teacup from Tara's hand and placed it on the small table. He turned back, inching closer. Tara swore she could hear his heart beating. Or was that just hers, echoing in this cabin? Jimmy tucked a few strands of loose hair behind Tara's ear, grazing her cheek with his thumb. Sparks exploded across her skin.

"Tá tú go h-álainn," Jimmy whispered to her.

"That's what you said at the platform, isn't it?" Tara had to will herself to speak, pulling the words out of her throat. She didn't trust herself to speak in complete or correct sentences in her third language right now. "What does it mean?"

"You are beautiful."

Tara's heart exploded. She reached for her book of poems, needing an anchor, so she wouldn't float away—a million sparks in the dark night. "Shall I read you some Rumi?" She didn't wait for an answer. "I'll have to do sight translation into English. Forgive me if it's a little rough."

Jimmy leaned back against the cushioned wall beside the bunk. He nodded.

Tara quickly opened to the page where she'd left off, a narrow, faded red ribbon marking her place. "'You have aroused my passion, your touch filling me with desire. I am no longer separate from you . . . I beseech you, don't let me wait.'" Her skin absolutely burned. My God. What was this? Tara gently replaced the ribbon and placed the book safely on the table. Jimmy drew himself up as she leaned toward him. A riot of thoughts ran through Tara's mind. Some of them were warning lights. Others were the white-hot lights of stars falling to earth. But they were all a jumble, really. And, for once, Tara led with her heart.

They kissed.

And it was slow and warm and everything and nothing she could have imagined. And it was fleeting. And it was eternity. It was a miraculous place without borders or words or wars. When they pulled apart to, at last, draw a breath, Tara bent her head, covering her eyes, an impossibly large smile spreading across her face.

Jimmy leaned back and pulled her toward him, so she rested her head on his chest. She could feel his heart beating. She felt the warmth of his arm as it rested across her shoulders. The train rocked back and forth as it clicked and clacked over the track. Dots of light like embers in the dark night sky rose up and faded in a blink. Tara's eyelids drooped to a close.

The train lurched forward, pulling Tara and Jimmy out of their repose. At first, Tara jerked her head up, then lay it back to rest when she saw Jimmy's smiling face. His body was so warm and his arm enveloped her perfectly. A second later, she flew out of the bunk.

"What . . . what time is it? What have I done?"

Jimmy leaped up and pulled her into a hug. "It's okay. It's okay. It's still night. Look."

Tara looked out the train window. The thread of dawn's light had not yet appeared on the horizon. She allowed herself to breathe. Jimmy smoothed her hair. And kissed her forehead and then her cheek and then brought his lips to hers. She wrapped her arms around him as her heart clenched and tears formed in her eyes and slid down her cheeks.

"What's wrong?" he asked.

"Nothing. And everything. I have to go. If my nanni wakes up and I'm not there, she'll worry."

"This can't be goodbye. No. I'm stationed sort of close to Shimla. I can see you on leave and I . . ." Jimmy's voice trailed off.

Tara's strength to leave him was slowly ebbing away. She knew she couldn't tarry much longer or else she would simply melt into the floor, cease to exist. She sniffled and wiped the tears from her face. Then looked up to see tears well in Jimmy's eyes. "You're a good man, Jimmy . . . ?"

"Daly," he added.

"I'm glad I met you, Jimmy Daly. Don't let this uniform define you. Remember what Yeats told you. And me." Tara chuckled a bit. "Remember what they died for."

Jimmy nodded. Tara raised her hand to his face. He leaned his cheek into her palm. She felt his tear trickle down the length of her index finger.

"Can I at least write you?"

"What would be the point?"

"To feel like I can still reach you. Because I met you for a reason. That this night meant something. That this fissure in my heart right now means something."

"It does. It will. Always. I know. I feel it, too." Tara wasn't sure how much longer she could stand it. "Rumi says, 'The wound is where the light enters you.'" If that were true, Tara thought, she'd be a million rays of the sun right now. She tried to say something else, but the words all caught in her throat and tears splashed across her face. She let out a deep, shuddery breath and took a step toward the door.

"Wait." Jimmy grabbed her hand. "Hold on. It can't be like this." He reached for his volume of Yeats with the unpublished poem tucked in its pages. "Take this. So you'll have something to remember me by."

Tara clutched her hand to her chest, hoping it would stop the pain. "I won't forget you."

"Take it, please. I know what that poem is saying. I know what you are saying. If nothing else, please know I see you. I heard you. I won't forget." Jimmy pressed the book into Tara's left hand and placed his hand over the one on her chest. "I don't even know your full name."

"Tara Jahan Gazhi."

"Tara Jahan. It's beautiful. What does it mean?"

"'Star of the world.' My parents are obviously romantics."

"So am I," Jimmy said. "I'll remember it's your starlight filling the cracks and the broken parts of me."

Tara unclasped the small silver capsule she wore on a thick black thread around her neck and put it in Jimmy's palm, folding his fingers over it. "It's the Ayatul Kursi. The Throne of God prayer from the Quran. May it keep you safe, Jimmy Daly," she said and smiled.

He clutched his fingers tightly around the amulet. "May the road rise up to meet you, Tara Jahan."

Tara and Jimmy stepped to the door, her Rumi and his Yeats, together, under her arm. He opened it enough to stick his head out. The hall was empty. He nodded at her.

Neither of them moved. Could such strong feelings

seize her in a single night and then leave her, before dawn awoke, with a heart utterly shattered? She wasn't sure if this was madness or tragedy or foolishness. She wanted to stop time and the earth and the stars. She wanted all the things that could not be. She wanted a different universe where there were more possibilities for a girl like her and a boy like him.

Tara gripped Jimmy's hand. She didn't want to be the first to let go. Nor, she felt, did he. But one of them had to. And since she was the one leaving, the terrible task fell on her. She pressed herself close to him and inhaled him one last time—the cardamom from the chai mixed with sharp scents of his boot polish and shaving cream. They stared at each other until the door closed between them.

Days passed. And nights. Tara kept Jimmy's book of poems safely tucked under her pillow in Shimla and in Hyderabad, and when the tears came, she found herself reaching for the pages, hearing his voice recite the words until, weeks and months later, the echo of his voice slowly passed into a dimly lit corner of her memory. The longing faded, too, until the wounds simply became shiny scars. Until the sharp pain became a dull throb and eventually just a pinch. Until the raging bonfire of feeling a mere ember that she guarded and kept glowing.

A year later, the memory of that night, their fugitive time together, felt like a dream. An illusion. Still, on her return to Shimla the following summer season, Tara found herself lingering on the platform, searching, like a fool, for Jimmy's face, listening for his voice. Hoping that eventually one of the soldiers she passed would be him. Wondering, always, if he remembered her—if her voice and smiles were fading away like a photograph left in the sun. If he had kept her amulet or if it had been forgotten somewhere, small and insignificant as it was. She contented herself with life as it was because she knew no other way to live. But she always hoped, perhaps, for one more stolen minute, a glance, a wave, a sparkling jolt of recognition.

Tara understood, whatever seed of hope she carried, that they would never see each other again. That the watery image in her peripheral vision was not Jimmy, but a phantom. Her pragmatism made the days and nights more tolerable, but it could not insulate her from the stark cruelties of life. So on one bright July morning when she happened to pass through Shimla Town Hall, a passing glance at the day's newspaper left on a bench made her knees buckle. Tara's eyes fell to the headline, and the words jumped from the page, tiny daggers that drew blood: *Connaught Rangers Mutiny. British Put Down Uprising of Irish Troops in Solan. Court Martial. Fourteen to Be Executed.* And there in grainy shades of gray was his face. James Daly. And his words, "I will soldier no more for England."

She could not scream or let her tears overcome her. Not in this public place. Or fall to the floor like a widow, for she was not that. She was merely a girl who had met a boy. And for too brief a moment, they had dreamed.

The Coward's Guide to Falling in Love

Caroline Tung Richmond

My name is Juliet, but I'm definitely no Capulet.

I wish I'd grown up in a place like fair Verona, but I've spent my whole life in the same boring suburb of Washington, D.C. I'm not Italian either, and I don't live in a fancy villa with servants and stables and masquerade balls. My family is Chinese-American and my parents drive Toyotas. I do have my own bedroom at least, but it doesn't come with an attached balcony where a handsome boy can call up to me after midnight. I've never even been kissed.

But I *have* been in love. He might not be a Montague, but I'm kind of really hoping that he'll play the part.

I just have to be brave enough to ask him.

It's 1:35 on a Saturday afternoon, and I'm pacing inside the National Gallery of Art, waiting for Milo to arrive and wishing that I'd worn my comfy flats instead of the new suede loafers that I haven't had time yet to break in. Milo's birthday was three days ago, and I usually treat him to lunch at Bob's Noodle House because their fried pork chop over rice is his favorite, but this year I asked him to meet me downtown instead. There's a free concert here at two—a string quartet will play a selection by Adrian Gogic—and my heart did a little zing when Milo said that he'd come, even though I knew he would because Gogic is one of his favorite composers.

I've been anxious all week leading up to this non-date, and I even made my sister drive me into D.C. today because the Metro is always running late. But now I'm pacing around the museum's sunny atrium and wondering if I have the guts to go through with my big plan. Milo and I have been friends since we met in middle school orchestra, and I've had a crush on him for just about as long. It's the sort of secret that keeps me awake at night, aching from the inside out as I imagine him sweeping me into his arms and pressing his lips to mine so softly that Romeo himself would say, "Now, *that's* a kiss." And I'd think, *One day I'll tell Milo how I feel.*

I was going to do it at eighth-grade graduation.

Then at his parents' Christmas party our freshman year.

Then at the statewide orchestra competition this past winter.

I kept nudging *one day* down the calendar because I figured I had time, but then last month Milo found out that he got into the new fine arts magnet program on the other side of our county. Starting next school year, we won't play in the same orchestra anymore or study for biology together or swap snacks at lunch, trading his barbecue potato chips for my wasabi-flavored dried seaweed.

One day has to start now.

My phone buzzes, and I'm feeling so jittery that I nearly drop it. It's a text from my sister, Thea, who drove over to Eastern Market after she dropped me off.

Good luck with Milo, but I still think you should tell him flat out that you like him. Or maybe go in for a kiss? Seize the day, sis!

My cheeks flush like little ovens. Thea says that I should

come right out and declare my love for Milo, not because she's a dreamy-eyed romantic but because she's the most practical person on the planet who thinks that I've already wasted five years pining after Milo in silence. But there's no way I'm taking her advice. What does she want me to do? Run up to him and shout, "Surprise, I love you!" into his face? I might as well tattoo his name on my left butt cheek and moon him while I'm at it.

Thea might not approve of my methods, but I want to work up to my big reveal, which is why I've come up with a step-by-step plan to woo Milo with my charms. I'm not going to *tell* him how I feel—I'm going to *show* him instead, starting with the museum today. After the concert I'll ask him to our sophomore spring fling, and I'm pretty sure he'll say yes since he doesn't have a date yet. I already have a dress in mind, too—with a cinched waist that flares out into a tulle skirt—and during the last slow song I'm going to lock my arms around his neck and pull him in close enough that it'll make him think that his old pal Juliet is looking rather cute and, hey, maybe she could be something more than just a friend.

"Jules?"

My eyes jerk upward. "Oh! You're here!" I squeak to Milo. I didn't notice him come in, and now he's standing in front of me, all six feet and two inches of him, and I'm scrambling to turn off my phone before he sees Thea's text about how I should kiss him.

"Didn't want to be late. This was an awesome idea of yours, by the way," he says, blinking up at the enormous Alexander Calder mobile that hangs from the museum ceiling before glancing at me again. "Everything okay? You seem a little jumpy."

I don't know if "jumpy" is the right word. More like absolutely mortified. My stupid phone screen has frozen on Thea's text, lit up for the entire capital to read. I shove it in my purse, where I restart it. "Too much coffee this morning," I blurt out before I notice he looks different from when I saw him at school yesterday. "Did you cut your hair?"

He glances at the floor, rocking back and forth in his sneakers. "My mom made me do it last night. It's too short, huh?" His hair had been getting long enough for the ends to curl and cover his eyes, which forced him to do this little head flick in orchestra so that he could read his sheet music. It was adorable then, and it's still adorable now, albeit an inch shorter.

"I think it looks—" I'm about to say "cute" but I swallow it back. "Cute" is too flirty, but what should I say instead? I need to come up with something fast because Milo is starting to look at me funny. What about "nice"? Or "good"? I only have to pick one of them, but my brain mushes the two words together, and it comes out, "—nood."

Which sounds a little like *nude*.

Oh, God. Did I tell Milo that he looks naked?

"Good! Your hair looks good!" I say, trying to recover. Ugh, I should've said that it was cute and been done with it. I better change the subject fast, so I reach into my bag and fish out his card. "For the birthday boy. There's a gift certificate inside to Bob's Noodle."

"Really?" He grins extra wide, and my stomach twists because the corners of his eyes crinkle when he smiles like that. "Thanks, J. You'll go with me, right? My birthday isn't my birthday without you and Bob."

His request makes me feel all gooey inside, but I try to play it cool. "I don't know. You always try to steal my fried pork chop."

"That's because you never finish it! You shouldn't waste food like that. Think about the environment."

I give him a little push, and he laughs and pokes me in

the side; and maybe I felt gooey before, but I'm now melting into a puddle. A thought tickles at the back of my mind that I should ask him to the dance right now. He's in such a good mood—and maybe he was flirting with me a little?—but my palms start sweating and I feel light-headed, and then my flicker of bravery fizzles out, like it has done countless times before.

It's okay, though, I tell myself. I'll ask him after the concert. That was the plan anyway, which is still a definite go.

The string quartet enters the atrium and gets seated by the expanse of front windows where they'll be playing. The concert is casual, standing room only, and Milo claims a spot near the musicians. I make sure to position myself a little in front of him so he can notice my outfit. I went through four options before I settled on a cream blouse with a Peter Pan collar and a pair of navy shorts with a scalloped hem. Thea said that I look like an anime sailor, which is kind of true, but I wanted to dress up fancier than usual. This might not be a date, but it's shaped like one, so I want to look the part.

Finally, I feel Milo's gaze land on me, and I'm grateful that the air-conditioning is turned on full blast because otherwise I'd be a sweaty mess.

"Do you think you'll challenge Asma for first chair next year?" he says.

Wait . . . what? I was hoping he'd mention that I looked nice today instead of bringing up the fact that I've been second-chair viola to Asma Aziz since our freshman year.

"Why do you ask?" I say, frowning a little. Did he even notice that I'm wearing mascara *and* lip gloss?

"Just saying you should think about it. You've been practicing so much and you're as good as Asma now."

I warm at the compliment, but I'm not as convinced as he is. "Challenging for first chair is a big deal, though." Milo doesn't have to worry about any of this because he has been first chair cello since forever. He's symphony-caliber good, but he's never flashy about it either, which is a big part of his appeal. (Sigh.) But if I were to challenge Asma, I would have to do scales and sight-read and perform an assigned piece of music in front of the whole class. Thinking about that makes me want to shrivel and hide, which is why I've never done it.

"I'll help you with the sight-reading if that's what's holding you back," he offers.

"Yeah?"

"Definitely. You deserve that spot." He bumps shoulders with me, and I try not to smile too widely.

A decent crowd has gathered for the concert. A few minutes past two, the first violinist greets everyone and tells us about Adrian Gogic, a nineteenth-century composer who was born in what's modern-day Montenegro. I know most of this already because Milo is obsessed with Montenegrin music. His parents emigrated from Kotor to attend grad school in the US, just like mine, who moved from Shanghai to go to Georgetown. That's something that connects him and me, being first-generation kids. Milo might blend in with the other white kids at school, but he understands what it's like speaking two languages at home and having parents who don't always get the nuances of trick-or-treating or the tooth fairy.

The quartet strikes up their first piece, and Milo's attention immediately shifts toward them. The two violinists may carry the melody, but his eyes zero in on the cellist, tapping his fingers against his thigh to pick out the notes. I don't want to stare but it's hard to look away.

I think my crush on him started the first time I saw him play, way back in the sixth grade. Even then he was impressive— his technique already on its way to perfect—but that wasn't what hooked me in. It was watching him with his cello, how he touched it with so much care. It gave me shivers. It made me think, *I want someone to love me the way that boy loves the cello.*

The quartet goes through three more pieces before launching into their finale, Gogic's interpretation of a Serbian folk song. The tune is so infectious that the audience claps to the beat, and a young couple starts to dance, twirling to the melody. The first violinist uses his bow to motion for others to join in, and more couples pair off around us. Even the little kids start shaking their hips.

That's when the old woman next to me elbows me and whispers, "You should ask your young man to dance!"

I balk and whisper back, "He's not my young man." I mean, I wish . . .

She doesn't miss a beat. "I sat out too many dances at your age. I hope you don't mind if I try to make up for lost time."

She proceeds to tap Milo's shoulder and asks him something that I can't hear, but it makes his eyes widen. Then he's grinning and he holds out his arm for the woman to take, like they're in a Jane Austen novel.

"A dance, my lady?" he says before they join in with the others.

I clap as I watch them, but my heart isn't quite into it. It's fun watching Milo dipping his septuagenarian dance partner, but now I'm kicking myself because I should be the one getting dipped. His hands could be on my waist right now, our bodies only inches apart, but that dancing grandma beat me to the punch.

Soon the song ends, and it's showtime for me. I can do this. I've been practicing how I would ask Milo to spring fling all week. I even wrote out the lines: *Did you hear that Ingrid asked Ben to spring fling? I was thinking that it could be fun if we went together. You know, as friends.* Thea told me not to say that last part, but I'm keeping it in because I need to take baby steps and I'm definitely a newborn when it comes to dating.

"So," I say to Milo, my pulse galloping off the racetracks. Hold on, what was my line again? *Did you hear . . .* something, something?

Oh no.

Milo waits for me to continue. "Sooo?"

I should just ask him to the dance—there's no need to get fancy—but I get a panicky feeling in my chest and my brain is shouting at me, *Abort! Mission abort!* So I say the next thing I can think of: "Want to get gelato at the food court?"

Milo loves sweets in any form, including gross stuff like stale Peeps, so he's quick to say, "I'm game. Do you know the way?"

I lead us down the staircase to the basement level while Milo talks animatedly about the concert, but I can only nod along. I totally blew my chance back there! I'd practiced for days, but I still froze up when it counted. But I can't beat myself up too much. There's still time for Attempt #2. What happened before was a practice round.

Down at the gelateria Milo opts for the Nutella flavor while I choose peach, and we sit at a table by the gift shop. In between bites of gelato Milo raves about the cello solo during the concert, but my nerves are getting to me again and I only catch every other word. I tuck my hair behind my ear, then let it fall. Gosh, I'm nervous. Why does asking someone out have to be so hard?

Milo stretches out his long legs under the table and taps his shoe against mine. "This is random, but can I ask you something about spring fling?"

My gaze snaps up to meet his. Oh my God. Is he going to

ask me to go with him? Okay, I can't get too ahead of myself, but why else would he say that? All right, act normal, Juliet. Be cool.

"Sure. Ask away," I say, shrugging like this is no big deal.

"Do you think corsages are still a thing? Like, are they expected?"

Hmm, this is a weird way to ask someone to a dance, but I say, "For homecoming and prom, I would say yes."

"Right?" He looks at me like we're on the same page, even though I have no idea what book he's reading from. "I told my mom that spring fling is more casual, but she's bugging me that I should order a corsage for Elena."

I almost drop my spoon. "Wait . . . you're going to spring fling? With Elena Greenbaum?"

"Yep, she asked me two days ago. Didn't I tell you?"

"Um, *no*." He certainly didn't mention this Very Important Development at all, and neither did Elena, who plays violin in the orchestra with us. That traitor.

"What do you think, though? Yea or nay on the corsage?"

I stuff a big bite of gelato into my mouth so I don't have to answer him right away. My brain is still processing that Elena asked him to the dance and that he said yes. I've been tying myself into an emotional pretzel all week, but I'm two days too late.

Well, crap.

Milo waves a hand in front of my face. "Earth to Jules? Where'd you go?"

"You should get a corsage," I blurt, because I would definitely want one if I were Elena, but then I wince because that corsage should've been mine. I would've saved it and dried it after the dance, too, because it would've been my first and it would've come from Milo.

Ugh. I need more gelato.

With my mouth half full, I ask without thinking, "So do you *like* Elena? Like more than a friend?"

He considers this. "I mean, she's sweet and all but I've never really thought of her that way."

"Oh, okay," I say out loud, but on the inside I'm like, *Oh, thank God!*

But my relief doesn't last long. My grand plan to show Milo how I feel hinged a lot on going to the dance together. I had everything plotted so carefully, but what am I supposed to do now? If Thea were here, she'd tell me that there's an easy fix for my dilemma, but I shut her voice out of my head.

Milo glances at his phone. "I have to head home in an hour. Want to walk around a bit?"

I say yes because of course I do, and we wander into the West Building of the gallery, where we enter a special exhibition about post-Picasso cubism. I drift a step behind Milo, thinking hard about how I might use our upcoming class trip to Kings Dominion to my advantage. The bus ride will take over an hour, so I could claim a seat next to him. Then I could grab his hand on the Flight of Fear coaster—only for a second or two but long enough to get him thinking. That might actually work, but it does little to chase away the sinking feeling in my stomach. What if Elena grabs a seat by Milo on the bus ride over or on the roller coasters?

Suddenly Milo turns around and dips his head toward mine. "What's with all the cats?" he whispers.

Oh, right. I'm supposed to be looking at art. I squint at the paintings in front of us, nine of them in total and arranged in a neat square, three in a row. Sure enough, each one depicts a deranged-looking cubist cat. There's a green one in the middle and another with big, googly eyes and yet another painted in shades of gray. It's like peering into a pet store if you were on LSD, not that I have firsthand experience with recreational drugs.

Milo has already moved on to the next painting, but his question has made me curious, so I read the little placard next to the kitties.

Joseph Preston
Canadian, 1902–1961
Street Cats: A Study
1926
Oil on canvas

Born in Vancouver, Preston settled in Barcelona to attend art school. He specialized in depicting common life, in particular stray dogs, birds, and—in this series— stray cats. Instead of signing these paintings with his initials, he used the letters "LJC," whom scholars believe to be a young woman that Preston wished to marry and for whom he painted this study. His personal letters reveal, however, that the woman became engaged to one of Preston's colleagues before he could gift her with this work.

My first thought is: *That poor guy.*

My second thought is: *Hold on . . . This sounds a little familiar.*

Joseph Preston wanted to woo LJC with a grand gesture, but he took too long and she ran off with someone else. My mouth goes dry at the parallels. I always thought that I had tomorrow or next week or next month to ask Milo to spring fling. I thought I had so much time to ask him to be my boyfriend or even to challenge Asma for first chair but I've put it all off because I was afraid, and now look where it has gotten me.

Joseph Preston should've set aside his paintbrush and told LJC how he felt—flat out, no beating around the bush. Maybe she would've turned him down, but at least she wouldn't have been the one that got away.

And if I don't say something now to Milo, I don't know if I ever will.

Seize the day, Thea would tell me.

The exhibit is empty save for Milo and me and the security guard checking his phone in the next room. Milo is standing in front of a bronze sculpture, and I'm terrified but I walk right next to him.

My voice trembles. "Hey."

"Hmm?"

"Can I talk to you about something?"

He pries his eyes away from the sculpture, and I'm so anxious that I feel dizzy.

"What's wrong?" he asks, alarmed.

"Nothing! I just—" Actually, I'm not sure anymore if I want to seize the day right now. "Seize the tomorrow" has a nicer ring to it, doesn't it? But then I notice Joseph Preston's paintings in the corner of my eye and I know that I can't end up like him, growing old with only my cat portraits to keep me company until my bones turn brittle from a lack of calcium and romantic love.

With that horrifying future in mind, I say, "I like you."

Milo blinks really fast. He looks confused.

"I *like* like you," I force out. "I have for a while."

His eyes fly wide. "Wow," he says after a couple seconds, as if it has taken that long for my words to travel through his ear canal and into his brain. He says softly, "You like me?"

I nod because I don't know what else to say. I chew my

bottom lip, waiting for him to smile at me or kiss me or tell me he likes me, too, but he keeps standing there, looking like a statue himself. His eyes won't meet mine either.

"Aw, Jules," he says.

In those two short words, I hear everything he wants to convey. The nerves. The discomfort. The undertone of how-am-I-supposed-to-tell-her-that-I-don't-feel-the-same-way. My hopes promptly drive off a cliff.

"Stop," I say quickly, because I don't want to hear what he'll say next. "Can we forget what I just said?"

He looks at me with gentle eyes. "Thank you for telling me. I mean that, but I—"

"Forget it, okay? Please?" My voice pinches higher and higher with every syllable, and I don't know how much longer I can stand here.

This is so awful.

Then it gets worse.

Milo hugs me.

"I'm so sorry," he whispers. His chin dips onto the top of my head, and we're pressed so close that I'm sure he can feel the lump in my throat. "Come on, let's grab another gelato. My treat."

I don't want a pity gelato, though. In fact, I'm feeling kind of nauseous, as if my body has been turned inside out, like my heart is on exhibit, beating and breaking apart.

"I better go," I say.

"But . . ."

"I'll see you later. Please don't follow me."

I get the hell out of there, dodging around the tourists until I finally find an exit. I manage to make it out the door before I crumple onto the stone staircase that leads down to the grassy lawn of the National Mall. People are walking their dogs and playing Frisbee, oblivious to me as I bury my face into my hands.

I sit like this for a long while, my arms hugging my knees to my chest. Milo doesn't come looking for me, and I'm grateful for it. I don't know how I'll face him at school on Monday, and I'm seriously considering taking residence at the museum to avoid him. I'll fit right in with Joseph Preston and his cats.

My phone pings. Is it Milo? I hate the burst of hope that rises inside me, that maybe he likes me after all, but it's a text from Thea.

How'd it go? Did he say yes to spring fling?

I groan and write back: I took your advice. I seized the day.

Ahem?!

My feelings are too tender to spell out everything in detail, so I send her a single emoji—the broken heart.

She replies in three seconds flat. God, I'm sorry. Meet me on Constitution, and we'll get milkshakes. By the way Milo is a bastard and I hate him forever.

Through my tears, I laugh, even though Milo isn't a bastard. He's smart and kind and cute and . . . he just doesn't like me as more than a friend.

Miserably, I wonder if I'm more like Juliet Capulet than I'd realized, doomed to a life of Shakespearean tragedy, except that she had her Romeo's love while Milo will never think of me that way. My heart hurts. Not metaphorically but physically. It literally *aches* with every beat.

My leg is starting to cramp, so I pick myself up and walk down the sidewalk, glaring at my shoes the whole way because they're leaving blisters on my heels. I wish I hadn't worn them today. I wish I hadn't come to the museum at all. I wish I had kept my mouth shut and never told Milo that I liked him in the first place.

I pause to rub my throbbing foot, and that's when a stray tabby darts out in front of me from under a trash can. I yelp as the furry ball of lightning scurries into a clump of bushes across the street. Then the thought hits me:

At least I won't end up like Joseph Preston. I won't spend the rest of my day painting street cats and pining after my LJC, wondering what might have been if I'd only been brave enough. Despite my hurt and humiliation, I know where Milo stands.

Maybe that's something I do share with Juliet of fair Verona—that we put ourselves out there for love—but that's where our similarities end.

I'm a second-chair violist who might one day take first.

I'm a natural-born coward who's learning to seize the day.

I'm Juliet of House Wu, owner of a pair of really painful loafers and a nonexistent love life, but I will survive these blisters and eventually this heartache.

So take *that*, William Shakespeare.

Death and the Maiden

Tara Sim

Parvani had never imagined facing death while dressed for a wedding.

Specifically, dressed for *her* wedding.

The mouth of the cave yawned before her, a condemned hole at the very edge of the world. The soft roar of waves rolled in from the ocean they had crossed to get here. This corner of the earth was wild and forgotten, and she felt like an intruder, a drop of ink or blood on an old, crumbling page.

No, she had not imagined death this way at all—a slow descent like wading into water, swallowed by a darkness stained with verdigris.

Her mother's hands rested on her shoulders. Parvani's vision of the world was stained crimson through her long wedding veil, embroidered at the edges with golden suns. Mehndi climbed her arms like vines and wrapped like lace around her feet. Gold and pearl and ruby sat at her throat, a weight that pulled her neck down, as if forcing her to be reverent to a god that was not hers.

Her mother's hands tightened on her shoulders, the bangles on her wrists chiming. "You know what to do," she whispered in Parvani's ear.

And she did. She would petition a foreign deity for a death.

She would avenge Ranya.

Parvani swallowed. Turning slowly, she took in her mother's face, the tired lines at her mouth, the grief already settling in her eyes. Blinking her own watering eyes, Parvani hugged her.

"I'll find a way back," she said. *Somehow.*

Her mother cradled her head and through her veil kissed the thumbprint of vermilion on her forehead. The sign of one about to be wed. About to be lost.

About to die.

Parvani turned back to the cave and took a deep breath, potentially her last. She would not look back at her mother. She wanted the last of her to live in the feeling of her kiss, warm and safe on her brow like a blessing.

This is my choice.

She took one step, and then another. The hem of her dress whispered eagerly against cold stone. Another step. Another.

The shadows swallowed her feet. She lifted her ink-stained hands and let them also be fed into the gathering dark. It was hungry—it wanted her. A shudder rolled down her spine, a strange sort of ache settling into her limbs, in her lower belly.

As she wandered farther down, a weight began to grow around her. Dread seeped in like water through porous rocks. Breathing became difficult, and her heart faltered in her chest until, eventually, it stopped beating altogether.

She panicked. Clutching her chest, she cast around for someone, anyone, to help her. There was only the darkness, its tendrils caressing her face as if telling her it would be all right. Parvani sobbed. A shadow wiped her tears away.

Is this what Ranya had felt, right before the end? This steady and terrible knowledge that she was about to become undone?

You know what to do.

This is my choice.

Vengeance was a fragile word she held beside her now-still heart, but it forced her to keep stumbling blindly into the dark.

Her hands grazed the sides of the cave. Here and there she caught a glimmer of tourmaline, amethyst, adamantine. A breeze fluttered her veil. Whispers caught her ear. On the air was a scent of marigolds, thick and cloying. It almost reminded her of home.

When she lifted her head, she saw that she had left the path. Before her was a cavern lit with soft blue, and somewhere beyond was the sound of rushing water. She drifted to an outcrop of stone in order to find the source of that water before a voice stopped her.

"The new queen finally arrives."

She turned her head. Three women stood on the other side of the cavern, under a patch of algae that seemed to be giving off that ethereal blue glow. Their skin was ebony and their heads were shaved, their bodies crafted with long, elegant limbs and curves that would make a mountain range envious. Gold glittered upon them—on their shoulders, on their bellies, even on one's face—as if a foil had been grafted onto their flesh.

They didn't speak any further, not even when she stood there and waited. They had called her *queen*. Did they know where she ought to go?

She opened her mouth to ask, but they retreated into a crevice, lips turned up in cruel smiles. It was in their black eyes too: something more predator than human, a terrible rage contained.

Parvani shivered. Out of the darkness, she finally began to feel the cold, and she wrapped her arms about herself as she headed away from the three women and toward the sound of water.

Queen. She did not come here to be a queen. She had come for only one thing: to end a man's life.

If her request was granted.

She emerged on a sandy bank that met the side of a flowing river like a hand cupping a cheek. Waiting on the shore was a long, sleek boat of gray wood, its sides painted green and orange. Swirling, intricate designs sprawled across the wood like the dye on her hands and feet. Hanging from the prow was a garland of marigolds.

It stunned her. Had this been done for her? Did the god know of the cultures of her kingdom?

Parvani kept shivering, but she forced herself to approach the boat, to carefully get inside and sit on the bench. There were no oars and no ferryman, but the boat smoothly launched itself into the rolling water, taking her onward.

Time passed, but she couldn't tell how much. She sat in her wedding vessel with her hands tightly clasped upon her lap, head down, eyes closed, drawing upon her waning strength to do what must be done.

The sloshing song of the water began to ebb, and she opened her eyes. The boat had carried her all the way down the river into a small pocket of a lake. It berthed now at a rocky shore, beneath a growth of pointing stalactites.

Pointing at the figure of a woman.

Parvani swallowed her gasp. The woman was dressed in dark threads, a gown of onyx and raven feathers. A black veil hung from a crown made of a stag's horns, shockingly white, as if bleached by the sun.

The woman stood silently, waiting for her to approach. When Parvani found that she could not move, the woman drifted to the side of the boat and raised a hand as pale as ash.

It took a moment for Parvani to unclasp her hands, now clammy and aching. She put one against the woman's palm and felt herself drawn up by a strength that surprised her. She somewhat clumsily got out of the boat and felt the sharp chill of the rocks beneath her soles.

The woman studied her a moment. Through the veil Parvani could see a pale face, long and thin, exquisitely beautiful. In fact, this close, she didn't seem a woman at all—she looked not much older than Parvani herself.

But of course, the subject of age was trivial when you were talking about a god.

Parvani forced herself to swallow. She dipped her head and body in respect, fanning her crimson bridal gown around her.

"Hades," she whispered to the river-cold rocks. "I have come to be yours."

She had grown up with the stories of other nations' gods, told in excited whispers as if wickedly divine on the tongue. One of them was Hades and the Netherworld, the realm of gamboling spirits and memory. How a bride was routinely given to the cave's maw, a girl swallowed whole to appease the sovereign of the dead. That was how Hades found the strength to keep the Netherworld in balance; without that power, the bridge between worlds would fade, until the living might as well have been called the dead.

Parvani had never imagined volunteering to become one of those girls. Now as she stood within a cluster of marble pillars, Hades herself before her, she still couldn't quite believe it.

They kept their veils lowered. They were alone in the open-faced portico, its columns choked with creeping vines and jasmine. Beyond, she again heard the rush of water. It seemed to be everywhere.

She couldn't stop trembling. When she'd first had this idea, she had been so certain, so determined. Now that it was unfolding before her, she wondered if she could truly accept an existence under the earth, where breath cut off and hearts were still.

She would not let this sacrifice be in vain. For Ranya's sake.

Her mother had wept when she revealed her plan, because she knew her daughter loved to run and climb, to feel the wind in her hair, to wade through the shoals of the river that cut through their city like a lazy serpent.

Her forehead still felt warm with her mother's blessing. She allowed that to calm her as Hades stepped closer, lifting her hands. In one rested the seductive curve of a mango. In the other, a knife.

Parvani knew the stories, but it had always been different fruit than this: figs, peaches, pomegranates. Was the god giving her another homage to her home? She forced herself to take up the knife, its bone hilt oddly soft in her grip. Next she took the mango, already smelling its familiar perfume.

The scent was an attack. Summer mangoes in the garden, dropping to the ground as if they were falling stars. Ranya up in the tree among them, grinning down at her from the very center of the universe. She would try to aim for Parvani's head as she threw them down, her laugh following like a comet's tail.

Her lips couldn't determine whether to smile or tremble. Pressing them firmly together, Parvani expertly cut a vibrant orange moon from one side of the mango. Peeling away its skin, she raised the flesh to her lips.

"Once you eat it, you can't return."

The words were soft, musical. Parvani raised her eyes to Hades's. She couldn't make out all her features through the veil, but she thought her eyes might be gray, the same churning coldness of the river she'd traveled to get here.

Keeping their gazes locked, Parvani fed herself the mango. Its nectar filled her mouth like a kiss.

Hades lowered her head in recognition. She took the mango and the knife from her hands and cut off a bite, which she ate soundlessly.

And then it was done.

Parvani was now a bride entire, with nectar heavy on her tongue and her mother's blessing turned cold.

Hades's palace was surrounded by asphodel.

The white stone building was built into the side of what looked to be a mountain, and for a moment, Parvani forgot that they were supposed to be beneath the earth. There was a sky here, dark and gray, with winking lights that could have been stars or jewels.

The valley was mostly barren, not verdant like the valley beyond her city's walls. Except for the asphodel; they swayed in a light breeze, their white palms open, tinged with purple.

Parvani followed Hades inside, through more columns and down long hallways, past crumbling statues missing heads and arms, over veined marble floors. Her shivering grew worse. Her mouth and fingers were sticky with mango juice.

Hades walked through an archway, and Parvani saw a large bedchamber beyond. The bed was a wide and foreign thing, draped in black and scarlet silks.

Hades bent her head and silently walked back out. Parvani stood there a moment, uncertain, but when it was clear Hades wasn't coming back, she finally let her shoulders sag.

She twisted her bangles off, lifted her veil, and carefully removed her bridal jewelry. She was wondering how she would get out of her clothes when the shadows in the corners of the room moved toward her. Fear clutched her throat, but these shadows had the same gentle caresses as the ones in the cave, so she forced herself to relax and let them assist.

Out of her heavy dress and jewelry, she could breathe. A white nightgown was laid out on the bed, and she slipped it on before turning to a large, silver-wreathed mirror on the wall.

She paused. The vermilion mark was still on her forehead, the last vestige she had of the world of the living.

She took a moment to memorize herself like this, still caught between one world and the next. Then she moved to the water basin and washed the mark off.

When Hades returned, Parvani was sitting on the edge of the bed. Hades had removed her veil and bone crown so that Parvani could gaze freely upon her face. It was as cold and beautiful as the marble surrounding them, her cheekbones high and her mouth sinfully red. Her eyes, when they rested on Parvani, were the blue-gray of agate.

Parvani shook. She tried to think of Ranya's smile, her laugh, her stories.

You know what to do.

This is my choice.

Slowly, carefully, as if trying to avoid aggravating a snake, she lay back upon the bed.

Hades watched without a shift of expression. But she came to the side of the bed and sat there, her presence like the first breeze of approaching winter, or the clean, cold air of night.

Parvani attempted to hide her uneven breathing. Her heart would have pounded, if it were still capable of doing so. Her nightgown was thin, and Hades looked down, as one starving looks at a feast.

Fingers as white and cold as bone came to rest upon her chest.

Parvani flinched.

Hades froze, then slowly removed her hand. She stood, as fluid and dark as water.

Parvani sat up. "Where are you going?"

Hades stopped in the archway and looked over her shoulder. "I do not touch the unwilling."

She left, and Parvani battled with relief and despair. She held her head in her hands as she finally allowed herself to weep.

She dreamed of her city. How it used to be—how she wanted to remember it. Cramped houses along winding dirt roads, bright jewel-colored kites flown in spring, the comforting lights of autumn festivals.

She slept deep and undisturbed.

She didn't see Hades for a few days. Still gripped by an instinctual fear, Parvani was fine with this arrangement, but once the fear wore off, she grew bored. She took to wandering the palace, wiping her fingers over dusty mantels and listening to the solitary echo of her own feet against marble.

No one else resided in the palace, from what she could see. It was only her and the shadows, which trailed after her like a lady-in-waiting. Parvani found clothes for herself in a grand bureau in her bedroom—their bedroom?—and was startled to find that they were in the style of her people: long tunics embroidered with silver and gold thread, silk pants, trailing fabrics in colors that could rival a parrot's plumage.

Had Hades done this for her?

It was also a surprise to find food and drink whenever she required it. She was sitting on a balcony overlooking the asphodel when she suddenly craved her mother's tea, and turning to the small table beside her chaise, she was startled to find a silver tea tray. The tea tasted almost as good as her mother's, creamy and spicy and sweet.

And every night she was greeted with dreams that left her aching in the morning. Dreams of home, her mother, Ranya, the adventures they would never have.

Eventually boredom gave way to annoyance. She had come here with a purpose, and it was her duty to see it through. She couldn't do that if Hades was avoiding her.

When her mehndi was mostly faded, she finally found Hades sitting in the dining room where Parvani liked to take her meals. It had an open wall framed by arches that oversaw the valley below. The sky was pearlescent, giving everything a monochrome look, but the lanterns inside provided much-needed color.

Hades sat at the head of the table, hands folded in her lap. She wore a demure black dress with long sleeves that tapered into gloves that covered only her palms. Her antlered crown was perched on her head of dark hair, which fell in hypnotizing waves.

Hades looked up when Parvani entered. She didn't say anything—just sat there and watched her with those steady agate eyes.

Parvani bit the inside of her cheek and sat on the opposite end of the table. Her plate was already filled with the things she loved: spinach and potato pastries with pomegranate chutney, chewy flatbread smothered in butter and garlic, chicken in a rich, milky sauce studded with peas. Mint tea had been poured for her, as well as a glass of garnet-colored wine.

They were silent a moment. Then Hades began to nibble on some flatbread, and Parvani laughed. Hades lifted one perfectly arched eyebrow.

"Sorry," Parvani blurted. "I just . . . didn't know you ate."

Hades put the piece of flatbread down. "I don't have to. I like to, though."

"Oh." Now feeling guilty that she'd made her self-conscious—was it possible for a god to feel self-conscious?—Parvani took a long sip of wine and began to eat her own food.

It was delicious. It was always delicious here.

The silence turned heavy, a storm cloud about to shed its rain. Parvani swallowed more wine and peered at Hades through her lashes.

She couldn't afford Hades running off again. She needed a strategy.

You know what to do.

"I'm sorry," Parvani said softly. "About how I reacted that night. I've never . . ."

Hades inclined her head knowingly.

"I'd like to, though," Parvani went on, her voice a little high in her ears. She swallowed, getting up from her seat. Hades tracked her movements with her eyes, hands still folded in her lap as she came closer. "I would."

Parvani reached out an unsteady hand and touched the side of the god's face. It was smooth, soft, a surprising contrast to something deadly, like the bone knife in her hand had felt.

You know what to do.

Framing the god's face with her hands, she leaned down to kiss her.

It was cold at first, her lips a little numb from the wine. But then she felt Hades touch her waist, and heat darted through her unexpectedly, making her gasp.

Hades began to kiss her back. Soft, a little uncertain. She smelled like jasmine blossoms at midnight, cold and tempting, a secret hidden sweetly in the dark.

Then Hades pulled away, distrust in her eyes.

"Not like this," she murmured, her lips even redder than usual, her face faintly flushed. "You've had drink."

"That doesn't matter."

Hades took a good long look at her, registering the frustration in her voice. Her eyes narrowed slightly.

"You want something," she deduced.

Parvani backed away, holding on to one wrist with a hand that still burned from Hades's touch.

Tell her. Ask her. Beg her.

"Well?" Hades demanded. "What is it?"

Parvani took in a breath and lowered herself to her knees, head bent. "Hades, please, I beseech you. There is a man—"

A soft snort above her. "And you'd rather be with him?"

Parvani flushed. It was true there was a boy back home she'd once been sweet on, but he'd had his sights set on the tailor's daughter.

"No," she said heavily. "It's . . . my people are in trouble. This man, Hajan, rules over us, but he is corrupting us, turning us against each other. My city was once rich, and is now becoming impoverished. Wars are being started that we do not want to fight." She closed her eyes, but a tear escaped anyway. "Please, Hades, you must help me. As your wife, I beg of you. You must—"

"No."

Parvani's head snapped up, her tears drying. Hades met her gaze levelly.

"I do not kill men for sport," Hades went on. "Especially those who are not in my domain. I merely tend to the souls who come here. That's all."

Parvani clenched her fists against the marble floor. "You don't understand." Her voice was a ragged whisper. "He took her. My friend, Ranya. Her brother was killed in the war Hajan started."

They had sat for hours upon Ranya's bed. Parvani had held her, rocked her, cried with her. Grief was a weight, and Ranya had carried a world of it.

"One day, Hajan's heir was in the city with his guards. They passed Ranya's house. In her grief, she . . . she ran outside with a kitchen knife. She tried to harm Hajan's son. But she was caught, and . . ."

She could not forget it: her friend's body swinging from the gibbet among the thieves and traitors, her beautiful face bloated with blood, her smile forever gone.

Her tears began again. "Please, Hades, I'm begging you—"

"If you've come to the Netherworld solely for this, you should have trained to become an assassin instead." Hades stood with a growl of her chair legs. "My duty will not be tarnished. Not for your revenge."

She left, and Parvani once again found herself alone and bitter, not even the shadows coming in to comfort her.

Her jaw tightened as she looked out one of the archways. Fine, then; if Hades would not help her, she would find a way to avenge Ranya herself.

She wore her anger like armor as she wandered into the mist.

"Wayward girls shouldn't wander," Ranya would whisper at night as they sat under the protection of a blanket lit from within by the irregular glow of an earthen lantern. "They're hunted, snatched up, and never seen again. There are things that grab them in the dark and never let go."

This time, Parvani was the one who would do the hunting.

She walked barefoot through the asphodel, past the chalky valley, down into the catacombs of her new domain. Strange that she should be considered queen of a place she hardly knew.

Wayward girls were snatched up even if they didn't wander. Hajan had an appetite for war, wine, and women, and his son was no better. More girls than Ranya had gone missing in the past year. Parvani liked to think they had escaped the city, rather than imaging the numerous other fates that could have befallen them in a territory turned to decay.

Parvani followed the sound of water. There were rustles in the shadows, under cave awnings and between columns of overgrown crystal. Who else lived in the Netherworld? She tried to remember the stories. It was said to be not only the home of spirits, but some lesser gods as well: the Bringer of Night and her children, Dusk and Dawn. The Lord of Memory. The Maiden of Songs.

She wished she could remember her own gods. But Hajan had burned all the texts long ago, converting temples to armories and pleasure houses.

Parvani found a river, the sluggish waters gray. A bend up ahead curved into an open space studded with barren, ashy trees.

The longer she walked beside the river, the heavier she felt, until some of the cold water splashed up onto her ankle. An unspeakable pressure grew beneath her breastbone. It was the feeling of letting go of someone's hand, the sting of being forgotten, the ache of losing something irretrievable. Tears fell from her eyes, and they somehow seemed to roll toward the river, becoming part of its somber current.

Get away from this place.

She staggered as far from the water as she could, crossing a threshold of loamy rocks that rose into craggy hills. It was almost like exploring the terrain outside the city, but with no sun to warm her back. Parvani was breathing harder by the time the landscape shifted yet again, this time into an orchard of sky-black trees with star-silver leaves. Through the dark shapes of twisting branches she spotted another river, ice caps floating on its surface.

Parvani felt a gaze upon her and looked between the trunks for its source. Those three dark-skinned women were back, watching her in the orchard's shadows. They didn't seem to mean her harm, but the gold on their bodies glittered like a threat.

She edged away from them, toward the river. Her throat was suddenly hot and tight, aching for water. Would it be safe to drink? This one didn't seem to be affecting her, filling her with that terrible sadness.

Biting her lower lip, she sank to her knees on the bank. She skimmed her fingers through the freezing current. Still no reaction. So she cupped her hand and brought the water to her lips to drink. The water was cold and sweet and hazy in her mouth. She reached for another draught.

Hands burst out of the water, skeletal and made of ice. They grabbed her by the arm and, before she could scream, pulled her into the river.

The world turned to ice and darkness. Her lungs frosted over. She opened her mouth and felt the last of her breath leave her, and with it, something intangibly crucial, rendering her incomplete—a book without its binding, or a forge without its fire.

She stopped fighting. The skeletal hands let go. She drifted through the river, content to do nothing. She may have always lived down here, in the murk and gloom.

Then the hands grasped her again—only now they weren't made of ice, but flesh.

She was pulled out of the current sputtering and coughing. Parvani found herself lying on a shore of black sand, glittering like the afterthoughts of diamonds.

"What are you doing?" growled a voice above her.

She looked up, wet hair sticking to her face. The voice belonged to a beautiful young woman, pale and irate.

"Wh-who are you?" Parvani choked out. Her mind tickled, as if she might know the answer, but she was curiously blank.

The young woman hauled her to her feet and pulled her away from the bank. Parvani followed at a leaden pace. Eventually they came across another river, the water bright turquoise. Without ceremony, the young woman pushed Parvani in.

She splashed and yelped, accidentally swallowing some of the warm water. Coughing, she managed to stand on the riverbed, where the water laughed over her thighs. She glared up at Hades, who stood with her arms crossed on the shore.

"What are you doing?" Parvani demanded.

"That's *my* question," Hades said. "You disappeared, and I found you drowning in the river of forgetfulness."

It came rushing back now: the grasping hands in the river. Parvani hurried out of the water.

"You're safe in that one," Hades drawled. "It's the river of memory. If you wanted to explore, you should have told me. It's dangerous otherwise."

Parvani crossed her arms, pretending she didn't look like a thing drowned. "After you chastised me?"

Hades's eyes flashed. "It was deserved."

Parvani pressed her lips together, beginning to shake in the chill. Hades noticed and sighed, unfastening her cloak to settle it on Parvani's shoulders.

"If you want," the god said, eyes fixed on the cloak's clasp as she snapped it closed, "I can show you something better than the rivers."

This intrigued Parvani, so she agreed. They began to walk through the Netherworld, Parvani holding the cloak to her. It smelled like midnight and jasmine.

"Who are those women I see lurking about?" Parvani asked. "The ones with gold on their skin?"

Hades smiled a little, without mirth. "The Furies. They

have a duty here as well. They punish those on earth who have committed grievous wrong and often drag them down here, to the lowest reaches of the Netherworld."

As they walked, Parvani began to grow warmer, until she realized they were passing a rivulet of smoldering lava. She followed the trail with her eyes to a crag where the lava spilled over in imitation of a waterfall. Farther on, a geyser of fire shot out of the earth, limning the edges of a monstrous pit.

"That is where they go," Hades said.

Parvani shuddered. "But they haven't taken Hajan. Surely he's evil enough. Why haven't the Furies done anything?"

"Who can say? They have their own way of doing things. Perhaps he hasn't done enough wrong yet."

She scowled, thinking of the wars being fought in Hajan's name, Ranya's body on the gibbet. "Who are they to judge such a thing?"

Hades's eyes cut to hers. "Who are you to judge the same?"

Parvani shrank into the cloak, keeping silent as they walked. Eventually they arrived at an open valley, the glowing algae high above their heads mirroring the light of dusk. Veins of glowing lapis spiderwebbed across the rocky valley, and twinkling specks of dust—perhaps fireflies, or drifting algae—floated through the air.

A large stone archway stood in the middle of the valley.

Hades walked toward it, and Parvani followed. The closer they came, the more Parvani realized the archway was emitting a strange, soothing hum, a lullaby she felt in her chest. She hid a yawn behind a hand, and Hades smiled.

"This is the Dreamers' Gate," the god said once they stood a few paces before it. The archway was lovingly crafted from an ivory-like material, etched with vines and elegant corbels at either end of the scalloped roof. "This is where I send dreams to the living. It's . . . a comfort, compared to what else I'm expected to do."

Parvani's lips parted. "The stories didn't mention this."

"Your people do not pray to me. I doubt you've heard every story." Again, another quirk of her eyebrow. "Otherwise you would have known about the rivers."

Parvani flushed. Still, she found herself in awe that Hades, ruler of the dead, found some small solace in this task, when the living gave themselves over to sleep and the night, which was a gentler sort of death. Perhaps this was Hades's way of repenting for her grim existence.

And then she understood. "You've been giving me my dreams," Parvani whispered. "That's why I haven't suffered nightmares in this place."

Hades did not look at her, but her silence was enough. Parvani felt something welling in her, a tender gratitude that took her by surprise.

"Everything else too," Parvani said. "The food and clothes and tea."

"Shouldn't I wish for my queen to be comfortable?" A hint of wryness in her words.

"I'm sorry. I tried to use you, and that was wrong. It's just . . . I'm desperate to help my people." Parvani swallowed, still tasting the remnants of the river in her mouth, wondering if it would simply be easier to forget. "To avenge my friend."

Hades kept looking at the archway. She reached out and touched one of its columns. "Would you like to see?"

Parvani nodded.

The empty space between the columns shimmered and warped. Parvani made a small sound of amazement as it cleared into an image of her city, the quaint downtown sectors and the markets highlighted with bright awnings, the sandstone palace that, by its beauty, seemed to ignore the disease hidden within it.

The image shimmered again, and Parvani took an involuntary step forward. *Mother.* She was there, asleep in her bed, the lines at her eyes deep and cutting. Parvani brimmed with tears, which she furiously blinked back.

Hades touched a pale fingertip to the center of her mother's brow. Then they were somehow inside an abstract space, a place of light and dark, shapes and sounds and color. Hades pressed her palm to the barrier of the archway, and the dream spun out of her like wool. Parvani and her mother walking hand in hand through the saffron fields, laughing as the wind tried to tease away her mother's scarf.

Hades withdrew, watching her reaction. Parvani managed to smile, a shaky thing that was nonetheless true.

"Thank you," she whispered. The god, looking a little flustered, simply nodded.

On their way back to the palace, an idea tapped its finger on Parvani's shoulder—a sudden, sickening idea that made her stop in her tracks. Hades turned back to her.

"I know what to do," she said. "About Hajan." Hades waited, so Parvani took a deep breath. "We give him dreams. Bad dreams, nightmares, the kind you can't shake off in the morning. The kind that haunt you throughout the day."

"What would this accomplish?"

"It would make his life difficult. I want to make him as miserable as he's made my people. It's not much, but it's something."

Hades considered it, her agate gaze steady but not scornful. It held the same surprise that came with summer storms, a little wild and a little delighted and a little afraid.

The silence that followed should have made her nervous. But Parvani had danced through enough summer storms to know what would come next.

"This is what my queen desires?"

My queen. Parvani drew herself up to her full height.

"It is."

After a moment, Hades put a hand to her chest and bowed. "Then it shall be done."

They began with small things. The knee-jerk fear of a spider on his hand, the breath-constricting choke of a snake around his neck. Parvani stood and watched as Hades wove the dreams into being, a maid at a loom, mixing nightmares as if mixing colors, creating patterns out of fears.

The first few times, it was disconcerting to watch Hajan jerk out of the dreams, breathing hard and shaking his hands as if to dislodge the spiders, scratching his throat as if to throw off the snakes. He was a large man with a graying mustache and the beginnings of a potbelly, an ex-soldier gone to seed and corruption.

"It's not enough," Parvani said after a while.

Hades lifted a sleek black brow but suitably altered her creations. After that came more terrifying landscapes: the city sinking under the earth, the palace invaded by foreign raiders, a plague descending upon the kingdom.

Eventually, the dreams began to take their toll. Hajan was irritable and twitchy. His eyes were rimmed with the bruises of the sleepless. He backhanded his eldest son, the one he was grooming to be his heir. The one Ranya had tried to take her vengeance on, and who had laughed as she was dragged away screaming by the palace guard.

Hajan was miserable. It wasn't quite the retribution Parvani had intended, but it was something, and she felt cruelly better for it.

When they weren't at the Dreamers' Gate, they were at the palace or exploring the Netherworld. Hades showed her sights more wondrous than the rivers: caves of amber and emerald, a forest of bone trees, a field with tall stag-looking creatures that allowed her to pet them between their wildly twisted antlers.

The more time she spent in the god's company, the more she came to anticipate their next walk, their next meal together, the tiny smiles she managed to coax on her carmine lips.

One day—night? It was hard to tell—they were sitting on the balcony overlooking the asphodel, sharing a pot of tea. It was the kind that imitated her mother's, and Parvani wondered, not for the first time, if Hades had somehow teased this from her dreams.

"It's quite good," the god said, peering down at her clay cup. They sat side by side on the chaise. "I can see why you miss it often."

Parvani smiled sadly, fiddling with the edge of her scarf. "It's more than the tea I miss." She hesitated, the words crammed behind her tongue. Eventually she blurted, "Is it possible to return? To visit?"

Hades looked at her, unsurprised and perhaps a little resigned. "I've had others ask this of me. I've even had some ask to break the contract altogether, though that is impossible. Is that what you want as well?"

Was it? Her first few days here had been miserable, but now . . . she was learning to keep her eyes open to the strange wonders around her. More than that, staying here meant feeding Hajan nightmares. If she went back home, she'd be powerless.

"No," she said truthfully.

Hades set her cup down. "You are allowed to visit, but only twice a year, when the borders between the worlds of the living and dead are thinnest. When summer fades into the deepest stretch of fall, and when winter thaws into spring."

Twice a year. Parvani took a deep breath and nodded.

They sat in silence, appreciating the simple calm it brought. Then Hades turned back to her.

"You truly want to stay here?" she asked quietly.

Parvani's face heated. She met Hades's eyes, nodding again. What else could she say to the one who crafted comfort just for her, who had read the stories in her heart and let her live them in her dreams?

They were leaning in closer, jasmine and cardamom and the sweet, crisp air of night. Hades touched the side of her jaw, a tangle of a lightning storm caught in her fingertips.

Their lips met, a softness and a sweetness. Her kiss was the last star before dawn, one small torch against the dark that heralded the coming of a greater light.

They murmured the secrets of the world into each other, hidden in the press of heat and hands. Parvani wondered if this was how the sun would feel if the moon ever caught up to it, a coming together of light and dark, a warmth that was eclipsing.

Hades's lips skimmed down her throat, onto the shelf of her exposed collarbone. Parvani shivered and ran a hand through the dark glossy falls of the god's hair. Her body was made of a million exclamations, all of them begging for touch.

It was the first time Hades entered their bedroom since their wedding night. This, Parvani knew, was their actual wedding night. Fabrics sliding away from skin, semi-frantic kisses. She marveled at the smooth curve of Hades's hip. The soft inside of her thigh. Her own body was somehow more beautiful next to hers, and they were more beautiful together, a fusion of memory and creation. *This is better than any dream*, Parvani thought.

And as if Hades agreed, her sleep that night was blissfully blank.

The Netherworld seemed brighter and more wondrous than ever. It was a living thing, thriving off passion. As winter hardened the world above, Parvani was resplendent in her love and curiosity.

Except when they stood before the Dreamers' Gate, carving out the dark seeds of nightmares.

It happened during the last of winter's choke hold. Parvani had been observing Hajan these last few months, quietly demanding that the nightmares turn more vicious, more unrelenting. She had turned bold in the light of Hades's affections, powerful in body and purpose. Eventually she'd come to savor that twilight merging of pleasure and pain, love and darkness at war with each other even as they entwined.

So they gave him dreams of treason and subterfuge. Spies and assassins and foreign conquerors. Dreams of grave illnesses, poisons, gangrenous diseases that peeled the flesh away from his bones. She could see their effect through the window of the archway—Hajan reduced to an ashen, trembling mess of a man, bloodshot eyes constantly shifting in suspicion. Parvani sometimes stumbled away to be sick, though she did not ask Hades to stop.

Perhaps, if she'd known what was coming, she would have.

Hajan had become wilder, more unstable in his demands. He broke into sobs and threw goblets of wine at the walls. He beat his wives and sons (Parvani clenched her fists and teeth, feeling responsible) and ordered more than one of his advisors to public execution for doing little more than cautiously questioning his decisions.

And then one day, his fragile shell shattered.

He was shaking after a nightmare about a usurper, faceless and young and mocking. He'd been forced naked before the city, then drawn and quartered. Hajan paced his chambers, mumbling and frantic, clothes practically falling off his emaciated frame.

A knock on the door. He spun around, gripping a knife from the table. His eldest son came in, face drawn tight, an heir about to overstep his bounds. Parvani almost recoiled, remembering the sadistic glint in his eyes as Ranya had been taken.

"Father, you must come out. You cannot stay in here forever."

"No. I won't let you lead me astray." Hajan breathed like a bull, eyes wide and terrified. "I will not go! You will not take my throne from me!"

His son frowned. "Father, that's not—"

Hajan couldn't distinguish between nightmare and reality. The young man before him was an enemy, the one who had laughed at him from the gallows. With a yell he darted forward with a speed that heralded his past as a soldier, plunging the knife into his son's chest.

Parvani gasped. Hades's eyebrows rose. Hajan stepped away and watched as his son sank to the floor and gurgled over the blood in his mouth, gaze incredulous. He twitched a few times, then was still.

Hajan's lips trembled. He laughed haltingly. "See? See! I am ruler. *Me*. I will not—you will not—make me—"

Shadows in the corner of the room grew darker. They coalesced into the forms of three dark-skinned women, the gold on their skin gleaming like malevolent eyes. They walked on soundless feet, surrounding Hajan. Hajan looked between them, teeth bared.

"You will not take me! You cannot!"

The Furies closed in. They grabbed Hajan as he began to scream, his voice raising to a sharp, terrified pitch as the shadows swirled and consumed them. All that was left was a flare of sparks, and a scorch mark where Hajan had stood.

Parvani thought of that dark, fire-spewing pit and shuddered.

She stepped away, pressing the heels of her hands to her eyes. There was a hesitant touch on her arm.

"It is what you wanted," Hades reminded her.

Was it? She had wanted a solution, to rescue her people, to avenge Ranya. The possibility of a brighter future.

"This is not solely your doing," Hades went on. "He is responsible for his actions. The Furies knew that. They wouldn't have come for him otherwise."

They punish those on earth who have committed grievous wrong. That's what Hades had told her. Parvani lowered her hands and met Hades's eyes. They were soft in their understanding.

"I feel wicked," Parvani said softly.

Hades smoothed back some of her hair, tucking it behind an ear. "It's all right to feel wicked sometimes, so long as you don't remain so. Sometimes a field must burn before it grows wheat."

Those words stayed with her for days as she wandered the Netherworld in a fugue. Suddenly it didn't look so beautiful or bright, but that was because she felt so ugly inside, so poisoned with vengeance. It was no longer a pale word within her, but a stark, ragged scar.

Ranya, I'm sorry. Is this what you would have wanted?

But Ranya couldn't answer. Her soul was already in the furthest reaches of the Netherworld, where Parvani couldn't follow.

She stood at the shore of the river of forgetfulness, debating whether or not to take a sip, to let herself be taken. But she never again wanted to feel the gray slush gripping her ankles, those skeletal hands of ice dragging her down to a silent place that wasn't meant for the living. It had been a world frozen over, without breath or thought or memory. A world without meaning.

If she was going to be a part of this world, she wanted to give it meaning.

She had burned the field. It was time to grow her wheat.

As winter began to melt away, Parvani asked Hades a question. The god hesitated, then agreed and accepted her kiss. Their bed that night was warm and filled with the soft, restless sounds of two worlds merging.

Parvani wept at the feeling of sunlight on her body.

She wept again at the sight of her city, full of voices and laughter and children running through the streets. The gossip she heard in the crowds was that Hajan's second-eldest son had taken the throne, a young man often teased for his love of poetry and astronomy. His first decree was to return funding to the temples, funding that had been redirected to his father's wars, which were now undergoing peace negotiations.

Her mother wept, too, when she saw her.

Parvani felt as safe in her mother's arms as she felt at Hades's side. With her mother stroking her hair, she told her what she'd done, feeling again a guilty stab between her ribs. Her mother kissed her brow, a blessing reapplied.

"Is it right?" Parvani asked later, drinking her mother's tea. "What I've done?"

"It was what you set out to do."

At the reminder, shame flooded her again. But her mother continued to hold her, and she hoped, somewhere, that Ranya's family now felt some measure of peace.

Before she'd left, Parvani had asked Hades if she could

help bring dreams to the living. Not nightmares, but sweeter things, the sort of dreams that made you sigh upon waking and made your heart beat calm and steady.

Sometimes a field must burn to grow wheat. This would be her way to atone.

Her mother combed fingers through her hair as Parvani told her this. "And will this make you happy?"

Parvani glanced at the empty mango tree behind their house. "Yes."

Her mother smiled, and her eyes were shining. "Then you know what to do."

They spoke of gods as immortal, eternal, a strength to be feared. What, then, would they say of the goddess who walked barefoot into death, baring her skin to grief and mortality? What stories would they tell of the girl who repeatedly lived and died and lived again, a phantom traveling between worlds, the pale horizon between spring and winter? She was neither warm nor cold, alive nor dead.

She was the queen of death and dreams and memory, and she was coming home.

# Faithfull

Karuna Riazi

At my mother's wedding reception, I had a tough time finding the right dish that embodied "Yulia has decided to become a cougar."

It was troubling, as I usually had a gift for eating my feelings. I could figure out if a really bad day warranted something with a ton of cheese pulls, or a mug cake with a few extra guilt-free shavings of chocolate around the rim. I knew how to feast out of spite for the douchebag who swerved around me at the red light. Out of relief in passing that physics test I did not study for. Out of . . . something . . . for my cougar mom?

One of the old ladies, a face I did not know in a sea of faces I did not know, cleared her throat, and I snapped back to the present.

Guilt churned in my stomach.

I had a feeling it made me a very bad daughter to contemplate food at my mom's wedding, but how else was I supposed to cope? That was my thing, just as much as Yulia's thing was apparently tossing herself headlong into marriage.

"I'm getting married, baby!"

When she'd told me a few nights ago, my first thought was that she'd committed herself to a convent. Was that the right word, *committed*? My experience with nuns was a black habit of uncertainty, stitched together by way of *The Sound of Music*, *Sister Act*, and a single lyric from a Death Cab for Cutie song. Yulia definitely wouldn't make it in there past two hours. After all, she was allergic to the word *commitment*. And also, she couldn't hold a tune, and to achieve happiness in a convent, you apparently needed to be ready to belt out an inspiring ballad or two at a given moment.

But then I remembered that the Catholic phase was over before I was born, back when Yulia actually kept in touch with my grandmother and tried to be a good daughter and go to Mass.

I stared at her, mouth still pursed around an errant spaghetti noodle, trying to appropriately comprehend what she had just said.

Married.

"It's not Dad, is it?" I finally choked out.

That was enough to shut off her glow, like a light bulb. We didn't talk about Dad, not outwardly. Dad was an equal-opportunity vampire. He liked to aim for your jugular, but suck more than your blood.

"No," Yulia said gently. "Of course it's not Dad. It's a brother from the halaqah I've been in—the learning group, at the masjid? You'll love him. He's really sweet. Moroccan."

"Didn't you join that two weeks ago?"

"*Three* weeks, Em. Honey." Yulia reached out and covered my arm with her hand. Her voice was soft, in that tone she reserved for conversations about what had happened at school that warranted an entire sheet cake and half a container of frosting ("No judgments on that at all, honey, but if you need me to call someone . . .") or, well, about Dad.

"It's going to be different, this time," she said.

(I'd heard that one before.)

"*He's* different this time."

I looked her in the eyes. There was that glow again. I couldn't protest at all.

"I'm happy to hear that, Mom," I said, and patted her hand back.

Yulia beamed from ear to ear.

"So, tomorrow, some of the sisters are coming over to help me figure out decorations for the masjid. Don't worry about coming down if you have homework, okay, but they really do want to meet you."

"Sure." I was already looking down at my plate and wrapping noodle tendrils into a neat nest around my fork. I never bothered to meet her friends unless it was by accident. They didn't linger once she got tired of their activity of the week, and we both liked it that way.

All of this was normal.

All of this was the way it was with the two of us.

Until, of course, it wasn't.

The buffet table stretched out in front of me, a jumble of homemade treats and cultural delicacies. I was lucky to put names to some that I'd had with old friends—friends that might as well have been swept out the door with Dad after I became a "child of divorce": chicken tikka, lamb biryani spiked with juicy raisins and shimmering prunes, and a large plate of syrupy orange jalebi sweets.

I moved slowly down the line, popping a little taste from each tray in my mouth as I went and shaking my head.

No, no, no. It's not right. I hadn't meant to say the words out loud. Maybe I hadn't.

"What about the spinach offends you so badly?"

I flinched, startled. A very cute, twinkle-eyed boy stood beside me. He smirked at the flaky pastry in my hand. He was probably my age, lean in a way that suggested athlete instead of gawky beanpole. He was also—genuinely—tall, dark, and handsome, with a gentle dusting of black stubble over his chin and the slight suggestion of dimples. Out of all the things I choose to get hungry over, I try not to make boys one of them. They are more likely to give you indigestion, and they never taste the way they look at first glance.

"Nothing," I said shortly. I turned back to the table, dropping the pastry and settling on a piece of naan. "Isn't there a line for the guys over there?"

The boy seemed entirely unruffled by my dismissal. "Food ran out, so my mom told me to wait here while she sends over another tray. Brother Khalid has a lot of friends."

Brother Khalid. Right. My new stepfather. I peeked over the boy's shoulder, my eyes quickly settling on the now-familiar face: as always, grinning so you could see his snaggle tooth, and framed by a wild tangle of curls. Brother Khalid was Moroccan, had never been married, and, according to my dreamy-eyed mother, had "*such* a way with words."

"Anyway, you didn't answer my question, Goldilocks."

"Goldilocks?" I snorted. "Really?"

I couldn't help but reach up and touch the scarf on my head, though, hoping it hadn't slid back. I knew a lot of girls at the masjid didn't wear hijab at all, but Yulia had been dead set on me making a good impression on her new friend circle. I was pretty sure I looked more like a frazzled babushka than the all-American Muslim girl Yulia wanted to pretend I was going to be, but whatever. It wasn't like this was permanent.

"You know: 'Too salty!' 'Too sweet!'" The boy paused dramatically and then slipped into a deep baritone. "Mm. Just right."

That was enough for me.

"Ah, I see. Okay. Well, if you'll excuse me . . ."

"Rehan," he said brightly.

"Pardon?"

"My name is Rehan. Nice to meet you, Sister Emmeline."

"Oh, God, no." I held up a hand, flushing. "No, I didn't mean you. Emmeline is my grandma. Literally. I'm named after her."

The last of my mother's attempts to be a good daughter, tacked on after the agreement to marry my dad. Neither had done either of us any good, and even though, honestly, if you pared it down, none of it was my grandmother's fault—or what she even asked my mother to do outright—it felt better for Yulia to make it one and the same.

"You can call me Em."

"Sister Em." He nodded seriously. "So, think you'll find anything here that suits your fancy?"

"It's not like I'm a picky eater," I mumbled. "It's just . . . I was looking for something a little more filling, that's all."

It didn't help that, apparently, Brother Khalid was not only the new stepfather but also the new chef.

"I didn't want to make trouble," he apologized as I stared down at a plate laden with sweetly filled nut crepes. "These are just the way my mom makes them."

"They are so good," gushed Yulia.

I wanted to ask her when she'd had the opportunity to taste her new husband's crepes when she hadn't even had enough time to tell me about *meeting* him, but I decided against it.

This was the first morning they were back from their honeymoon, and though I'd considered bracing myself with a stiff cup of black coffee against the gooey banter and sheep eyes, they were being tame. I hadn't seen so much more than a quick pat on the shoulder.

That was comforting. That was normal. Maybe Yulia was already cooling off from her recent exploration into cougarhood. If he wasn't going to stick around, I could allow him a small victory and his presence in my kitchen, even though I wasn't a sweets person in the morning at all.

I thought Yulia knew that. Even at my lowest, it had to be savory, something that crisped up around the edges or was dense and peppery and dripped with melted cheese. I shoved sliced strawberries to the rim of my plate like they were skaters reluctant to touch the ice, and let Yulia and Khalid's chatter buzz around my ears, until two words Yulia said made me rear my head up.

". . . Sunday school."

"What did you say?"

"Sunday school," Yulia repeated patiently. "We thought it would be good for you to pop in today. You might make some friends!"

"Saying it that way implies I don't have any."

"When was the last time any of them were over here?"

"I like to compartmentalize my life. You know that."

I hoped my glower at her transmitted everything else I wished I could say if there wasn't another witness: that we both compartmentalized our lives. She ventured into kickboxing, decided she was going to get certified to become a day-care owner, or attended an MLM meeting and came home laden down with tacky leggings and stringy, cheapsmelling shampoo.

And I went to school, chose my lunch with care, hung out at my friends' houses, where if their moms had hobbies, they indulged in them reasonably—wading in so that their passions sloshed just over their knees and didn't immerse their faces, plunging in only to clamber out, gasping, because they went too far down too fast.

I put aside the kickboxing gloves when they started to gather dust on the coffee table, tore down the class brochures or told the pleasant-sounding secretary who kept calling that my mother had decided to drop her certification classes, and poured the shampoo down the drain.

But that was it. I didn't get involved myself.

And up until now, I thought we understood each other about why that mattered, and how it worked well.

"And I'm not sure I'm a good fit . . . for Sunday school," I managed, this time in Brother Khalid's direction. He was still smiling, eyes downcast to focus on his crepe, dragging the tines of his fork through a smear of Nutella.

"You are. You will be," Brother Khalid said. "The girls will love you. A change is always good."

I took a bite of my crepe. It was too sweet, cloying on my tongue.

Everything was wrong.

He was wrong.

A change wasn't always good, particularly when nothing tasted right anymore.

Before Yulia and Emmeline, my grandmother, parted ways with a final vicious phone call and a ceasing of Christmas cards, I had a faint understanding of what it meant to attend church. I think I went to a distant cousin's wedding once, staring up in awe at Jesus etched out in glass panes—beautiful and patient as he hung on the cross—and shifting back and forth on a wooden pew.

Again, I would be in a church-like atmosphere because of a marriage, and I assumed it would be more of the same: hushed voices, hand clamped over my knee so I didn't get any ideas to rush up and down the aisle out of turn.

I was wrong. Sunday school at the masjid meant being

back up in the women's section, which jutted like an unhinged upper jaw over the lower men's chamber. It was packed with girls, separated by age and presided over by weary teachers who hardly looked old enough to drive, much less come up with reasonable lesson plans.

My mom, gushing and glowing, soaked up all the congratulations by several giddy moms. I got introduced to them, but their names passed over me like the hems of their gauzy scarves. And of course, once she had done her part of maneuvering me over the crossed legs and outstretched hands on the floor, she disappeared.

Great.

I got sandwiched between two girls, Sabrena and Hala. They were obviously sisters, or else the type of best friends whose devotion could be reflected in how their jaws, noses, and even slight bands of sun-freckles seemed to mirror each other. I only knew their names because they kept popping them into conversation, like I would forget if I didn't hear them pointedly every few minutes. It was obviously a setup from the get go.

My stomach grumbled. I could have used a breakfast burrito, or maybe just skipped over the rational pattern of meals in the days and gone to town on a burger and fries. Brother Khalid had been infiltrating my kitchen a lot recently, scorching pans in his determination to make us the perfect couscous and chicken peppered with bitter pickled lemon or an elaborate cooked salad that would, in his words, "take us right to Casablanca."

It was hard to remind myself that this would be over soon when Yulia was still looking at him with those wide moon eyes and . . . well, I was here. Next to Sabrena and Hala, who were as subtle about their mission to "make me feel welcome" as if they were acting out a comedy routine on Open Mic Night.

"And then there's . . . oh, but *Hala* could tell you more about that, right, Hala?"

"*Sabrena* really likes our weekend camps. You should join us sometime."

Not if I could ever help it.

The only really interesting thing happened around lunch, when I was being dragged downstairs to the kitchen in the basement. A familiar name rang out.

"Brother Rehan!"

I looked up. Sabrena was waving giddily. Hala rolled her eyes.

"Since when did you give your own cousin that much respect?"

Sabrena rolled her eyes right back. "Since I realized it totally annoyed him. And so does what he's wearing, by the way."

The last part was to me, but she didn't need to add it. Brother Rehan, as she called him, looked quite miserable and awkward in one of those long white dress outfits a lot of the guys wore to the masjid. I think Yulia called it a thobe.

At the sight of me, though, he beamed and waved.

"Hey! Goldilocks!"

"Goldilocks?" Sabrena asked curiously, but I was already backing up the stairs.

"I'm not hungry right now. You can go on without me."

There was no way I needed to give them—or him—the impression that they would be seeing more of me. But after that first day, I seemed to run into Rehan, Sabrena, and Hala everywhere.

My house was still the last frontier, and that was enough to keep me from reaching for the real hard-hitters—elaborate noodle recipes borrowed from a classmate's Chinese grandmother, or complicated French cakes with doughs that needed to be carefully whisked and blended and flavored. But the driveway was fair game.

"Let's go shopping!"

"We're having a party tonight. Wanna come?"

"Rehan's taking us to the movies!"

I was embarrassed to admit that the last request was hardest of all to really say no to. Rehan was just . . . cool. He never said too much, as much as he had at the wedding. He just raised his eyebrows and smirked at me, in a way that always made me subtly reach up a hand and touch my ears to make sure they weren't obviously red—uncovered, because in spite of Sabrena's and Hala's neatly done turbans or carefully pinned wraps, they never seemed to care that I didn't follow suit.

At the latest superhero flick we snuck into, Sabrena's and Hala's pockets overflowing with dollar-store-variety chocolate mixes that they crumbled into our shared popcorn bucket during the previews, Rehan managed to sit next to me. I honestly didn't realize, trying hard not to laugh too obviously at Sabrena and Hala's jokes, until he nudged me during one of those quiet "he's just like you" scenes action movies always try to sneak in.

"That look appetizing to you?"

I blinked, trying to focus on the screen as the protagonist waited in line at a Halal cart on some nondescript city corner. I rolled my eyes.

"No white sauce. Probably dry as heck. Pass."

He chuckled, and the warmth of it spread over the nape of my neck as though he'd placed a hand there.

"What do you find so funny about that?" I hissed.

The next moment, the theater was alight with a fight scene, and I blinked rapidly as blue sparks flickered across the screen.

"Nothing at all," Rehan murmured, and I managed to hear in spite of everything else going on. "I like the fact that you notice that much."

I tried not to dwell on that, or what that could mean, or why the heck I even cared what Rehan thought about me. Compartmentalize. Compartmentalize.

This would be over soon.

It was hard to keep compartmentalizing, though, when Sabrena and Hala weren't so bad. They steered me to their table at the community dinners I was inevitably dragged to nowadays, filled with girls our age. Some of them gave me a side-eye or two, but most of them were chill. A few went to my high school, and we exchanged thoughts on biology teachers and end-of-year exams.

I started learning more about the community than I expected to ever know. Sabrena's older brother's best friend was slated for medical school even though he had a secret burning passion for hotel management, but there wasn't a doctor yet in the family and *people would talk*.

Some other girl's cousin eloped with the boy her parents least expected her to ever be interested in, and it was all very dramatic because *people would talk*.

By the fifth or so story, I could understand the fear about people talking because . . . well, all the people around me at the table were. But it was fun. It made me feel welcome. It made me feel like it was crucial to actually know these things about people, to be able to make a little grandma smile by asking her about her family by name and if her son had managed to open that new restaurant yet so I could check it out. I was getting comfortable.

I was feeling full for the first time in days. If not years.

And in a lot of ways, that scared me.

Because I knew it wasn't going to last. It never did.

Later one night after a community dinner, Yulia knocked on my door.

"Honey, do you have that sweater you borrowed from me?" Yulia said, peeking into my room, a pashmina unraveling from around her head and a pin sticking out from her lower lip.

I looked up, trying to blink math formulas out of my eyes. "Yulia, that describes half my closet."

"The teal one with the heart pattern. Come on, check for me! Sister Reshma is going to be here any minute."

"And you need the teal sweater with the heart pattern because she won't be happy to see you otherwise?"

Yulia rolled her eyes at me. "It matches this scarf, okay? Come on. Now."

"Fine." I made a show of shuffling through my closet: my usual clearance-rack frocks and cardigans and the occasional concert T-shirt and one or two of Yulia's phase cast-offs: some long, shapeless smock that I used for weekend chores and a pair of her college overalls.

"Nope. Not here."

"Check my closet for me."

"Remind me again who is the mom and who is the daughter here."

"Em."

"Okay, okay. Sheesh." I got up and stormed past her into the hall.

Yulia pursed her lips in an air kiss. "Thanks, my love."

I yanked open Yulia's closet, grumbling to myself and pushing through the piles of clothing. It took me a few minutes to realize how much trouble I was having wading through it, shoving aside stray sweaters and scarves like they were clumps of tangled seaweed complicating my treading through a current.

And then I realized nothing had been tossed out.

Usually when Yulia got tired, she'd clear things out. That

meant it was over, that I could get rid of the Tupperware boxes of her special diet or move out the prayer books she had ended up collecting. But it was all still there.

Brother Khalid was still there, bustling about in what was previously my kitchen, clanging my pots, and asking anxiously if I would mind lamb for dinner.

Yulia wasn't moving on.

It was weird, but for once, I wanted to go up to my mother and ask her if she knew how to sate this hunger in me: if something about the way she was kneeling and turning her fervent gaze to the carpet strewn over the grass could soothe me too, in a way that food never seemed to be able to reach.

I didn't.

I just left the sweater on her bed and went back to my own room and curled my arms around my knees.

When had things reached this point?

The next weekend at Sunday school, Sabrena knew I was in a foul mood. I didn't want to join in on the conversation like normal: asking whose relatives were having beef and whose engagement might be on the rocks. She separated from the rest of the cluster and put an arm around my shoulders.

"Whatever it is, it's all right," she soothed. "Really. Want to talk about what's bothering you?"

But my stomach just felt hollow. I was both gnawingly empty and entirely without an appetite. We milled to the basement toward a makeshift prayer area used when the normal section overflowed, where some masjid aunties were already lined up next to each other—sock heel stretched out to meet sock heel—with arms crossed, devoutly murmuring supplications under their breath. My heart lurched when I saw a familiar scarf: navy blue with a blush flower print.

Yulia.

Should I try to nudge my way in next to her now, grab her aside, and confide all my turmoil to her? I could see a glimpse of her face, eyes closed, lips moving. She looked so peaceful.

Before I could move any farther, though, or follow Sabrena, a woman blocked my way.

"Sweetheart, what are you doing here?"

"Huh?" I blinked. She did not have a face I recognized, in terms of features, but the expression already had my heart sinking. It was the type of look I got from Dad when I used up all the hot water or flipped away from his favorite channel: not just disliking what he saw, but dismissive of it. I didn't even warrant the vitriol he saved up for Yulia. She got the "you never learn" and "you could do better." I got the "it's a waste to even try when you're not worth it" and tried to be grateful for even as little as that.

The woman shook her head impatiently. "Did you take Shahadah yet?"

"Oh, um"—I fumbled as I racked my brain, sifting through random Arabic words like I was about to hazard a guess on *Jeopardy!*—". . . greetings?"

Her lips pursed. It was the wrong answer. "Do you at least know how to wash up properly? You can't stand here and pray if you haven't done that."

She looked me up and down, like something about my frayed jeans and American Eagle sweatshirt implied dirtiness.

In all the years my parents' divorce had volleyed back and forth, nothing was worse than the awful days when I crept in from a friend's house to see my father sprawled over the couch with that sneer on his face—eyes taking in the frayed cuffs of my jeans, the oversized and cheerily gaudy sweatshirt with some animated movie character plastered across the front, and summing it, and me, up as useless.

Tacky.

Not fulfilling, for his life and his world.

Not impressive enough to be presented via wallet picture to his boss and coworkers or boasted over in those later days when he openly cheated on my mother, leaving Tinder dates in the passenger seat of his car and running inside because he supposedly forgot something.

I hadn't felt that way in a long time, utterly scraped out and useless. Until right now.

"What's going on?" Hala asked from behind me, and I could feel the weight of Sabrena's hand on my arm as she shouldered up toward this lady I didn't even know, who passed judgment on me, whose eyes softened as she took in the both of them with their neatly wrapped scarves and kind, whole families.

I couldn't take it anymore.

"It's okay," I mumbled, or something close to it, and I turned, ignoring their calls, and made my way outside, not stopping until I was sitting on the curb of the parking lot. I didn't cry. I just sat there.

It was over. The way I waited for it to be since the first day I softened under the smiles and thought, hoped, it might be filling enough to be here.

The other shoe had dropped.

As soon as the prayers were over, I wove my way through the crowd outside the door to Yulia. I snagged her elbow, ignoring the woman she was excitedly in conversation with.

"Yulia, I want to go home now."

"Em?" Yulia blinked down at me. "Honey, there's a lecture we're staying for, remember? What happened to your friends?"

She tried to turn her back, but I wasn't having it. I yanked at her arm again.

"I mean it. I want to go home."

"Em . . ."

"Now. Right now."

Yulia smiled tightly at the woman she was speaking to. "I'm sorry. Can you give us a minute?"

"Oh, oh, sure!"

As soon as she moved away, Yulia turned on me. "Why are you being this way, Em? Did someone say something to you?"

"Did anyone have to say anything?" I snapped back. "I'm not comfortable here. I want to go back to my own house and my own bed."

Yulia's lips thinned. "Please don't tell me you're throwing a tantrum right now. Is this how you're supposed to be with your mom?"

"Seriously?" I snapped. "Is this how any of this is supposed to be? Do I look like I want to be here? And am I always supposed to be the person who makes it easy for you?"

My voice rose several octaves. A few heads turned. I could see Sabrena, brows furrowed and eyes concerned.

Yulia looked panicked. "Em . . ."

"I'm sick of this place and I'm sick of these people. I'm sick of you trying so hard for them, when you can hardly try at all for me." My fingers dug into my palm. I wished spewing this out would feel better, satisfying, wipe away the sense that the woman from earlier was looking from afar and nodding decisively as I confirmed her judgment of me—and why shouldn't she? I didn't belong here. I never belonged here. I was fooling myself.

"Why am I always the one who has to compromise for you? Aren't you bored yet? Shouldn't you be ready to move on?"

"Em!" Yulia's voice snapped in two, and she cleared her throat.

"Aren't you tired of pretending that you feel full?" I shrieked. "Because it's not going to work, Yulia. It never works. You just get bored and you move on. It doesn't matter how I feel about it. What matters is you taking a bite and then spitting it out, the way you always do. And I'm tired of it!"

Yulia took a step back, crossing her arms over her chest. No, that was wrong. She folded them there, as though she was trying to hold herself together. If it were any other time, I'd feel terrible for making her do that. Now, though, I was trying hard to breathe. And keep my lunch down.

"I want to go home. I just can't do this now. I want to go home."

A small crowd began to gather.

Someone asked, "Sister Yulia, is everything okay?"

Yulia didn't answer. She gave a small sigh.

"Okay, Emmeline. I'll take you home now."

I tried to feel sorry, but I couldn't.

It didn't matter that I'd said everything in front of her friends. They were temporary, after all. Now she'd probably remember that this was the point when everything ended, when she was supposed to get tired of collecting prayer beads and started looking toward, I don't know, prayer wheels or those peaceful types of communes where everyone ate whole-grain breads and meditated at certain times. We'd go back to our normal routine. It didn't matter that Brother Khalid, too, seemed to start coming home late and leaving early over the next few weeks. That was his business, right? If Yulia had told him what I had said, and he had taken it person-ally—because, you know, I implied his wife only saw him as a flavor of the week—that was his problem.

And maybe it was time for him to realize that, too.

I skipped Sunday school, but that didn't help me feel less empty.

Eating well-balanced meals—making sure to try variants on brussels sprouts and broccoli instead of dishes that oozed cheese and carbs—didn't seem to be the right solution, either.

Junk food just cast an oil slick on my skin and made my friends, the ones from school, the ones who knew me for my food-indicated mood swings and large casserole dishes of delectable leftovers brought to sleepovers, eye me worriedly when I suggested going for tacos or fried fish instead of staying in and layering lasagna or frying up sweet and sour chicken to be doused in tangy sauce.

What was missing?

Some part of me thought I knew.

But I didn't want to listen to it.

Not yet.

Yulia wasn't talking to me, so when my masjid friends—or at least, the people I thought were becoming friends, as much as it scared me—turned up, I had no one to blame.

At least they weren't inside. They were all huddled on the porch, quickly rising up with wide eyes as I approached, my steps slowing as I reached up to awkwardly adjust my backpack.

"Sabrena. Hala. And . . ."

Rehan gave me an awkward wave from where he was seated on top of the bannister.

"We've come bearing gifts," he announced, and I saw that on his lap was balanced a covered aluminum tray. Sabrena and Hala held up plates, smiling hopefully.

My lips thinned.

"Sorry, guys, Yulia and Khalid aren't home," I muttered, trying to sidestep them.

"Look, Em, please?" Sabrena asked. "I know you're hurt and I can't tell you how much I hate that you had to experience that. But could you please talk to us?"

"I'm sorry that you had to deal with that, too," Hala chimed in softly.

"Why, though?" I blurted out. "I'm not sorry. That's exactly how it should be. Don't you guys get it? She was right. I don't belong there. Neither does Yulia. We've never been those type of people. It was only a matter of time."

"Why does it have to be that way?" Rehan asked, and I turned to him, eyes narrowed. "Just because there are jerks out there who might shove you aside and challenge your seat at the table, you're going to get up and walk away hungry?"

"I'm always hungry, Rehan! I'm never full. This is absolutely normal for me, because this is how life is."

Tears stung my eyes. I was mortified by them, by the fact that I'd blurted that out, in front of a guy whose voice alone filled me with the most warmth I'd ever experienced in my life, in front of the girls who had never pried about my father or our life before Brother Khalid's marriage brought me into their lives.

For a moment, the air was close and still around us.

And then Rehan lifted himself off the bannister with a sigh. The wood creaked.

"I don't think any of us feel full or content or satisfied all the time," he said. "But what matters is being around people who try hard to remind you that you're a person who deserves to feel full, to be cared about when you're hungry. And, whether you believe it or not, to us, you're that type of person, Em."

"Yes!" Hala burst out. "Forget that auntie and people like her. It's not like we want you there to convert you. We want you there because you're our friend."

"What is this, a Disney movie?" Sabrena mumbled.

I let out a watery giggle in spite of myself, and she reached out and gathered me to her side.

"Come on, Em," she said firmly. "Tell us. What are you in the mood for, Goldilocks?"

I glanced over her shoulder at Rehan, who was doing his usual look at the ground, but whose lips were obviously stretched in a smile.

"Pasta," I said slowly. "Gooey, cheesy pasta."

Hala's and Sabrena's smiles matched Rehan's.

"Well, have we got a surprise for you."

So apparently, I had my friends back.

My mom would be a little harder—mainly because I didn't feel like taking her back in some ways. After years of us going it alone, the two of us, it was hard to realize that we both knew very little about each other and the ways in which we tried to fill the hole inside. Sabrena, Hala, and Rehan had all promised that even if I ditched Sunday school classes—which I intended to—they'd keep me in the loop of hangouts, movie nights, and weekend hikes.

But I wasn't sure if Yulia would promise the same thing, or want to. It was still very quiet between the two of us. She smiled, and pressed her hand against my head in the morning, but that was it.

It would take time.

Brother Khalid was another thing. He was hardly at home. I was pretty sure that, if Yulia hadn't told him about my outburst, he'd otherwise heard about it or been able to put together the pieces of my frustration with the ways in which my life changed—most of which could be led back to my mother, but also him, and their marriage.

At first, I didn't care. But then I felt guilty. I thought about all the mornings he eagerly slid a plate in front of me, waited for me to take a bite while pretending he didn't.

That, I thought I could do something about.

Monday night, Brother Khalid came home late. I was in the kitchen. I had planned so many things to say to him, but now that I was looking at him, none of them would stick in my head. I turned my gaze down to the holey tops of my Converse and shifted uncomfortably.

"Um . . . I thought you were done with work around nine."

It wasn't the least bit relieving that he looked just as uncomfortable. He rubbed the back of his neck. "Well, yes. But then I stopped by the masjid to pray Isha, and some of the brothers were there, so we got to talking."

"Oh. That's nice."

"Yes." There was a pause, and then he started, "Em . . ."

"Are you hungry?" I blurted out. "We had tacos. DIY tacos. I can warm up a tortilla for you."

His eyebrows shot up. "Really? Don't you have homework? I thought your mother said you had a project to pull an all-nighter for."

"It can wait." I bounded toward the kitchen without looking back.

It was ridiculously awkward in the small space, hemmed in by the stove and the refrigerator. I focused on laying out the sour cream and shredded cheese.

When I finally had a plate together, Brother Khalid stood slightly from his seat anxiously. I had to do it right this time. I tried to focus all my energy on that: not the feelings, not the constant knot of worry or fear, but the need to do right, to make this better. I had to be Goldilocks. For my mom.

"Here you are," I said, setting the plate down in front of him.

It was simple, if you compared it to what he could whip up with a half hour and a hot stove. I might have added a little too much taco seasoning to the ground beef, and the salsa had gotten a little mushier than I had hoped, but it was food, and it was Halal. Seeing the way his eyes lit up, I hoped he wasn't so hungry he'd miss what I wanted him to taste in it.

I care.

I do.

And I'm sorry if you thought I didn't.

His eyes widened as he took his first bite.

"Wow. Em, this is really good!"

"You like it? Really?"

"Best tacos ever."

He ate in silence, but it was a warm silence, and I was happy enough to just sit there and watch him eat.

He did say one thing, though, at one point.

"You did eat too, right?"

The warmth of that moment—of his eyes, as anxious as Yulia's when she asked the same question—made my stomach feel a little too full.

"Yeah," I said, grateful that my throat didn't catch on the word.

"Good." He took his last bite and smiled. "I'm glad."

We sat there together, and then he cleared his throat. "Well, uh, you should probably go up. You have school in the morning."

"Oh. Uh. Yes. Right. Good night."

I turned to leave. I could leave it there. We were at peace with each other. I knew he wasn't a phase, or a replacement for Dad. He was my stepfather, and the man my mom chose, and we could live in harmony with each other.

It wouldn't be the same as before, but it didn't have to be.

But something made me turn.

"Brother Khalid?"

He startled. "Oh. Yes, Em?"

"Do . . . do you want to make breakfast in the morning together? I'm in the mood for French toast."

There was a long pause, and then, slowly, he smiled. "I would like that."

I thought I would, too.

And afterward, maybe I would tell Rehan he was right. I felt fuller already.

Gilman Street

Michelle Ruiz Keil

To the Bubble Lady Julia Vingograd,
poet laureate of People's Park

The days plod on like a pair of ugly shoes, the kind my mom wears to the hospital. Today is no different, except maybe my undereye circles are a little darker than they were yesterday. A long weekend of sleep will help, but there is still Friday to get through.

The kitchen table is cluttered with insomnia art projects, but cleanup can wait—Mom is doing a double shift and won't be home till early tomorrow morning. I finger the pile of hacked-up photos I found last night in the back of the art cupboard. After the divorce, when my mom went to therapy, she'd do a weekly mood board. I found them on a closet-snooping expedition when I was ten. Many featured erupting volcanoes and dismembered photos of my dad, which explained the lone torsos in the envelope.

Not all the pictures were mutilated, though. There was a series of photos of my mom and dad I didn't recognize. I don't know how long I sat there gazing at the ginger-ponytailed hippie version of my now totally absent father and my supercute sixties mom, her brown legs long and glossy under a hot-pink miniskirt. Without thinking, I cut them out, two tiny finger-sized paper dolls. I made them dance a little to the college radio station I'd discovered at the end of the summer, bopping their paper brains out to the Ramones. Then, before I realized what I was doing, both images were laid out for surgery. When I was done, they were shiny with Mod Podge and sparkling with a light coat of glitter.

Now, even though I'm borderline late, I grab my tiny glittery parents like my fingers know something I don't and bore holes in the tops of their heads. In the cigar box of jewelry-making stuff are a pair of earring wires. I pop them through the holes and slide the earrings in my ears. A month ago, I would never have gone to school like this: unbrushed hair in a messy bun, yesterday's eyeliner traced over with a second coat of black, paper-doll earrings, and my mom's old army jacket—but honestly, I could probably show up for school naked these days and it would be third period by the time someone even noticed.

I snag my backpack, put on my headphones, lock the door, and walk. At the end of the block, my once-white sneakers lean left like a dog pulling hopefully toward the park. I shake my head no and move past Kelly's street. I'm late enough that I should be able to avoid my second-least-favorite part of Kelly's new status as a girl with a boyfriend: the moment when she and Ben zoom right past me in his VW Bug, the windows already clouded with smoke. Like most of the popular guys, Ben believes in wake-and-bake. I tell myself this is why they don't stop for me. Kelly knows I hate the armpit smell of it.

I hit play on my Walkman, but the batteries are dead. Didn't I just change them? But no, that was yesterday morning. And yesterday had been bad enough that I wore them as much as possible, playing my saddest mix over and over.

Headphones in the hall aren't allowed, but the teachers left me alone. It was as if, without Kelly beside me, I'd become invisible even to them.

Kelly-and-Ben. I hear them paired everywhere now in the mouths of people in the hall, Jolly Rancher sweet. Even I see the perfection of them, their combined shades of gold creating an aura of sainthood, like the statues lining the wall of the cathedral where my mom's best friend was married—the only time I've ever set foot in a church.

"You must really love Camilla," I remember saying to my mom's tight neck from the back seat of the car. If she'd been a cat, her fur would have been sticking straight out.

My mom is an atheist. She doesn't believe in God or Hallmark holidays or True Love. "All love is work," she says. "And that's okay."

But it was never work with Kelly. Not till now.

Without her the halls at school are grayscale dim like those famous photographs of the Dust Bowl during the Great Depression. I remember sitting in history class the week after the Kelly-and-Ben convergence, thinking that perhaps this was my Great Depression. My time of natural disaster and desperate lack.

That first week of hand-holding official couple-hood, Kelly had dragged me to lunch on the quad with Ben's friends. "Alex is cute," Kelly said. "Maybe we could double date." Like her, I wanted to believe our story could be a light romantic comedy where everything turned out great. I smiled, tried to flirt. The boys were nice the way you'd be nice to someone's sister.

Later, walking to the parking lot after Ben insisted on giving us both a ride home—something he did in the early days when they both worried about my feelings—Kelly asked Ben about Alex. "I saw him looking at Tam," she'd said. "It

would be so cool if we could all go to homecoming together!"
My mouth dropped. Last year homecoming was, according
to Kelly, "an archaic ritual."

But then Ben said something that closed my mouth for
the rest of the day and the next day too. Finally, my mom
demanded to know what was wrong.

"This guy—" I started. "Kelly's boyfriend. He said his
friends were talking about me, like, wondering if I was . . .
hot." Mom was doing her best to be casual, but I could see
her ears prick up, the tension in her shoulders, that slight nar-
rowing of her eyes. Part of me wanted the angry-cat mom on
my side right then, so I spilled.

"He said they couldn't decide. Like, they debated it. But
then Ben goes, 'For what it's worth, Tam, I think you're
a total babe. I bet those idiots would think so, too, if you
weren't Mexican.'"

Just like that, Mom was detonated. When the swearing
was finished, she grabbed me. She always showered off the
hospital smell right when she got home, so the hug was a
hundred percent mom: coconut lotion and sunshine. I let
myself rest in her arms.

"Oh, mija," she whispered. "I'm so sorry."

I love it when she calls me "mija," but she hardly ever
does. She says her Spanish sucks, but I've heard her use it at
work, the plump syllables softening her face as she speaks.
I remember calling my mom "mamacita" and my Irish dad
"papacita." I remember him laughing. I must have been three,
definitely younger than four. My mom left my unfaithful dad
when I was in kindergarten.

"Wait," she'd said as the hug transitioned to a trip to the
freezer for shitty-day ice cream—what we call the huge tub
of rocky road we make sure to have on hand for emergencies.
"How did he say it? The part where you're a hottie?"

I thought about that. "Not creepy. More . . . nice. I hate to say it, but he's kind of okay. He's got good taste to like Kelly."

Mom likes Kelly too. They are both newspaper readers, debaters. They used to love talking politics together. "I bet Kelly gave him an earful about his friends."

"Umm, yeah," I said. "Totally."

But I was lying. In the moment there'd been a weird pause. Even Ben felt it. Then Kelly had laughed, a weird throaty sound I didn't recognize, and leaned across me to kiss Ben on the mouth. That was two months ago. Now she and Ben eat lunch off campus every day, drive to and from school together, and I'm left in the Dust Bowl of Edenrock High to fend for myself.

The cloudy sky turns darker as I approach Eden Boulevard. The thought of the day ahead, seven hours of Trying to Look Fine, of superficial encounters with Kelly in the hall, of the shiny, Caucasian, clearly hot student body fluttering past me like a flock of the same kind of bird stops me in my tracks. And then my shoes stage a mutiny. My jeans are all in. My backpack is ready, and even my hippie-parent earrings are on board. I am overridden, not clued in to the plan, just following along as I cross the street and get on the bus heading away from school.

When it reaches the BART station, I look at the clock. Something must happen when a student skips school—a phone call, a note sent home. I would have to explain and Mom either would be pissed and silent or, worse, she'd be worried. In a month of double shifts that I know are the result of the amazing summer camp she sent me to this year, the first time I'd been able to attend with Kelly, I would be a total dick to add any stress.

But it's too late now. First period is almost over.

I take a deep breath and let my mom's jacket lead the

way. With its peace patch and embroidered doves and hole at the hem from an escape from the cops during my mom's farmworkers' rights activism days, there is only one logical destination.

The train ride to Berkeley passes quickly. Kelly was always the one in charge on BART. She was always good with directions, with maps. I was good at not losing Kelly. Or I used to be.

But now it seems I can do it on my own. I remember to change trains in Oakland and stand to get off at the Berkeley station like I do it every day. Without Kelly, I actually blend in—just another brown girl with a backpack and messy bun. I let myself pretend to be a college student.

I ascend from the station into the sunlit October morning. The streets have a half degree of strangeness, a shine I never noticed before, like a city in a portal fantasy that is almost but not quite like the regular city on the other side of the magic door.

On the lookout for fire lizards and fauns, I walk toward the campus in the storybook light. I have the twenty bucks my mom left for my school lunch and pizza for dinner. I see her tired face as she heads out the door for another double shift. I cringe but determine to spend it, clearly corrupted by my seditious sneakers and my favorite bookstore's siren song.

Ahead of me, sitting on the steps of a handsome shingled house, I see the Bubble Lady, an older woman in Renaissance fair garb who's blowing soap bubbles into the air. Almost every time I visit Berkeley she's here, blowing bubbles and selling her poetry chapbooks from the embroidered bag slung over her shoulder. Sometimes she's peaceful, but other times she seems confused.

Today I smile at her and she smiles back, offering me the plastic stick with its hoop on the end. I accept, dipping into the small pink bottle. In the iridescent soap circle stretched across the hoop, I see my own reflection: dark eyes, dark hair, a rainbow across my cheek. I blow, turning my features into a dozen bright orbs that drift into the high blue autumn sky.

At the Other Change of Hobbit, I discover the pleasure of browsing a bookstore alone. How had I never done this before? I wander the shelves, pleasantly dizzy, and wonder if this is what it feels like to be drunk.

My stomach is growling by the time I reach Blondie's, where the slices of pizza are the size of your head. In front of me is a girl pulling her pockets inside out, rummaging through her bag.

"I know I have a five," she says. "I'm so sorry!" Her brown skin is a shade darker than mine and splashed with red as she hunts through the pockets of her jean jacket.

"I've got it," I hear myself saying. "Can you add a slice of cheese and a root beer?"

"Are you sure?" The girl is Mexican, probably, with eyes as soft and dark as my mom's brown velvet coat and the coolest way of putting on eyeliner I've ever seen.

Slice in hand, the girl smiles like a movie star and says, "Want to go eat on the steps?" She must mean the steps of Sproul Hall, the scene of so many sixties protests. My mom and dad had met at an anti-war rally—not here but in Sacramento, at the state college. Now, in the eighties, the protests are still about financial morals—students want the university to divest from South Africa because of apartheid. Kelly explained it the last time we were in Berkeley together at the end of our freshman year.

The girl clears her throat. "Or I can just, you know, go . . . somewhere else . . . all by myself." Her attempt at sad-orphan eyes fades into another grin, showing perfect white teeth and a single band of silver retainer.

I laugh. "I'm Tam."

"Lourdes," she says, grabbing the sleeve of my jacket since my hands are full and pulling me through the crowded street, always finding a clear path, making it just in time so we don't have to stop at any lights. I wonder if she's good at Pac-Man too.

On the sun-glazed steps, I find out everything about Lourdes all at once. She is also cutting school, not out of bitterness like me, but for art. "My band got asked to fill in at Gilman Street. We're opening for Bikini Kill." She says it very casually, like it's something she does all the time. Then she bursts out laughing. "Dude, you have no idea. It's such a huge big deal! Like, *beyond* beyond!"

"That's so cool!" I say. I have no idea who Bikini Kill is, but I love their name.

"It's our first gig ever," she says, jiggling her leg so the safety pins pegging the ankles of her jeans glint in the sun. "I'm the drummer." She holds out her fists, showing me her scraped knuckles. "Hazard of the profession, ma'am," she says in a sort of cowboy accent, then rolls her eyes at herself. "But enough about me—tell me about you."

To my surprise, I do—all of it.

"Assholes," she says when I come to the part about Ben's friends. "And was that Ben guy hitting on you in front of his girlfriend?" Wow—her and my mom both. No wonder Kelly doesn't want me hanging around with them. "But also, dude, what's with this Kelly? That's no way to treat a friend. Girls should have each other's backs."

I start to protest, but then, all of a sudden, I know she's right.

"Some girls go dick-crazy," she says. "Not me, though." There's something almost . . . flirtatious about the way she says it? Or not. Probably not.

"I don't know if it's that . . ." I lower my lashes and glance sideways at Lourdes. She's my favorite kind of pretty, tall and strong like she could easily play sports, with messy braids and red lipstick and a cut-up T-shirt that reveals one perfect bronze shoulder.

"Hey," Lourdes says, standing up and holding out her hand. "Want to come put up the rest of these flyers with me?"

"Okay," I say, my pulse suddenly racing. "I don't really have anywhere to be."

"Oh! Then you're coming to the show?" Lourdes says. "We can get ready at my house."

I consider it. My mom won't be home till morning. I've never gone out while she's at work before, except to Kelly's. She might call, but probably not. On Friday night, the ER is always busy.

"I need to get back to BART before the last train." I try to recall the small print of the schedule. "I'm pretty sure it's at midnight."

"C'mon, Cinderella," Lourdes says, holding out her hand to pull me up. "I'm sure we can find you a ride."

We get off the bus on a quiet leafy street. Lourdes trots up the steps of the prettiest house on the block, pink stucco with a red-tiled roof. She shoves a key into the door and bangs it open.

The hallway is long and airy, with a tiled floor and a little alcove molded into the plaster walls holding a vase of fat pink roses and a candle I recognize from my grandmother's house: La Virgen de Guadalupe, serene in her blue robes. I think about the last time I saw my grandparents. There'd been tears then, and anger. I was too little to understand what they were saying, but I think it had to do with my parents' divorce.

"I brought a friend, so no one be naked!" Lourdes yells.

"Nudists?" I ask.

"Just my youngest little brother. He's five. I used to say,

'Miguel, put your clothes on, a girl is here,' but he doesn't want people to know it's him that goes around starkers."

"How many brothers do you have?" I hang my hoodie on a hook next to Lourdes's jean jacket. The whole wall is lined with antique-looking hooks in different shapes— birds, arrows, animal heads. Mine is shaped like the head of a fox.

"Four," she says, like a horde of brothers is the most normal thing in the world. "Two younger, two older. I'm the only girl."

"Only child," I say to explain the look on my face.

"Lucky," she says. "Come on."

I follow the swing of her two thick braids up the shiny wood stairs, my shabby sneakers not feeling as brave as they had this morning. The stairs open on a large landing full of afternoon light, framing a window seat surrounded by book-shelves. "You guys read." My voice bounces off the high slanted ceiling.

"Nah," Lourdes says. "Those are there for the cleaner to dust. My parents are lawyers. Well, Dad's mostly a profes-sor now. All they read is the paper. And, like, work stuff. They're into politics. MECHA, MAPA, city council—you know. Always going out."

I don't know, but I nod anyway.

Lourdes's room is a post-glitter-tornado disaster area. Clothes are everywhere. Shoes. Dried flowers glued around the mirror of a beautiful antique vanity. Mardi Gras beads, like the ones my mom has hanging from her rearview mirror from a college trip to New Orleans, stretched at odd angles from the high ceiling like the web of a giant Skittles-eating spider. Posters cover the rose-papered walls: the Slits, the Waitresses, the Go-Go's, the Bodysnatchers—the last one a xeroxed flyer.

"Good taste," I say, nodding to the flyer. I just discovered The Bodysnatchers a week ago on KPFA.

"You're the first person I've met who knows them." Lourdes beams. "They totally inspired my band."

She goes to her record player and hits the button, blasting the EP of my favorite Bodysnatchers song. We both yell the lyrics, me on the bed, her at the door of her walk-in closet, which is bigger than the bathroom Mom and I share in our condo.

She throws me an item of clothing that might be a dress or might be a long black T-shirt with the words *Las Pochas* spray-painted in acid green. "Please consider wearing this and pretending to be an official fan," she yells over the music. "I will totally be your friend forever." But as she says "forever" the song ends, so she's yelling it into the quiet house.

"Lolo?" someone calls from downstairs.

Lourdes goes to her door and opens it a crack. "In my room. Studying. Math test!" She shuts the door again. "My parents don't know about Las Pochas," she says. "They would not approve."

I hold it up to my chest. "What's a pocha?" I ask. "I thought it was a bad word, like pinche?"

"It means 'not Mexican enough.' Like, Mexican American. My parents would freak if they knew—they hate that term. But, like, I don't care if they make us speak Spanish and stuff. I'm not as Mexican as they are, you know?"

I nod. She's more Mexican than I am, though, and I'm jealous of that.

I try not to watch her as we get dressed—her in ripped leggings and big boots and a marker-graffitied Madonna T-shirt that I'm thinking is probably ironic, her bangs teased and swooped up over her forehead in a pompadour and tied into a high ponytail, her eyebrows fierce, thick-winged eyeliner perfect. She leans close to me to draw the same wings on my eyes, a sweet honeyed scent slipping past the hairs-pray fumes.

She pulls back, considering her work, and I look up and see us in her vanity mirror, a study in shades of sepia—my eyes, her eyes, my skin, her skin. Hair the shades of brown you see in horses they call bays and blacks.

Unlike Kelly, who'd been counting kisses every chance she got since we were eleven, I'd only started to really feel desire when I turned fourteen. Even then, it was a personal thing, a walled garden of rare plants I liked to visit sometimes. Then, this summer, real desire rose in my skin like yellow dandelions bursting from cracked pavement. Every beautiful person I saw was gilded with possibility. Finally, I had my first kiss, the last night of camp. The tall dark-haired boy and I had been eyeing each other all week, and the moments under the stars with him make my body sing even now when I think of them.

But Lourdes makes me feel that way too. There is no denying it. I don't know anyone in Edenrock who's gay or bi except the choir teacher, and while he's known as beloved, behind his back people aren't as kind. Even my mom sometimes makes jokes about a guy being swishy or a girl being butch. The jokes aren't mean, exactly. Not hateful. But they lodge in my belly every time I hear them, like rocks I've been made to swallow with milk and can never digest.

Now, with the air between Lourdes and me fizzing like fancy water, I lean in closer, brave in my bird's-wing eyeliner and dark lipstick. Lourdes closes her eyes and we kiss, my wine-deep Shiv red on her brighter Ruby Slippers. My skin rings with sensation like the singing bowl my mom uses to begin her daily meditations. I pull Lourdes closer, kiss her harder.

There is a light knock at the door and then it flies open, but we only have to pull an inch apart to have our alibi, since Lourdes still has the mascara wand in her hand.

"What?" Lourdes says like a sitcom star, her tone perfectly bratty teen.

"Who's your friend?" The woman in the doorway looks like someone from TV too, a polished soap opera lady lawyer. She's light-skinned like me but clearly Latina, in a red suit and black pumps, her shoulder-length hair a stiff cloud of perfect waves.

"Tam," she says, "this is my mom, Pilar."

"Hola, Tam," she says. "Vas a la escuela con Lourdes?"

I feel myself going pale, my backward version of blushing. "I'm sorry," I say, trying to smile. "I don't speak Spanish." I kick myself for taking French with Kelly instead.

"Pero eres Mexicana?" she says. "You're Mexican, aren't you? I see that."

"Not everyone who's Mexican speaks Spanish, Mom." I realize that the Las Pochas shirt is still sitting next to me. I shift my leg to hide it.

"Of course!" she says. "Are you going somewhere tonight? Is there a dance?"

"Just the movies," Lourdes says, her voice suddenly younger. "Tony said he'd drive us."

At the mention of Tony, who I'm assuming is another brother and who I'm sure is not taking us anywhere, her mom's face relaxes. "Okay, mija. There's money on the mantel. I'm meeting Papa for dinner, and the boys are at Abuela's. Nice meeting you, Tam."

With her mother gone, Lourdes slumps. I wait for her to say something about the kiss, but she doesn't. I look in the mirror, unbutton my shirt, and put on the Las Pochas tee. It's big but cute somehow as it slips off my shoulder and shows a little of my black bra. "Here," Lourdes says, grabbing a fine-tooth comb with a skinny handle. She teases my fine, straight hair until the top is puffy and pulls it back tight into a high ponytail like hers.

"I've only seen, like, chola girls with this hair." I'm thinking of a small group of sleek black-jacketed girls in my middle school people called "lowriders," with their thin-plucked brows and high-teased bangs.

"Ha!" Lourdes says. "What do you think a chola is, Tam? It's a Mexican girl from California. It's *us*, honey! Just add a little punk." Her fun, zany, TV-girl voice is back. I wonder if it's been there all along just to hide the girl behind that kiss.

"If you say so." I close my eyes while she sprays the Aqua Net. "We'd better just stay away from anything flammable."

"Guess you can't watch me drum, then." Lourdes grins and pounds down the stairs, and I follow.

"Are we taking the bus?" I ask. Lourdes just twinkles her gorgeous eyes at me and sends me to the porch.

"Don't worry, princess," she says, waving a fan of cash my way and plopping down beside me on the front steps. "Mami left us this! Your coach will arrive shortly."

We sit together and wait, quiet in a way that feels sweet, the energy of the kiss returning with the rising moon, our pinkies almost touching on the cool stone step.

Then a taxi screeches up. Lourdes rises and bows and opens the door for me. We laugh and talk the entire ride. I think it's going to be super glamorous pulling up to the club in a cab, but Lourdes has it stop a few blocks away, and I get it—glamorous, maybe, but not punk rock.

Outside the club, her band is easy to spot—they all sport that ska-punk chola style but look a little older than Lourdes. "You're late!" a bleach blonde in suspenders and a tight white tank calls. Lourdes runs to the dirt-streaked van and starts unloading her drums. I go to help, but her bandmates and a couple of guys grab the gear with practiced ease and walk past me. "New girl, lock the van up, okay?" a guy with an impressive shoe-polish black Mohawk yells. I've never seen one that high in real life.

I lock the van and realize Lourdes isn't coming back out for me. I'm alone, stranded in a part of Berkeley I don't know with no ride home and a bunch of punks filling the sidewalks around me. I could go now—try to find a bus that will take me to BART. But I don't. It's not even my sneakers this time. It's my stupid heart.

As nervous as I suddenly am, I want to see Lourdes drum. I want to get her phone number. I let the crowd shuffle me to the entrance.

The sign at the door says:

924 GILMAN COLLECTIVE

NO RACISM

NO SEXISM

NO HOMOPHOBIA

NO DRUGS

NO ALCOHOL

NO VIOLENCE

And now I'm smiling, because how cool is that? I push my wadded ones at the Debbie Harry look-alike door girl.

Inside, Gilman Street is a living homemade comic book, an all-punk metropolis, a waking dream of spray paint and Sharpie-scrawled band flyers where all the superheroes are girls. There are guys here too, yes, but they're mortal compared to the bandit-eyed glitter-trash pantheon of girl power everywhere I look. It's the band, I'm realizing, as I see homemade Bikini Kill T-shirts on a trio of what appear to be zombie kindergarteners in pink ankle socks and holey canvas Mary Janes.

The crowd is so thick I can't even try to find Lourdes, but suddenly that's okay. For the first time, I know what it means to feast your eyes. The people around me are food—the sweet, salty things teenagers crave.

In the corner, someone catches my eye: a brown-skinned

boy giving the girls here a run for their money with his short, sharp Mohawk like the crest of the coolest tropical bird and bright blue eye makeup to match. He's wearing a short feathered cape around narrow shoulders, and his arms are decked in jingling bracelets from wrist to elbow. My heart catches—a boy like this could never, ever, walk safely down Eden Boulevard. He would silence the halls of Edenrock High to menacing whispers. Here, he's just a beautiful part of the carnival. And, I realize, so am I.

I turn to look for the bathroom and bump straight into Lourdes. "Hey," she says, grabbing my hand. She pulls me to the front of the stage. "You got the T-shirt, you get front row."

I'm about to ask about that ride home or maybe just try to flirt when a blond god of a boy pushes through the crowd, grabs Lourdes, and holds her, hand on the back of her neck, a gesture of careless intimacy a thousand times worse that a kiss. The energy changes in the crowd, and I know the boy is really someone around here—a band guy, probably. And Lourdes is clearly his girl.

It was only a kiss, an afternoon, an adventure. I want to be like the French women in the red-covered book of scandalous stories Kelly and I found at the library sale last summer. Instead I'm hollow, my insides whooshed down some infernal drain.

The band is tuning up now, the crowd gathering close to the stage. Punk Apollo lifts Lourdes to the platform, muscles bulging—maybe another drummer? They are adorable, the Gilman Street version of Kelly and Ben.

Las Pochas launches into their first song, frenetic ska-core that shakes my shoulders, a surprisingly good substitute for crying. The crowd churns like a washing machine, cycling me into the whirlpool center of the pit. A girl in a pink party dress and fishnets shoves me into a shirtless guy, who shoves me off

and then grabs me to steady me. In turn, I pull him into the
pit. A girl with knife-sharp eyeliner and no hair except for little
devil-horn tufts shoulders me to the edge of the crowd, and I've
got a mouth full of feathers. The boy I admired earlier grabs
my hands and we're dancing, laughing and careening into
everyone around us. I'm having so much fun I forget to even
look at Lourdes till the final song. Eyes closed, ponytail flying,
arms tense and strong as she hits her sparkly silver drums—I
wonder if she's the girl I want or the girl I want to be.

"You got it bad, huh?" The bird-haired boy nods toward
the stage.

I meet his eyes, about to admit the truth, but something
stops me. "Wait," I say, suddenly a little dizzy. "You look so
familiar."

"Dude, I go to your school."

"Oh my God!" Suddenly, something shifts into focus. I
think of those pale-feathered flocks soaring past me in the
halls and how, in Kelly's wake, I used to almost feel like one
of them. Now, seeing Marco—because that's his name, I've
actually known it since middle school—I realize that he can't
be the only brown face I missed. "Kill me now," I say.

"You and your girl were super tight, that's all. Best friends
can be like that." And like a photo in a chemical bath, his
best friend blooms behind my eyes, a Filipina with a cute
New Wave bob and rhinestone cat-eye glasses.

"Your best friend is Rosa?" I ask, worried that I got it
wrong.

"She's actually my cousin. She's grounded tonight," Marco
says. "She's so pissed she can't be here."

"I'm sorry I didn't recognize you," I say.

"I look pretty different at school." He grins. "But then, so
do you!" He looks at me with such obvious appreciation, I
start to blush. Silly, of course, because now that I think of it,

I remember people way back in middle school saying Marco was gay. I remember because someone was shitty about it and Kelly told them off.

I'm rescued from the Kelly vortex my brain is heading down when the second band starts playing. Marco shoves me into the pit, and we are all feet and elbows and sweat and swagger until they stop. A short pause for breath, and then the moment the crowd is waiting for: a skinny dark-haired girl in a twirly skirt and shit-kicking combat boots yelling, "Girls to the front!"

I swarm the stage with the other girls and here is Lourdes, jumping up and down like a circus girl on a pogo stick. She grabs my hand and I jump with her, the mess of our kiss less important than this moment when a tiny, powerful woman stands, feet spread wide, and the crowd of boys parts for the shining, raging mass of girls.

"GIRLS TO THE FRONT!" she yells again, and she is pure magic.

After the show, Lourdes leans in to kiss my cheek. Her eyes say something I know I'll be trying to decode for the next hundred years, but she doesn't speak, just turns away and pushes through the crowd to catch up with her band.

I file outside, the high of the show still stronger than my anxiety about getting home. I have no idea what time it is—minutes or hours could have passed while I transformed in the cauldron of the pit, a different girl, surely, than I was before tonight.

Outside, Marco is talking to a gangly boy in a leather jacket. I walk past, but he stops me. "Tam!"

My hearing is fuzzy, my name slightly distorted. It's odd somehow that it still belongs to me.

"Want a ride?"

I laugh and nod and get in his car and talk about Lourdes

and the cute boy whose number he has written on Marco's hand in Sharpie. We talk about his parents, about Rosa. About how he's going to move to New York after high school because he needs the entire continent between him and his huge, nosy, judgmental family.

"What about your mom?" he asks.

"She's pretty cool," I say. We're on Eden Boulevard, close to my house. "Actually, do you want to come over for breakfast? My mom's at work—she's a nurse. She won't be home till later this morning."

Then we drive into our complex and I see something that makes me feel like barfing immediately. Our parking space is occupied. By my mother's car.

I turn pale. Marco offers to come in with me, to help me explain. I stare at him because this is the most honorable thing anyone's ever offered to do for me. I'm still sitting stunned in the parking lot when a face looms in Marco's window.

"Hi there," Mom says, looking almost . . . amused? "I got off early. Are you kids hungry?"

Marco looks at me like my mother is a miracle, which I'm pretty sure she is right now. "Sure," he says. "Thank you."

In the house, my mom is making French toast and veggie sausages, my favorite. "Why am I not dead right now?" I blurt.

"Ha!" Mom says, shrugging, making me wait for it. She turns the sausages. Gets out some orange juice.

"You're not going to tell us?" Marco asks, his grin showcasing his dimples. My mom happens to be a sucker for dimples and big brown eyes. She's also big on being polite to company, so maybe that's why she answers.

"If I'd been sitting here worrying all night, your ass would be grass," she says. "But lucky for you, I only realized you weren't asleep in your bed when the car drove up. I happened to be looking out the window. *I know that kid in the pas-senger seat of that little blue Honda. I made that kid from scratch.*"

I blush, but Marco just laughs and offers to set the table.

And so we sit, feasting, and I tell her everything.

"Las Pochas?" she says, looking at the T-shirt with one eyebrow raised.

"What's that?" Marco asks.

"Maybe it's you," I tell him, grinning. "Are you Mexi-can?" I always hate when people ask me what I am, but it feels natural here, and Marco smiles.

"Mostly Filipino," he says. "But a quarter Mexican too. Does that count?"

"You speak Spanish?" Mom asks.

"I understand it," he says. "When my abuela wants me to. And a little Tagalog."

I take a bite of sausage. "That's more than I can say—but yeah, you're probably a pocha too. Or a pocho?"

"Whatever," he says. "I'm not big on labels." He twinkles at me as he says this and I wonder . . . but no. The cute leather-jacket boy's number is still there on his hand.

Marco offers to do the dishes, and when he's in the kitchen, my mom touches my face in a gentle way that make tears spring to my eyes.

"Don't make me worry, Tam. Next time, we have to talk before you go out. And maybe we need to have another talk too . . ." She glances meaningfully toward the kitchen.

"*Mom!*" Now I'm the one who sounds like a sitcom girl. She just laughs and tells me to go get her purse. She takes out a pale blue envelope.

"It's a birthday card," she says. "From my aunt. She's pretty radical, for a nun. Lives in Oakland and runs an after-school program. She knows a lot about our family."

I open the card. It's a classic Hallmark about how my mom is an amazing niece, but the signature has a note: *Missing you, mija*, it says.

"She sends one every year." Now it's Mom's turn to look a little teary-eyed. "Maybe we should go and see her. She's not like—not like my dad." There is a pause like there always is when she mentions her father, short but Grand Canyon deep. As I get older, I see the outline of the broken story there, the something too hard for me to hear that lives in the space between her words. She takes a little breath and goes on. "I just assumed she judges me like my parents do, but maybe not. She sends a card like this every year."

"That's pretty sweet," I say, tracing the raised flowers on the card's face. "She sounds nice."

"She used to be," my mom says. "Maybe she still is."

"Only one way to find out," I say, squeezing her hand.

"Maybe Sunday," Mom says. "Now, go help that cute boy with the dishes. They are yours for the foreseeable future, some nice quiet time to think about how you could have given your mother a heart attack. And tell him he can stay till whenever it is his parents expect him home from wherever it was he told them he would be. But just this once. I can't be an accessory to minors lying to their parents." Her smile makes me remember stories of how strict her parents were, and how she and my dad used to come up with elaborate schemes to sneak her out.

In the kitchen, Marco makes me sit in the breakfast nook instead of helping while he finishes up.

"My mom says you can hang out till the coast is clear at home."

"I love your mom," Marco says.

We go into the living room and plop on the sofa. I grab my backpack from the coffee table where I'd dropped it and dig for my lip balm again—but find something that definitely wasn't there when I left the house a million years ago/ this morning. A glitter-crusted cassette case labeled POCHAS MIX in pink nail polish that gives me an instant flashback to Lourdes's bedroom.

"Let's hear it," Marco says, so I get up and grab some batteries from the junk drawer and pop them into my Walkman, propping my headphones on the back of the sofa between Marco and me.

It's an awesome mix of the musicians from Lourdes's bedroom walls and spare, soulful ballads in Spanish from a deep-voiced lady singer. I close my eyes, trying to find the way back through the wardrobe to my day in Berkeley, but all of me, even my Las Pochas shirt, seems to want to stay right here.

At the end of a stunningly beautiful song, I feel a hand on my hand, a spark of starstuff. I look up and realize that Marco has been looking at me for a little while. And suddenly, I realize something: Marco is like me. A little of this, a little of that. Not one thing or the other, but maybe all of the above. I lace my fingers in his, his brown and my brown, my bitten nails and his polished the bright blue of his eyeliner.

I scoot closer so that our legs are touching and lean my head against his shoulder. I feel his head against mine, our hair crispy with hair spray, our hearts beating at the same sweet frequency.

"The Boy Is"

Elsie Chapman

"Holly, wait—you're really breaking up with me over the *phone*?"

It says a lot that the note of incredulity in Kyle's voice leaves me satisfied instead of regretful.

"Yes, I guess I really am," I say into my cell. I'm lying on my bed, staring up at the glow-in-the-dark stars still on my ceiling that haven't glowed in years. "At least it's not over text, right?"

"Except that both are kind of shitty," he says.

They are. But he deserves it. And I couldn't find him after school to do it in person, spring break starts tomorrow, and it's as good a time as any to stop being a jerk's girlfriend.

"I heard about your list of tokens, Kyle. Seems you can now cross off yellow."

The echoes of him and Dev and Ross laughing their asses off from down the hall this afternoon still ring in my ears, a tinnitus of shame. "Achievement unlocked, Kyle!" Dev had chortled with a gross kind of slyness. "Asian girlfriend, check!"

I'd been around the corner, sight unseen, my face stiff with embarrassment even as my brain whirred. And all of it had spun neatly into place, a row of winning cherries filling up the display window of an old-fashioned slot machine—the recollection of how Kyle had gone out with Jasmine before me, Jasmine, who's black; how before Jasmine, it was Lissa, who's brown. I'd thought of his uncle who'd just been visiting from somewhere in Tennessee, who asked Kyle right in front of me if I spoke English. Of his father, who thinks he's being nice each time he starts talking to me about Jackie Chan movies (he settled on Jackie after he decided I had to be a *Star Trek* fan because of Sulu and I pointed out that George Takei is Japanese).

"You heard us—" Kyle laughs, never getting it. "What? *Tokens?* C'mon, we were just kidding around."

"Okay, so let's say you were just kidding around." My cell is pressed hard enough into my cheek that it hurts. "But how does that make it any better?"

"I have literally *zero* clue what you're talking about, Hol."

"I know you don't. Have a nice spring break, Kyle."

I disconnect, still facing the ceiling. I really should clean up those old stars.

"Holly, dinner's ready!" my mother calls from the kitchen.

I swing my legs off the bed to get up, rubbing my cheek to make it go back to feeling normal.

"Holly? You coming?" My mom's voice is growing needled the way only it can, even when she's yelling out of love.

Holly?

Are you listening to me?

Why don't you listen?

"Holly!"

I sigh. "Coming!"

Since Chinatown's just over the bridge and all my father's best card and drinking buddies own restaurants or diners over there, we usually end up with some kind of takeout on the table. Tonight it's classic barbecue pork, thick slices of it laid over rice in a large Styrofoam container.

My dad nudges the food toward me. "From Foo's. Eugene says hi, by the way."

"Tell him hi back next time." I take some pork. My parents have known Eugene for years, ever since we moved to San Alejandra from San Santos when I was a baby so Grandma wouldn't have to live alone after Grandpa died. She'd declared Foo's the best Chinese barbecue house in the Bay Area and directed us its way.

"Eugene also says to tell you Nathan's single again," my father adds. "Nathan, remember? You and he are good friends."

Nathan is Eugene's son, and he's seventeen, a year older than me. We're friends in the way that a lot of parents who are friends like to think their kids are also friends. Which is to say, we barely know each other. I mostly just remember us watching shows like *Parks and Recreation* and *Breaking Bad* on the small TV in the smoke-filled kitchen of Foo's while across the room our parents played games of mahjong. And our conversations rarely went beyond the typical go-tos, such as "Can you turn up the volume?" and "Pass the chips?"

I snort. "Dad, I haven't seen him since I was, like, ten." At eleven, Nathan had been shorter and scrawnier than me, and full of smirks because he somehow always won at Rock, Paper, Scissors each time we couldn't agree on what to watch.

"Has it really been that long? Well, he's a nice kid. Taller than me now, and Eugene says he's on his school's volleyball team. You should get back in touch."

"He wouldn't even know who I was."

"Sure he would."

My mother's laugh in my father's direction as she eats salad with chopsticks is breezy but pointed. "Holly isn't right for Nathan, and he's not right for her. Besides, shouldn't he be busy making plans for leaving for university next year?"

Nathan's university plans don't have much to do with why my mother says he's not suited for me, while him being 100 percent Chinese does.

My mother's kind of a puzzle this way, the Old-School part of her tangled up with the Progressive, so it's hard to figure out where one ends and one begins. She's fiercely proud of being Chinese, but she wears her pride more like a bruise instead of a badge, earned through some kind of odd suffering. She says being Chinese is both a blessing and a curse, depending on which part of the world we're in, which era of time we're talking about. *Holly, why would we leave China if not to make sure you weren't just going to be us? Why are we here all the way across the sea if not for you to become someone new, someone who can shine even as they fit in?*

Maybe if she and my father had been able to have more kids, she might not care so much about who I end up choosing to date. Or if they hadn't already been nearly forty before I came along, so that my mother's mind was already too crowded with trending sitcoms starring white people, with popular books filled with white characters, for my voice to be heard. So that hers was lost too. Or if I'd been born with any other birthmark instead of the splotch of brown on my neck that she says is in the shape of America, of a part of the world that lies far from the East.

This, Holly, is a sign that you're of the West.

I think it looks like a whale (to be fair, I'd been six when I'd declared this).

No, it doesn't.

Then a man wearing a cape.

No.

A ballerina with a huge, fluffy tutu?

No.

And I've never dated a guy just because he was Chinese

or just because he wasn't. The first because I don't actually know that many Chinese guys in the first place, and the second because people like Kyle and Dev and Ross—who then lead to people like Kyle's uncle and Kyle's father—can get kind of tiring.

Grandma died last year at the ripe old age of eighty-two. You'd think she would have been really old-fashioned and told me to date only Chinese boys because only Chinese boys would ever understand what it means to be in a Chinese family. *How could a white boy ever really know you, Holly? Know our ways, our traditions and duties?* But she would only ever just shake her head at my mother's advice and whisper to me in the kitchen as she made me help her with dinner.

That birthmark's not America, Holly. That birthmark's just you.

I had no clue what that meant. She had to explain.

Your mother wants the best for you, but she forgets how that should mean choice.

I'm not sure if my having had three boyfriends total quite measures up to the grandeur of that declaration.

Still, it's a fact that Kyle, Aaron, and Zach had each fit my mom's idea of a guy suited for me.

Hey, Grandma, I'd say to her now if I could, *how about my choice of dating* no one *for a while?*

"Nathan's planning on UCLA, actually." My father scoops up gai lan. "Eugene says he wants to stay local, but it's also the money. Too expensive to head out of state."

"Hmm." My mother's picking at her rice, frowning. She's considering a diet because her best friend, Amber (whose blonde hair now comes from a salon, my mother reports, but whose wardrobe still comes from all the right stores and online sites), recently dropped five pounds by cutting out bread. "Yes, well, Holly's still dating Kyle, so you can tell Eugene that the next time you see him."

"Except I'm not," I say. "Still dating Kyle, I mean."

My father stops eating. "I'm sorry, Holly. You okay?"

I shrug. "We only went out for like two months, anyway." And what's two months in the grand scheme of things? I've had scars from falls last longer than that.

My mother's clear distress makes up for my already being over it, for my father already helping himself to more food because he has nothing else to add. She sets down her chopsticks. "Oh, Holly, what happened? You liked him so much."

Not as much as you wanted me to, though. Footballer Kyle Bergeron with his corn silk hair, whose white-collar parents could have been cast in any one of her beloved dramas. "Nothing happened. We just broke up."

"Oh, Holly," my mother says again, like someone's died.

I'm working my entire two-week spring break, the 10 A.M. to 3 P.M. shift at the Chinese restaurant in the mall. The Luckiest Wok in the Main Food Court has a menu that offers everything from noodles to stir-fries to spring rolls. It's okay that I still can't cook any of it because I only ever work the till.

I'm pretty sure Adam—he's the manager—hired me to lend some credibility to the place, given that I'm the only Chinese person on staff and everyone else is trained to handle customers at the counter *and* be able to work the kitchen. Vera—she's one of the other workers—told me she heard the Brentwood branch up north was in danger of closing before they hired a Chinese guy for the counter. Then all of sudden, The Luckiest Wok was the one restaurant in the area known for serving truly authentic Chinese.

I should probably be insulted, but the work is mindless, Adam's really good about giving me whatever shifts I want (during the school year it's Sunday mornings, and Tuesday and Thursday afternoons), and I get hefty discounts for the rest of the mall.

My parents have only ever eaten here once (not while I was working, thank Christ).

Well, this place has nothing on Chinatown, that's for sure (my dad).

There are worse things in the world than orange beef made with canned Minute Maid frozen concentrate, you know (my mom).

The morning after my not-so-soul-shattering breakup with Kyle, I show up right on time for my shift. Just as she always does on the Sundays when we're on together, Vera's already there at The Luckiest Wok, making coffee in the back and readying the tills. Louis and Anton get there minutes later and get the grill going. It's early, and our half of the food court—all the breakfast and coffee places are on the other side—is still mostly empty.

"I saw the schedule, Holly." Vera clucks her tongue and shakes her head so that her dyed red curls bounce, gray roots peeking out. She opens her till and cracks open rolls of quarters. "Spring break and you're here every day. Sweetie, why aren't you somewhere fun with your boyfriend, or on some road trip with your girlfriends?"

I grab the mini display chalkboard on the counter to change the day's special—spring rolls are two-for-one today to kick off the break—and give her a grin. Vera's never had kids, and almost everything she knows about teenagers comes from watching Everything '80s, her favorite channel to stream on Flicked.

"I don't have a boyfriend," I say, doodling spring rolls with happy faces in chalk, "and all my girlfriends are also working."

Vera's penciled eyebrows lift. "What happened to Kyle?"

More like, what happened to me? "I guess I found out he's kind of an ass."

"Huh. Only wanted one thing, right?"

I laugh. "No, not that. Just a case of yellow fever."

"You dumped him over an *illness*? Is yellow fever the new mono these days? Is it just as contagious?"

I laugh again.

Vera huffs. "I'm old, hon. You're going to have to elaborate."

"You know, like Asian fever. Wanting to go out with someone *just* because they're Asian."

Her eyebrows lift even higher so they disappear behind her bangs. "Oh my. How . . . ungentlemanly."

"Right? So gross." I adjust the display chalkboard so customers walking by can see it. I hope Vera doesn't think of me as a hypocrite, since I've told her my guess as to why Adam hired me in the first place, and here I am, still working at The Luckiest Wok.

But then again, Adam's not laughing with Louis and Anton when they all think I'm not around to hear.

"Anyway," I continue, "no doubt my mom's already counting on the next white guy being the one, so I'll be able to truly Embrace the Way of the West. Meanwhile my dad's about five minutes away from trying to set me up with the son of his best Chinese friend. Fun times."

Vera shuts her till and leans back against the counter. "But what do *you* want, sweetie?"

I rub chalk from my fingertips and mull over the simple-yet-far-from-it question. Between enduring another Kyle and endless Jackie Chan questions, and reconnecting with Nathan only to then deal with my mother's outright disappointment (*Such a nice boy, has always been, but he's not for you, Holly*), there's only one answer that calls to me right now.

I step out from behind the counter of The Luckiest Wok. "Doughnuts over guys, nearly each and every time. Got the front for a minute?"

The best things that can be said about the Batter Up! on the other side of the Main Food Court are that it's close by and the doughnuts are still mostly vintage instead of trendy. A dieter's nightmare, the menu ranges from crullers to fritters to long johns. The smells of fried dough and sugar hit me in rushes as I near the counter, so I can't tell if I'm more sleepy or buzzed.

"Help you?" the bored-sounding server asks when it's my turn. His hat's a giant paper doughnut (everyone who works at the food court agrees Batter Up!'s uniform hats are the most humiliating). "Spring break special is a free doughnut hole with the purchase of a dozen doughnuts."

(Everyone also agrees Batter Up!'s manager is a cheap ass.)

"Oh, yippee," I say. "I don't know how I'm going to resist."

"I'm supposed to recommend the jelly-filled ones."

I love jelly doughnuts, but Peak Dough—which closed months ago—was the only place in San Alejandra's south end that still made them right, true classic style with lots of strawberry filling before rolling the balled dough in sugar.

While Batter Up! here in the mall uses a *grape* filling. And a *cake* base instead of yeast. Two strikes.

(It's also supposedly their worst-selling doughnut, so I guess I'm not alone in being a hater.)

"Why don't you guys start making them with strawberry?" I ask the server.

He shrugs, still bored. "I'm just recommending what I'm supposed to recommend."

"Have you even *tried* your jelly doughnuts?"

"No. They're made with grape filling."

I roll my eyes. "Can I just get four sour cream glazed?" It's Batter Up!'s least messed-up kind, even if they go too light on the glaze. And Vera, Louis, and Anton would never forgive me for returning empty-handed. "Thanks very much."

The server turns to grab my order from the display case.

"The new shake bar that's just opened in the Upper Food Court has some pretty amazing ones," someone behind me says.

I glance over my shoulder. It's a guy around my age, dressed in black jeans and a dark blue T-shirt that says EARL OF SHAKE on the chest pocket. He's smiling, hazel eyes on me, messy hair the color of sand on a beach, and he's cute as hell.

My mother would approve.

Well, *damn it*.

"Amazing what?" I ask Hazel Eyes. "Shakes?" I look pointedly at the words on his shirt pocket.

He grins. "Yeah, those too. But I mean jelly doughnuts, which we also make. Sorry, I felt like I had to say something since you were just talking about them."

He's got the kind of smile that really spills over into the eyes, and before I can help it, I'm grinning back at his dangerously cute face. "Can you beat the ones Peak Dough made, though? That's the real question."

"They used premade jelly they bought in boxes from Costco."

Whatever my expression, it makes him burst out laughing.

It's a good laugh, deep and kind of husky. I feel it somewhere in my stomach, swimming and fluttering and utterly pleasant, as I pay the Batter Up! server and take the bag of doughnuts.

Not a good sign.

Holly, you're taking a break! You're tired of explaining that kung fu, karate, and tae kwon do are actually different things, remember? And how if one more person thinks you're lying about having never been to China, you swear you're going to scream?

"Help you?" The bored-as-ever server asks Hazel Eyes now that I'm done. I slide away from the counter to make room.

Instead, Hazel Eyes slides away with me.

"Right, well, I'm kidding about Peak Dough," he says, clearly not caring that he's lost his spot in line. "But I'm not kidding about our jelly doughnuts being better. Earl of Shake, right upstairs."

Now I *am* smiling back, and I kind of hate myself for it. But oh, he's totally flirting, his cheekbones are *fine*, and all the sugar that I'm breathing in definitely isn't helping.

"See, that's a challenge," I say.

"You challenged first, don't forget."

I laugh. "Fair enough."

"A mutual challenge, then?"

"Impossible, since Peak Dough's gone."

"Come by, anyway? Food will be on me."

"I don't know . . ."

Hazel Eyes leans over Batter Up!'s counter and calls out to the server, "Hey, got a pen I can borrow?"

After he gets the pen, he fishes out a small card from the pocket of his tee, scribbles on it, and hands it to me.

"My mom's the owner and it's grand opening week, so everything's still kind of chaotic. But come on by tomorrow and I'll buy you lunch—shake, grilled cheese with cheese of choice, and the best jelly doughnut you've ever had."

The Devil Is in the Design is on, and I'm sitting beside my mother on the couch, pretending I'm watching.

It's this super useless but admittedly fun show about this group of friends who all work for the same designer house in Los Angeles. Ramie is one of the designers, Isa is the in-house photographer, Dove runs the monthly magazine, Tash keeps the celebrity clients in line, and Clary is the stylist. Everything's opulent and shiny and draped in glitz. No paint color is allowed to exist unless it's also a shade of gems and jewels, of satins and velvets. Characters earnestly ooze words like *posh* and *alluring* every five minutes.

Other than Ramie and Dove being the two guys and the literal differences between everyone's jobs, they're all really just the same white twenty-something-year-old, living the same shallow life and dealing with the same superficial problems.

Which girl to date this week, which guy to sleep with? Which celebrity to style, which one to gossip about? Which dress to design, which outfit to showcase? Which spa to visit, which bistro to eat lunch at?

I get that the show being so ridiculous (on the practical level) while also relatable (on the emotional level) is exactly why it's so popular.

But my mother's kind of missed that memo.

She thinks it's popular because it's so very white.

In tonight's episode of *The Devil Is in the Design*, Ramie and Tash are dating in secret, Isa is fighting with the celebrity she has to photograph, Dove's worried about a bunch of lost photographs, and Clary can't decide between Braden with the tight butt and Erica with the pillow boobs.

Meanwhile, my mind's on the very real Hazel Eyes and how I now know that his name is James.

He'd scrawled it right beneath where his mother's name had been printed (it's her business card: ABBEY THORNTON, OWNER AND MANAGER, EARL OF SHAKE). The card's still in my wallet.

I probably should have just tossed it before heading home after my shift, given that I'm taking a break from dating.

I'm pretty sure James Thornton is like the whitest of white boy names.

I don't want to Google to find out.

I also don't want to analyze why I don't want to find out. Or why I'm actually considering going by tomorrow just like he asked, instead of reminding myself how it sucks that Jackie Chan movies might be ruined for me forever.

How am I supposed to prove my mother's wrong about so many things by doing exactly what she wants?

Maybe it's because the sound of James laughing is way nicer to think about than the sound of Kyle and Dev and Ross laughing.

"See, Holly, this is what I want for you."

My mother's peeling and eating fresh lychees as she watches the television. She's found out the fruit is low-carb and has filled the fridge with bags of them.

For a second I think she's talking about feeding me a lychee before I drag my mind from the trouble of James and really look at what's happening on *Design*. It's Clary making pros and cons lists for both Braden and Erica.

"You want me to go out with two people at once?" I ask.

My mother gestures impatiently toward the screen. "No, I want you to have the world that is this show. This show is about finding success here, on this side of the sea. Happiness. Privilege. You deserve that."

"Um. All the main characters are kind of pathetic, Mom."

"Pathetic in what way? They live in big houses and shop whenever they want. How is it bad of me, wishing my daughter to want those same things?"

"What I mean is, Clary's literally weighing the virtues of butt against boobs while weepy-drunk."

"She's showing her emotions. It's liberating."

"She's drinking wine from the bottle with a straw."

"But that looks like very fancy wine. You can't buy anything like that in Chinatown, even if you wanted to."

My mother deftly peels open another lychee with her strong fingers, the painted tips of her nails carefully filed.

I feel the dig of those fingers in my own chest, trying to guide my heart, wanting to set its course.

Right before bed I get a text on my cell.

Hey there Holly, it's Nathan Lau of Parks and Rec on an old TV in Foo's restaurant kitchen, remember? (And I honestly hope you do because otherwise this text is going to be really weird, and if we ever run into each other let's both pretend it never happened. Deal? Deal.) Anyway, it's been a while, and I hear our dads thought it'd be cool for us to catch up. So here I am, texting hi, wondering if you'd like to meet for coffee one day (and I can finally confess in person how I cheated each time we played Rock, Paper, Scissors). Nathan

My dad says Nathan's grown even taller than him, but other than that, I have no idea how he's changed. I click on his profile photo to blow it up.

Okay, unreal shoulders, amazing hair, a grin instead of a smirk and it's a grin that's a mile wide. There are hints of the smug boy I'd known, a sense of familiarity that only makes me more curious of what's new about him.

Seriously, he's *cute*. Cute enough that it makes me pause. So that Grandma's words come and fill my head.

Your mother wants the best for you, but she forgets how that should mean choice.

Maybe I was too quick to laugh at Clary's pros and cons lists.

Maybe I should have made them from the start and then Kyle and Aaron and Zach would never have happened.

Fine.

But I'll make my new lists over hot tea and not wine. Because we don't really keep wine in the house, while a hurricane would probably hit San Alejandra before we'd ever run out of tea (fact: California doesn't get hurricanes; the Pacific Ocean's too cold, so storms just end up petering away).

And it's just as well we also don't have straws, because who drinks hot tea with straws, anyway?

Some things have to be universal.

I lie on my bed and open up the Notes app on my cell.

From above, old stars gone dark continue to stare down, and I wonder what they see.

It's the next afternoon, ten after three, and my shift at The Luckiest Wok is over.

After changing back into my jeans and T-shirt, I stuff my work uniform into my backpack and leave the tiny staff room through the side door. I head down the hall and into the food court.

I spot familiar red curls just up ahead.

"See you tomorrow, Vera!" I call out over the heads of shoppers.

Vera turns and waves, stopping so that I catch up to her. "Oh, I'm not leaving quite yet, sweetie," she says. "You know I always need some sugar at this time of day."

"Going for ice cream?" Vera lives for the gelato place across the food court as much as she does for Flicked.

"Of course. Need a hit yourself? My treat this time."

"No, I'm good today, thanks. Actually, I have to go meet someone."

She must sense the nervousness—tingling, excited, a bird going round and round inside its cage—that's taken over my stomach. She's nearly cackling as she pats my arm. I'm positive every teenage couple from every John Hughes movie she's ever watched is flashing across her brain. "Oh, you're meeting a *boy*."

I nod. A grin breaks free—at her glee, at my choice, at having no clue if it's the right one but knowing I have to find out anyway. Maybe it's a kind of mutual challenge, even.

Vera winks. "So who is he, hon?"

"The boy is James."

Sandwiched in Between

Eric Smith

It doesn't feel like the Thanksgiving season until I have a Gobbler hoagie from Wawa clutched in my hands. Forget the autumn leaves, the brisk weather, or the occasional odd decorations. It's that hoagie. Wrapped in crinkly white paper that quickly becomes translucent the longer the hot sandwich sits inside, it is a glorious mash-up of the staples found at my family's Thanksgiving dinner table. Turkey, stuffing, gravy, cranberry sauce . . . all crammed within a roll that is totally unprepared for its glorious contents. It's like the bread goes into shock, just totally falling apart. The Gobbler looks nothing like the advertisements plastered around Philadelphia, on buses, the SEPTA trains, on billboards . . .

"You're seriously going to eat that?" Amina asks as we sit down on a bench in Rittenhouse Square, a fancy park that just beckons you to have a picnic in it. Lush gardens with stone barriers perfect for perching on top of, and a fountain so old it has a landmark sign on it, the mosaic tiles lining the bottom glittering in the afternoon autumn sun. The square is bustling, the weather surprisingly warm. People are out and about with their dogs, and young couples with little toddling kids who dash after one another are laughing as they jet across large patches of grass.

The sandwich is warm in my lap, the paper gone clear after

walking several city blocks to get to the park from Broad Street. I unwrap it carefully, the contents precious, and glance over at Amina's plastic bag.

"You could have gotten one too, you know." I smile at her. "I mean, who gets a salad at Wawa?"

"*I* get the salads at Wawa," she playfully snaps, her nose crinkling in a way that drives me crazy. Her dark brown eyes flit down to the sandwich in my lap and back up at me, her winged eyeliner making her gaze feel even more penetrating. She smiles and my heart flutters. "That paper is gross. How do you have gravy on your jeans already? Look at your hand!" She grabs my hand and then tosses it back at me, like it's a filthy rag. "It's sweaty! *From carrying a sandwich!*"

I take a bite and audibly moan. The bread is soggy, but it's soggy with gravy, and the flavors just explode in my mouth.

"Sorry, I can't hear you over all this joy."

"You don't make any sense," Amina scoffs, taking her salad out of her bag. It's prepackaged neatly, and she peels off the plastic, mixing everything together. It's some kale and quinoa thing. She aggressively points at me with her plastic fork in an exaggerated way, to the point that her thick black curly hair jostles around her shoulders. "You are literally having everything in that sandwich at your parents' house in, like, five hours. And at mine in four."

"It gets me psyched. This sandwich is the hype man for Thanksgiving dinner." I take another bite and have to mentally force my body not to shudder. This sandwich is everything. A little kid hustles by us, chasing a tennis ball, his tiny hands outstretched in front of him the entire way. "Besides, does your family even do Thanksgiving like this? The stuffing and all that?"

"What? Of course!" She laughs. "Are you expecting turkey moussaka or something? Grape leaves?"

"No, I . . . wait, what's moussaka?" I ask, taking another bite of my sandwich.

I glance back at Amina when she doesn't answer, and her face is turned up in worry, looking straight ahead. It's the kind of expression she gets during tests in pre-calc, or when graded papers are getting passed out. Forward, eyes intense, mouth a straight line.

"Hey." I nudge her, and she shakes her head quickly, looking back to me, a soft smile back on her face. "Where'd you go?"

"Nowhere," she mutters. "Nowhere, I just . . ." She stops and exhales. "You told them I'm coming, right?"

"What?" I scoff. "Of course. Right after we visit your place. Pretty sure my mom would flip out if I brought surprise company; she takes Thanksgiving very seriously."

Me and Amina had only been dating since September, just these past three months after a summer of flirting through Facebook Messenger and Instagram DMs. But I feel like I've known her forever. We've been in classes together since freshman year at Central. So, maybe not forever, but three years, most definitely.

"You know I can't wait for you to meet everyone," I continue, my heart feeling full. "I talk about you, like, all the time."

"It's just . . ." She puts her fork down and sets her salad aside. "Look, Mike, I don't want to make this weird, but . . ."

"What is it?"

"It's just, have you ever brought home . . . someone . . . like me?"

I shift around on the bench and look at her, and she stares down into her lap, which is significantly less gravy-stained than mine. She's wearing tight black jeans and some kick-ass vintage boots that come up halfway between her knee and her foot. I reach out and take one of her hands, an array of bracelets jingling as I bring it closer to me, thick silver rings on several of her fingers.

"What do you mean, someone like you?" I ask, running my fingers over the top of her hand. She pulls her hand away slowly and sighs.

"Michael, you know what I mean," she says, shaking her head. "Look, I know your exes. Okay? Becca? Anne? And your parents, your family and all . . . they're sweet from everything you've told me, but you know, they're—"

"White," I say, nodding slowly at first and then a bit faster. "They're white. This again? That's what this is about?"

"I'm sorry, it's just—"

"*I'm* not white," I say. "They don't have any problems with *me* at Thanksgiving. Or Easter. Or Christmas!"

"Come on, that's not even remotely what I'm saying here, and you know that." She shifts around on the bench to look at me, and I realize we're not really sitting next to each other anymore, but across from each other.

"It's just . . . this feels silly," I mutter. "We keep circling back to this. Why?"

"Because we should talk about it," Amina presses. "All your exes were white girls. This is new." She points at herself and at me. "Do they know?"

"It's not like I'm hiding you or something." I get up off the bench and pace a little. "It's not like I told them, 'Hey, I'm dating Becca, she's a white girl' when I was seeing her. What's the difference now that I'm dating a brown girl? Did you warn your parents about me?"

"I didn't say you had to *warn* your parents. And no, I didn't, though maybe I should have."

"What's the difference between all that and saying I'm dating someone like me? They've seen photos of us!"

"Like you—" She starts and stops, taking a breath. "The difference is that they were white girls, and I'm not."

"I'm not white either!" I exclaim, heat brewing up in my chest. "And my parents are the last people in the world who are going to be racist. Would they adopt some ambiguously brown Middle Eastern kid if they were racist? Hell, my sister is from Honduras."

My family is like a Saturday morning television special, one of those old ones you can laugh at on YouTube, in grainy washed out colors with some powerful lesson about acceptance. The more you know.

"I'm just saying." Amina says, getting up, and I can hear her patience fading. "You should maybe tell—"

"There's nothing to tell! We don't even *see* color in my family, you know?"

There's a beat, a bit of silence in the air as Amina glares at me.

"Wow." She breaks the quiet first.

"What?" I ask.

"Nothing." She shrugs. "It must be nice."

"Can we . . ." I reach out and take her hand, but she shirks away from it. My chest tightens. "Look, can we just drop this? I hate talking about this. It's the only thing we seem to fight about, and I don't want to fight."

"It's a privilege to be able to drop things like this in the first place," Amina says, sitting back on the bench. "Not everyone can. Most people have to fight because of what they look like. Who they are." She grabs the little plastic container with her barely eaten salad and closes it up, tossing it back in the Wawa bag.

"Wait, where—" I start.

"I'm going to go help my parents get things ready," she says, standing back up. "Just come meet me at my house at, like, four, and then we'll head to see your . . . *colorblind* parents after."

"I'm— I'm sorry I messed up our lunch date." I reach out for her hands, and this time, she takes one of mine. "I just, what do I say? To make it better? I have no idea what to say to any of this."

She reaches out and pats me on the face.

"You don't have to say anything. You just have to shut up and listen more often."

Amina's family lives in the quiet Queen Village neighborhood of Philadelphia, where smattered among the charming row houses you can spot the occasional mansion tucked away in the brick. I've strolled by her home what feels like dozens of times, walking her there from class or after we've gone out, coming back from the movies or rummaging for used books in Giovanni's Room, my favorite bookshop-slash-nonprofit thrift store.

I look up at her house, dark copper stars hammered into the front, like most older Philly homes. It's a wide row house, a dark red brick that casts a strong contrast to the lighter brick houses attached to it, with dark green shutters on the windows and a bright yellow door. They're empty now, but over the summer, the window boxes on the bottom two windows overflowed with bright wildflowers. It's how we started talking, even after years of being in school together, after she saw me leaving comments on her Instagram photos of them. I keep trying to think of a more romantic story for how we met but haven't quite come up with anything yet.

I know there's a yard. The house has a thin iron gate off to the side, in a rounded arch that breaks the seam between her house and her neighbors'. I can always make out a spot of green beyond the brick walled alley. But what it looks like inside the house? With her family? No idea.

I take a step up on the stoop and ring the doorbell, a soft chime echoing from someplace inside. That's when I notice all the voices talking inside, blending together as footsteps sound off, making their way to the door.

It swings open, and there's Amina. She smiles.

"There you are," she says, motioning for me to come in. I lean in for a kiss and she backs away quickly, looking into her house and then back at me. "The hell are you doing? None of that. No way. Get in here."

I walk in, and the home is an explosion of color. Deep reds and golds are everywhere, and the air is heavy with delicious smells. Her family has furniture that doesn't look like it's been put together hastily after an Ikea visit, the "extra pieces" buried in a kitchen drawer.

"I thought you told them about me?" I ask as Amina hurries ahead of me, leading the way. Toward the back of the house is what looks like the kitchen, with a big sprawling table topped with piles of food.

"I did. Not everyone can make out in front of their family."

"I wasn't trying to—" I start, but she looks back at me in a way that tells me the conversation is over. "Fine, fine."

Amina's family is already gathered around their kitchen table, which is this gorgeous piece of furniture. Everything in here feels older than me, and it's as though the sentimentality of every object is just pulsing in waves. There's history laced into every object. A cabinet with large glass doors, full of little pieces of kitsch. Couches covered in sheets of plastic, like they're too valuable to sit on. Paintings on the wall that are actual paintings, not prints.

"So . . . this is Michael," Amina says, and I turn back to the kitchen table and watch as several conversations in progress stop, multiple sets of eyes looking at me expectantly.

"Hi," I say, waving awkwardly. There are two seats next to each other at a corner of the large dining table, and we walk over there. I sit, and the plate in front of me looks like it's seen some things, old with a few chips here and there, a fading illustration of some birds in the center.

"They were my great-grandmother's." I glance back up at . . . Amina's mother, I think, across the table, who nods at my plate and then looks around the table. "We bring them out for holidays and family gatherings."

"That's amazing," I say, looking back at the dish. "I don't think anything in our house isn't from Target or Ikea." There's some . . . strange swirling feeling inside my chest that I can't quite pin down. I shake it off.

"This is my mother," Amina says, my assumption correct, and then she gestures around the rest of the table. "My father, my sister Nalia, my uncle . . ." She continues talking, nodding to everyone, and I just can't help it.

This. This is the sort of family people expect me to have when they meet me. The sort I sometimes think about, when I'm alone and everything is quiet. Long bus rides. When I can't sleep at night or wake up too early, staring at the ceiling. And it's not that I want this. It's that I feel like I'm supposed to have it. And I don't. And it's a weird, impossible emotion to pin down.

Now I recognize that strange swirling feeling.

And why me and Amina keep having the same conversation.

And I really want to get out of here.

"So, Michael, where are you from?" one of Amina's aunts asks.

I glance over at Amina, and she immediately looks embarrassed.

"I mean, I'm from here. I was born in Philadelphia," I start, but I know what she's asking. And it's not like this is a bad thing; it's just hard sometimes. "But I'm Palestinian."

Amina's entire family erupt in *oohs*, looking at one another around the table.

"When did your family move here?"

"Are they first generation? Second?"

"From where in—"

"That's, um . . ." I look to Amina again, and she's physically wincing. "That's a little more complicated, I guess? I'm adopted? I don't know that much. Anything, really."

There's an awkward beat of silence, and I look around the table for something, anything, to talk about other than this. It's never easy. Being . . . this, on the outside, but feeling entirely different inside. I'm not the person people see, and I never know how to talk about it.

And then I see it.

"What is that?" I ask, pointing at something on the table.

"Oh, that's my pumpkin and sweet potato moussaka!" Amina's aunt exclaims. I look at Amina, trying so hard not to laugh.

"I'm sorry," she whispers, and then she looks at the moussaka. "Shut the hell up."

We're getting closer to Fitler Square, the neighborhood my family calls home. It's a bit like Amina's neighborhood in Queen Village—row houses and the like, the occasional stone building tucked in between, with large towering walls and big windows.

I love my little neighborhood. Really, that's what Philadelphia is: a bunch of little neighborhoods, scattered all about. There are tons of tiny side streets that are barely half a block in length, tucked away and hidden between blocks, with streets built in the 1800s that cars can't drive down, and homes so skinny I have no idea how they fit furniture through the doors.

Well, I do know. They shop at Ikea. Like my parents.

"Have I mentioned that I'm sorry?" Amina asks as my parents' tucked-away side street comes into view.

"There's nothing to be sorry about," I say, squeezing her hand. "I'm used to all that."

"I know but . . . I kind of thought my family wouldn't be like that?"

"Did you warn them about me?" I ask, grinning.

She smacks my arm.

"Those kinds of questions always come up. It's not a big deal." I sigh. Though it kind of feels like it is, I really don't want to dig into that. It's my weight.

We turn the corner onto my parents' side street, Rainey Court, a dead-end street that is hidden away in the middle of a small city block. There are a handful of homes on this street that look out of place—a large white mansion with an obnoxious gate for one, which is right across the street from my parents' simple row house. Amina scowls at the eyesore, and as we approach my family home, she stops me in the cobblestone street.

"Hey." She smiles and pulls me forward. She kisses me, and it's like all the tension from those questions in my back and shoulders flows out of me, my entire body sighing. She pulls back and we both exhale, and if I could blush, I would.

"I promise. They'll be cool," I say, hopping up the stoop to the front door. I jiggle the doorknob, but it's locked, so I wrestle for my keys in my pocket.

Before I can put the key in the lock, the door swings open. It's my mom, blonde hair and all smiles, her bright blue eyes wide and welcoming. They flit over to Amina, and her face turns up in an expression like she might cry.

"Mom—" I start.

"Aminaaaaaaa!" my mom says, skirting past me and down the three little steps to the sidewalk, her arms wide open. She hugs Amina, who is staring at me wide-eyed, like she has no idea what to do. My mom lets her go and holds her shoulders. "We've heard so much about you. Welcome to our home."

"Th-thanks?" Amina says, in almost a question.

"I'm here too, Mom," I mutter as she walks right by me again, leading Amina into the house.

"Oh shush, you," she says, shooing me away as the two of them go inside first. I follow quickly and close the door behind us.

My mom is smiling like someone who is hiding something, someone with a surprise. She turns to our dining room, which you can see right from the front of the house, just a little past the small living room. "Michael told us all about you, Amina, and well, his father and I wanted you to be comfortable."

"Thanks, Mrs. Becker," Amina says, still glancing back at me.

The table is already set, my father sitting at the very end. Some of my cousins sit around the living room, plates in front of them, gossiping about who knows what, while my aunts and uncles sit at the table with my dad. I pull out a seat for Amina and she sits down, and I settle in next to her.

"What can I get you?" my mom asks, clasping her hands together, so eager to please.

"Mom, it's okay, we'll just pick at stuff?" I look at Amina, who nods. "We ate a bit at her parents' house."

"Well, I hope you have room for dessert." She smiles

and hustles over to the kitchen, returning quickly with an apple pie.

"Oh! And how could I forget!" She dashes off again, and I look over at my dad, who shrugs and shakes his head.

"School okay?" he asks.

"Yup." I nod.

"We have hummus!" my mom exclaims, placing a platter down on the table, using the end of it to scoot the apple pie out of the way. And there it is, an impossibly large spread of store-bought hummus, a little dish full of olives, and some poorly chopped-up pita bread.

My heart sinks, and I glance over at Amina. Her mouth is open just a little, and she looks like she's trying to figure out what to say.

She looks at me, and I shrug. I mean, what am I supposed to do?

"Hey—" I start.

"Excuse me, Mrs. Becker, I, uh, have to make a phone call," Amina says before I finish anything. She flashes me a glare and walks out of the house, closing the front door behind her.

"I told you that was going overboard," my dad grumbles, shaking his head.

"Hummus? Seriously?!" I look from my mom to my dad, and my mother has a deer-in-headlights look on her face, like she can't process what just happened. I get up and walk toward the door. "I'll be right back."

Amina is standing in the middle of the tiny street, looking down at her phone, and catches me as I close the front door.

"Told them about me?" she asks, shoving her phone in her pocket. "That's what they think?"

"Amina, they didn't mean anything—"

"My family didn't have some spread for what they assume

your white family likes. A green bean casserole or, like, a platter from Panera Bread."

"That's not—" I close my mouth and snort, trying so hard not to laugh.

"You think this is funny?" Amina asks.

"Come on, that Panera Bread joke was hilarious. You're funny."

Amina digs the toe of her boot into the cobblestone street.

"I'm sorry," I say, taking a few steps toward her. "They really do mean well, I swear. And I did tell them about you. I talk about you all the time. Every day. They're tired of it. I'm the sorry one. I'm the one who never wants to talk about why this"—I point at myself and the house and then at her and then just gesture all over the place—"why this might be complicated and weird. My outside doesn't match the inside. And I can't help that."

Amina snorts.

"Oh, now you get to laugh?" I ask.

"Maybe." She grins. "It's just like that horrible sandwich of yours. That Gobbler mess?"

"I don't get it. What about it?"

"On the outside, you're sure it's just this one simple thing. A sandwich. And then inside it's a jumbled mess, stuff that doesn't belong together. Things you wouldn't assume based on what you see on the outside."

"Hey, I am not a sandwich."

There's a pause, a silence in the air.

And then we laugh.

Yuna and the Wall

Lydia Kang

It started with a wall.

It encircled Yuna's home and was built of good, thick red-stone, three horses high. Father had it created when he first immigrated to Silendar's hilly lands when he himself was a young man, bursting with ambition and secrets.

Yuna patrolled the inner perimeter of the wall in the early evenings, hauling a basket containing a pot of mortar, chisels of varying sizes, a hammer, and a trowel. Her dark eyes narrowed as she searched for cracks. She was careful to stay on the meticulously kept paths. Stray but a little, and a careless hand might brush nettles that could fell an ox with a single scratch. On the east end of their property, asps lived within carefully managed glass domes; by the center pond, jewel-bright frogs lurked. Yuna smiled fondly at them, for a touch of their skin could render an olyphaunt unconscious. Soon she would tend to the scorpion birds, thumb-sized wasps, dagger spiders, fire scorpions, and acid-spitting ants.

Even later, she would tend to Father, who worked tirelessly in his room, where he concocted one poisonous potion after another. These were sold to the most powerful leaders in Silendar. (Swords were for commoners; poisons were a far tidier method of obtaining status and inheritances.)

But first, there was this wall.

Yuna pushed her black braid over her shoulder, crouching to investigate sunlight shining through a crack in the wall. The mortar was crumbling. It needed patching, so she tapped her hammer against a small chisel, *tap*, *tap*, *tap*, to break up the old mortar. Suddenly, instead of the mortar crumbling, the stone it held shattered.

Ugh. Now she would have to replace the whole stone! From beyond the wall, the sound of ringing hammers on anvils broke the stillness of early evening. There was a particularly large smithy fifty yards away—a sprawling compound, her father had told her, though she'd never seen it herself. At a particularly loud clang, a patch of biting hemlock spewed their fang-like seeds, as they were wont to do with loud noises. Biting hemlock always flourished near forges.

Yuna knelt closer to clear out rubble. The broken redstone crumbled in her hand. She pulled more chunks out, reaching in over and over again, when suddenly her hand grasped something that was decidedly not stone.

Something softer.

Something warm.

"Oh!" she squealed, snatching her arm back. She peered through the hole in the wall.

A set of eyes met hers. Dark blue eyes, so dark they looked like the Tillen Sea under angry storm clouds. Black lashes blinked once, twice. It was a boy, her age, about fifteen. Like all Silendars, his hair was some version of honey-colored—old honey, new honey, tilberry honey. This boy's was medium, like a good clover honey. But unlike most Silendars, his skin was marred with scars everywhere. He was likely a victim of the poxplague that had run through the village when she was a child. Most children who'd contracted the virus died, and those who lived were scarred for life.

"Are you all right?" the boy's voice issued through the tiny passage.

Yuna said nothing. Father always told her to keep to herself. The less she said, the less trouble would find her. Father himself was quiet for days, surrounded by expanses of silence that made Yuna feel adrift, even within their enclosed home.

"I've seen you in town," he said.

It almost sounded like an accusation. Yuna thought, *Yes, I have seen you too.* She remembered him behind the smithy's booth in the market where knives were brought to be sharpened, twisted gates fixed. Only yesterday, he'd watched as several town children had thrown clods of earth studded with rocks. Like her, he stayed quiet. His own cloak had been stained too, from the town children's wrath.

"Kiss the Poison Girl!" the town boys had teased their friends, once they'd run out of dirt projectiles. She had tripped, and her basket of vegetables had tumbled to the street. "You'll die if you do! Don't touch her skin, or yours will peel off like a snake!"

People whispered, not nearly quietly enough, that the poisons Father brewed into bitter, tenacious concentrates had been fed to Yuna since she was a babe. They said venoms seeped into her very flesh until she was dangerous to even touch. She bled from the stones that hit her, just the same. And Himil had always stayed quiet.

People like Yuna and Himil traded turns on receiving the angry ugliness of others. A siblinghood of oppression. Tomorrow, it would be Himil's turn. Another day, the girl with one leg. Yet another, the children of the Gira family, whose skin and hair were lily white, eyes reddish, like their ancestors from the island of Korrs who shunned daylight. And yet Himil never spoke to Yuna. Yuna's own father had told her to stay far from the victims of the poxplague: "You don't need to become sick by associating with them. Stay away."

"Are you all right?" the boy asked again.

"I saw you at the market too," Yuna blurted out.

Silence. And then, "Yes. The Master Smith forbids me from speaking to anyone while I'm working in town. He thinks I'll do more harm than good, because I know nothing yet about tempering iron."

"Father forbids me from speaking to anyone," Yuna said. *Never draw attention to yourself, Yuna, or trouble will find you. You must be a shadow.*

"Why? Because you'll give bad advice about sword repairs too?"

Yuna snorted, nearly a laugh. A few more fang-like seeds rained down from the biting hemlock, ticking on the stone path.

"I actually thought there was a rakkon trying to dig through the wall," he explained. "You don't look like a rakkon." He chuckled. Rakkons were the size of puppies, with inch-long fangs and claws that could tear through a roof. They loved butter more than anything. They'd tear a hole through a house just to find the butter crocks in the cellar. "I'm Himil. And that was my hand you grabbed."

"I'm sorry," Yuna said.

"Your name is Sorry?"

"No! My name is Yuna. I'm sorry I grabbed your hand. I was clearing away the broken stone to repair the wall." She was sweating now. She had not spoken to anyone this much since she couldn't even remember. She'd probably exchanged fewer words with the rice merchant from whom she'd purchased rice weekly—for years. It was wrong, it felt wrong, and yet . . . it felt wonderful. And easy. She pressed her lips together, ready to flee back to the house, when Himil spoke again.

"And I have been ordered to burn away this hemlock that's spread onto the property."

"Oh. Yes, it's growing marvelously in the western sunlight. But you shouldn't burn it."

"Why not?"

She nearly snorted again. Didn't everyone know that biting hemlock regenerated after a good burn only to grow to twice the size afterward?

"Because—"

"Yuna!" Father called from the doorway of the glass growing house. "Where are you?"

Without a goodbye, Yuna jumped up and grabbed her basket. As she scuttled along, the wind blew in her hair and a hand peeped out from the hole in the wall. Himil's hand.

It was either waving her goodbye or asking for her to return. She didn't know what to think about that. But her face grew warm at the gesture.

That night, as Yuna slept on her pallet, Zizi the scorpion bird flew circles above her head, chirping. It didn't matter, because Yuna couldn't sleep. Zizi landed on her forehead, preening her flaming orange wings. Her scorpion hook bobbed merrily between her tail feathers. Yuna was never stung, because she never gave Zizi any reason to sting her.

Yuna could not stop thinking of Himil. She had touched a boy's hand today, and the boy hadn't exclaimed in fear, or protest, that he'd die from her touch. And Yuna hadn't suddenly erupted in blisters across her fingertips. With accidental effort, they had weakened two myths, watering them down like a poor man's soup.

After another hour of being unable to sleep, Yuna crept outside the cottage, past the room full of brown glass bottles of tinctures and potions, while Zizi stayed on her shoulder.

As a precaution, she grabbed an empty glass vial from the pantry and crept out into the moonlit garden.

She went straight to the hole in the wall. *Just to check for rakkons*, she thought to herself. Under the silvery light, the garden took on a purplish hue. The nightshade flowers were drinking in the cool evening, paper white and lovely. The trickling water of the irrigation channels sounded like bells in the darkness. Here she might recall the moments of her small adventure, to rethink the words that were spoken and knit them back together after a delicious unraveling.

She sat down by the hole, and Zizi nuzzled her cheek. The crickets sang merrily, the breeze calm. It almost sighed. Yuna sighed too.

And the night sighed louder on the other side of the wall.

Yuna froze. Tentatively, as if offering a small rice bun on her ancestors' shrine in the kitchen, she slipped her hand into the hole in the wall.

Her fingertips touched cool stone, solid and irregular beneath her hand. Rubble bits were there too. She reached farther. Her fingertips brushed something that was neither crumbled stone nor sandy mortar.

A hand.

A hand, waiting for her. A hand, ropy with scars that felt like twisted vines. On a tree, it would be beautiful. On a hand, perhaps beautiful too, now that she thought of it.

This time, the boy's hand quickly withdrew. She heard a small knocking sound, and then "Ow!"

"Oh! What happened?" Yuna whispered.

"You surprised me. I hit my head against the wall. I'm all right."

Yuna laughed low. She heard Himil rubbing his head rapidly to ease the hurt.

"I didn't think you'd come out again," he said.

"I thought the same."

There was a long pause. Yuna needed it, her heart was so full. Strangely full, and beating quickly.

They stayed in silence for a while. Finally, Yuna could bear it no longer. She was used to the disappointed glances of the Silendars in the town square when she shopped. She saw the boys and girls sneer at her, at the scarlet sash she wore under the cloak that was part of a traditional garment worn by unmarried women of Bando. "Like blood!" the sneering boys would say. "She's bloody poisonous! Stay away, and take your nasty wares back to your land."

Zizi sensed her tensing at the memory and cooed a burbling noise.

"What is that?" Himil asked.

"It's Zizi, our scorpion bird."

"Aren't they dangerous?"

"Only if you try to hurt them."

"You mean, they're like people?" Himil said. She could almost hear him smile, if that were possible, from the other side of the wall.

"Some people like to hurt for no reason."

"True." Himil sighed again.

"But just in case, I brought this." She showed him the glass vial.

"What is that for?"

"Watch." She put Zizi on the ground near the hole so Himil could watch. Cooing gently, she gently grasped Zizi's stinger from between her tail feathers and hooked it over the lip of the glass vial. Golden venom dripped into the vial until it slowed to nothing. Yuna corked it, pocketed the vial, then placed Zizi into the little hole in the wall.

"There. You may pet her now. It's safe."

Himil gently stroked Zizi's back. Zizi cooed and leaned into a scratch. "Hard to believe something so beautiful can be lethal."

"Ugly things are lethal too," Yuna murmured. "Most creatures can be, if you provoke them."

"You would know, I suppose."

Yuna startled at his words. Again, with the myth. Yuna was so tired of being the poisonous girl. Of being so unlike the other Silendars, of being considered so very unbeautiful. She'd never done anything to make anyone think she would hurt a mosquito, and yet the stories went on. Zizi noted her tenseness, and fluffed her feathers in anxiousness.

"I'm not poisonous," Yuna said, nearly hissing.

"No! I meant, I meant . . . you know so much. About the plants and animals on your farm."

"Oh."

"Anyway, I figured that you weren't poisonous. My hand didn't fall off after I touched you."

"Did you really think it would?"

"I wasn't sure. I'm not sure what to think when there's nothing but people saying the same thing all the time."

"Lies turn into truth when faced with silence," Yuna said. "Father has told some people the truth, that we're not poisonous ourselves, but he always said that it helped business to keep the lie going. So I never say anything."

"Does it help you?" Himil asked.

Yuna was silent—always silent. She was usually too shy to speak to anyone in town, and people avoided her, so it seemed like destiny that she'd live in a void. But the void was so very lonely.

"Well, the truth is out now," Himil said. "I'll ruin your father's business! Except that no one ever listens to survivors of the poxplague, so I guess your business is still safe."

"Between no one speaking to you, and me not speaking to anyone, we might as well be invisible."

Himil laughed quietly. It sounded like a warm fire crackling. He reached through the hole to pet Zizi again, and their hands brushed each other as Zizi hopped back to Yuna. "I should go. I'll get a thrashing if I don't stoke the night fires soon."

"So you're to be a smith someday?" Yuna asked.

"No. Not with this skin, I won't. I run errands and work as a cook. I like cooking more than forge work anyway."

Himil's hand was still in the passageway of the wall. She asked, "Does it hurt?"

"Yes. It was worse when I was growing. Like having ropes trying to hold you back while you're stretching to be taller. If I don't stretch and exercise, the scars grow tight and limit my movement. And it hurts when that happens."

"And the poxplague?"

Himil sighed, the sigh of someone who has had to explain something a thousand times over. "I'm not contagious."

"But Father said—"

"Rumors and lies. One only needs to see all the people I work with at the smithy to know I'm not contagious, haven't been for over ten years."

"I didn't know. I'm sorry."

"And therein lies everything wrong with Silendar and the lands beyond—not knowing the truth. Or maybe it's not believing the truth."

Yuna wanted to say, *Life is easier sometimes just being afraid.* But she was afraid even to say this. Zizi pecked at Yuna's cheek and yawned, shaking out her feathers and stretching her stinger. "We should all go to sleep."

"Yes. The fires need me." Himil sounded tired, but not in the usual way. More like his soul had been wrung out.

"Cooks need their rest," Yuna said, pretending to be wise. "Maybe I'll make you something sometime."

"I should like that," Yuna said.

"Come back tomorrow?" Himil asked.

Yuna had hardly any words left. As if she'd been compiling conversations in her head her whole life and had just spilled them all out. But she had one word left yet tonight.

"Yes."

The next morning, Yuna slept in so late that Father made the morning porridge with eggs and spicy cowcumber salad for breakfast, leaving the bowl outside her door. Still, she woke up at moonrise to steal away to the wall. Himil was there, also tired but with eyes open and eager to see her. He slipped her a delicious garlic chive bun through the hole, and after gobbling it up, Yuna stood up and patted the extra flour off her hands.

"Going to sleep already? Has my bun incapacitated you with such a full belly?" Himil teased.

"No, I'm not tired at all. But I'm tired of talking through this hole."

"As am I. Why don't you let me in through your gate?"

"The gate is always locked. Only Father has the key."

"You could climb over the wall. I could show you around the smithy! I could cook more for you in my kitchen."

"No!" Yuna said quickly. "If the Master Smith sees us, you'll be fired."

"They're all asleep. Nothing wakes them up—not even a rakkon licking butter off their faces. They sleep like boulders."

Yuna stayed stubbornly quiet.

"All right. Then I'll have to come over there."

"Oh! Can you climb over the wall?"

"I don't think . . . I can't," Himil said.

"Is it your scars?"

Himil said nothing, but she leaned down to the hole. She saw his face there, and he nodded. "I can't reach with my arms very well. But I can crawl well."

"I have an idea. Meet me at the west wall."

There, below grade, was an iron grating that covered the inlet of the stream that fed the irrigation channels and the pond. On the farm side of the wall, Yuna might pull the grating up. Father did this once a month to clear the dead leaves clogging the aqueduct. She did this now, though it was very heavy.

"I can come through," Yuna said.

"No, let me. I've always wanted to see your garden."

Himil tossed over his tunic, and Yuna captured it as it fell. It was warm and smelled like the sun on a wheat field. She didn't realize she had closed her eyes to sniff it.

Soon Himil could be seen treading the chin-high water. He dragged himself onto the dry grass on her farm. She watched him breathe heavily and handed him some dry cloths she'd fetched, then his tunic.

"May I do anything else? I'm not sure what helps," Yuna said.

"Thank you. I'll be a bit stiff, so walk slowly, please. But show me everything here!"

"You're the first Silendar ever to be here," Yuna said. "Welcome."

"Feels like an odd welcome when I've just snuck in. Underwater. At midnight."

"Let's begin." Shyly, she showed him the greenhouse first. Vines of fuchsia flowers blossomed over the glass, and pots of varying sizes held carnivorous plants, some with gaping maws with teeth and some aglow with sparkling, gummy dewdrops. She tugged Himil's hand toward the water garden, where he met the freshwater lionfish and prickly urchins that crawled slowly over the bottom, feeding on algae. Then to the storehouse, where plants were hung to dry and intensify their poisonous offerings.

"It's so odd," Himil said, his hand still within Yuna's, "how much these creatures want to kill us all."

"Oh, Himil." She took her hand away from his and he frowned, but only for a moment. For Yuna had only moved her hand so she could lean on his arm a little. This way, they leaned into each other as they walked. His frown vanished. "These creatures and plants don't want to kill us. Well, the carnivorous plants want to eat insects and birds for dinner, but aside from them, they aren't murderers. We are. The humans that blunder into their midst, not understanding them. *They* only wish to live. They're defending themselves in the best way that they can."

Himil only nodded. He said nothing for the next hour as they walked about the garden and the menagerie full of animals. Though Yuna enjoyed his closeness, there was something about the quiet that disturbed her. She was so used to the quiet. It was her armor. But now it dissatisfied her. Silence and hiding were no longer comforting. It wasn't a way to live anymore. Or was it?

Himil stopped walking when they reached the aqueduct.

"I have to be at work at dawn, so I must go." He put one foot into the cool water, then turned to grasp her hand. "If I see you at the market, I promise to say something, you know, if those boys bother you again. I'll threaten them with the poxplague!"

Yuna didn't smile. Himil seemed expectant. Why must he say such a thing? That would be a terrible thing to say. And she wouldn't want the attention. Why couldn't they simply keep going with their quiet nighttime trysts? Everything here was perfect.

"Yuna?" Himil pressed.

"I don't want to think of the market." She let go of his hand and stepped back.

Himil's eyes dropped to the ground. He massaged his hand where she had let go, as if the scars had suddenly welled with tight discomfort. Without a word, he waded back into the icy-cold aqueduct. He removed his shirt, bundling it in his hands and tossing it over the wall. His fingers were scarred but beautifully long and elegant. His torso, too, was twisted at its core even at rest. It reminded Yuna of a plant trying to reach the sun in a garden full of competition. The asymmetry took her breath away for a second. He turned back and blinked at her with those blue eyes that were as dark as hers in the night light. After a tight-lipped smile, he slipped below the water and was gone.

Himil did not show at the hole in the wall at moonrise the next night. Yuna slumped about her morning chores the following morning. The Bando-style house, with its sloped and tiled roof, seemed to frown at her.

"There's a hole in the wall I saw this morning," Father said at breakfast. "You should tend to it."

"I'm out of mortar" was Yuna's excuse. Father said no more words until the next morning.

The next night, there was still no Himil.

Of course, Yuna thought. *I can't expect him to get away every night. He's just a poor servant at the smithy. They probably drove him to exhaustion, shoveling ore or coal or wood. Cooking for all those workers.* She left a flower in the hole in the wall. A nonpoisonous one, of course.

Father said at breakfast, "I found a spare sack of mortar in the toolshed."

"I'm behind on pulling duckweed in the pond" was Yuna's only reply.

That night, the flower she'd left was still there, wilted. This time she left a bundle of rosemint and Bando citrus peel, tied together with twine. But yet again, Himil did not come.

On this next day, she went to town. A mile from home, a large gate of centuries-old oak stood, flying Silendar flags of gold and green. Inside, the vast market awaited her. A giant oval fountain in the center watered beasts of burden. Around the oval, booths of wood were squeezed together, covered under yellow oilcloth awnings. Bright vegetables of purple and red and orange were handsomely displayed, next to huge barrels of grain, plows, candy, and bolts of cloth. But Yuna hardly noticed the colors, the textures, the expressions. Her heart was bursting with expectation. Perhaps there would be an argument—one that wasn't about the price of pork. But she didn't see Himil at the smithy's stall. Even the little boys who teased her were nowhere to be seen. It seemed a letdown to not use the courage she had fought to bring with her today.

So she stopped by the rice seller. The old lady saw Yuna and crinkled a smile. Yuna held a coin in her hand. Usually she placed it on the table and pushed it toward the lady, but today she handed it to her. Her fingertips touched the old woman's wrinkled hand.

"Fifteen measures, please." She tried hard not to speak in a whisper.

The old lady took the money and motioned to a worker to bring the rice out. Yuna thanked her and did something she never had before: stiffly held out her hand to shake the old lady's. Silendars shook hands at every greeting, every good-bye, at the celebrations of babies being born, at funerals. But Yuna never touched anyone, because she assumed no one wanted to. It suddenly occurred to her that perhaps it had been seen as rude. The old lady raised her grizzled eyebrows in surprise, then shook Yuna's hand.

"Oh, your hand is so soft," she exclaimed.

"It's from the aloe plants. Not poisonous, of course. The aloe, that is. And my hand too. Not poisonous." Yuna was babbling, which was odd. It was as if her internal permission had opened a floodgate.

"Goodness. That's more words I've heard from you than in the last ten years." The old lady smiled. "It is good to hear your voice, my dear. Have a bright day."

The chicken seller refused to touch Yuna's hand. But he watched her speak to the flour seller and the spice merchant, and shake their hands. She'd never seen so many smiles answer hers before. She went home, grinning all the way.

Seven days into no Himil meeting her at the hole, she was having supper with Father. He stared at her furtively throughout their meal of chive and pork dumplings.

"You're quiet," he said.

"Isn't quiet good?"

"Not always." He bit a dumpling and chewed thoughtfully. "Not always."

Yuna's eyes went wide. Father had never said such a thing. She wanted to ask him a million questions but found she, too, was silent, thinking over his words that could have meant very little, or could have just changed the color of Yuna's sky from blue to orange. She looked up at the sky to check.

"I am getting old, Yuna. Someday this garden will all be yours, along with the business. I have always had you. But the garden isn't company enough. The quiet isn't, either."

So many words. So much. Yuna could hardly bear it. "I need to go to town," she said, standing up from the table.

She packed a bag. Taking her horse, she rode into town

quickly. She went to the smithy's stall. The wood beams of the stall were stained with smoke and grease. One of the junior smiths was there, clanging away on a crooked sword. Other workers were sharpening blades on spinning whetstones.

She went boldly up to the stall, though her ankles felt weak. Her face was sweating.

"Is . . . may I speak to Himil?"

"Himil?" The smith paused his hammering and wiped his forehead. "Somewhere here. He was oiling whetstones."

A clod of earth hit her back, and she turned quickly. A small group of boys held their handfuls high. Their jeering faces made Yuna quake with shame.

"Look, it's the poi—"

She spun around, standing tall. Her heart hammered so hard it might pop right out of her chest. "You disrespect me. And you disrespect this business by throwing dirt. The sand will mar their sharpening stones."

"And you disrespect this lady," a voice said.

Yuna turned around, and Himil stepped out from the back of the stall. He came out into the square to stand beside her.

The little boys stared at them and hooted. "Pox! Pox on all of us if we get too close!"

"Don't be ridiculous," Yuna said. "None of the smiths have gotten the poxplague. There hasn't been a poxplague epidemic in ten years. Have you not minds to think?" Her voice was shaking. Her mouth was so dry that she feared she would choke before she could get the words out. "And . . . I am not poisonous. A smith is not made of iron, and a master poisoner's daughter is not made of poison."

"Who says I am not made of iron?" One of the smiths bulged his bicep, and the small crowd about them laughed aloud. Yuna smiled, and the smith winked at her.

The boys gaped, their eyes round. Yuna stepped up to Himil

and took his hand in hers, her throat now too dry to speak. And the smiths hooted and clanged their instruments in cheer.

"Why stop there? Give Himil a kiss!" hollered the Master Smith. "He's been pining after you for a year now!"

Yuna blushed wildly. "You have?"

"Well now, maybe not a whole year—"

She laughed, and the Master Smith and his assistants laughed, and the little boys dispersed once their targets seemed otherwise engaged with the sword-wielding smiths. After the hollering died down, Himil walked Yuna to the gates of the town market square.

"I'm still trembling," Yuna said, laughing shakily, grabbing the reins of her horse.

One of the little boys scurried by and hissed. "Poxplague! Poison!"

Himil rolled his eyes. "Can't fix Silendar in a day."

"No. Nor can I fix myself in a day either," Yuna said. "Or my father." She mounted her horse. "Himil, I'm mixing mortar this afternoon. The wall will be repaired this afternoon."

"I see," Himil said. He stepped back a few paces, and Yuna strode forward on her horse. She passed him by but halted to look over her shoulder.

"But I will be sure the gate is open at sunset," she said with a smile. "Just in time for supper."

Something Gay and Magical

Adam Silvera

Everyone would be happier if books were gayer.

Okay, maybe not everyone, but Oliver Espinoza would be. He only has twenty more minutes in this bookstore until his mother picks him up.

Oliver hasn't spent a single dollar yet. He's always been aggressively sentimental, sometimes to a fault, but he got this gift card for his eighteenth birthday and he wants to buy something special for once. He already tore through all the popular books about magical academies, battle arenas, and underground societies like everyone else on the planet because duh, he's not walking into any movie theater without having read the book first.

But would it really be so impossible for these heroes to be gay and make out in between all the world saving? Not to be dramatic, but he would cry so hard that he would solve the world's water crisis.

He has been very vocal about all of this at school, mind you. When his classmate Richard told Oliver that he was spending too much time online with social justice warriors, Oliver promptly unfollowed Richard on Instagram. When his friend Diana (bless her) went on about the single shelf that her local bookstore has for "gay stuff," Oscar got the message: he was supposed to sail across the city in a big gay arc on his private rainbow ship to worship at this shrine of a shelf.

It's not fair that the Richards and Dianas of the world get the rest of the Young Adult section to themselves. Or that Oliver is left only with "contemporary realistic" or "issues" novels—as if it's impossible to imagine what coming out and first crushes are like otherwise. He wants other worlds, too. He wants stories he hasn't lived, stories like the ones everyone else has read so often they don't even appreciate an invented world for the miracle that it is.

Fan fiction has been great for Oliver to see some favorite ships sail across that arc. Harry Potter and Ron Weasley. Frodo and Sam. Batman and Robin. Superman and Green Lantern. Wolverine and Cyclops. Captain America and Bucky. Han Solo and Lando Calrissian. Jon Snow and Robb Stark. He can go on and on.

But it would be lovely if he could walk away today with a book that could give him those same epic feelings.

Maybe if the fantasy section wasn't in such chaos, Oliver would have an easier time finding this white whale of a novel. Time is running out, but Oliver can't stop himself from putting sequels in their proper order so some reader doesn't get screwed over. During the shuffle, no titles intrigue him.

Right as Oliver is ready to give up and spend his gift card on some café treats, he hears the magic words:

"You need help?"

There's a gorgeous boy with dark brown skin pushing a cart of books toward him. His name tag reads WINTER. He's a little shorter than Oliver but his curly hair gives him the illusion of being taller. Oliver wonders if he's a bookseller by day and a runway model by night.

"You don't have the book I want," Oliver says.

"What book do you want?" Winter asks.

He shrugs and blushes. "I don't know."

"I need more than that."

"I don't know if it even exists."

"If what exists?"

Oliver is a breath away from screaming "SOMETHING GAY AND MAGICAL!" but he collects himself and says, "I want a book with a gay hero who saves the day and flies off into the sunset with a beautiful boy."

Winter smiles, just for an instant. Then he pretends to be serious. "Is flying into the sunset a must?"

"Negotiable."

Without a word, Winter leads Oliver to a table stocked high with fantasy fiction, all sun-kissed from the bay window. He hands Oliver a paperback.

The Swordsman and the Boy-King.

It's love at first sight.

Oliver hates insta-love in books except when they're about queer people. He can skip the slow-burn romance and instead race straight to marriage and fighting over which Hogwarts House onesie their kid will wear. But this cover feels like a breath of fresh air. The Swordsman is white or white-passing like Oliver with a crystal saber, and the Boy-King is brown like Winter with a big gold crown that's sitting crooked on his head. The Swordsman and the Boy-King are flirting with their eyes as the sun sets over a kingdom that Oliver couldn't wait to enter.

"Sunny enough for you?" Winter asks in a dry voice.

"You're an actual wizard," Oliver mumbles. "You straight-up conjured this book."

Winter laughs. "Not a lot of people know about this one, but it's one of my favorites. I wish I could show you the Spanish edition I bought when I was in Argentina visiting family because it's so beautiful."

Oliver would make a total ass out of himself if he tried to string together a sentence in Spanish right now to impress Winter. He's so jealous of everyone who talks about how they learned a language simply because their parents spoke it around the house while they were growing up. His mothers are always speaking to each other in Spanish, but when they brought him to Puerto Rico last summer to see the town where they first met and fell in love, Oliver wandered away at one point and got lost under the stars and felt powerless when no one understood him. He's still indebted to this lovely local, Mariana, who helped him find his way back to the hotel; best believe he'll honor his promise to name his firstborn after.

"I wish more people actually bought the book," Winter says. "I hype up the plot and they're sold on the quest to solve the murder of the Boy-King's father but then they see the cover and—"

"They put it down," Oliver finishes.

"Exactly."

It's totally okay for Oliver to read every book about every heterosexual hero, but God forbid someone be a good enough human for long enough to see what it's like on the other side of the street. He turns back to the book and sighs, shaking his head. "People are the worst. I feel like this cover was made for me."

"Same," Winter says. "I dressed up as the Boy-King last year for Comic-Con and Halloween."

"Really?"

"Yeah. Not everyone knew who I was, but it's not every day I see someone who looks like me on a fantasy cover."

Now Oliver feels like an idiot. Embarrassment consumes him as quickly as his love of the book cover. In all his rage about never seeing enough gay heroes in books, he completely overlooked how he could always see white or white-passing people in TV shows and movies and pretty much any book cover. If Oliver wanted to dress up as Harry Potter or Luke Skywalker at some convention no one would bat an eye, whereas Winter would probably turn heads as the Hispanic Captain America or the brown Jon Snow.

"You sold me on it, Winter," Oliver says with the paperback in one hand and the gift card in the other.

There goes his bright smile again. "Really?!"

"It's everything I want," Oliver says. "Minus the Swordsman and the Boy-King flying off into the sunset."

"You'll have to come back and tell me what you think about the ending," Winter says with his eyes cast low. "I work afternoons every weekend."

"I'll be back this weekend," Oliver says, his chest soaring with the promise of seeing Winter again soon and dropping when he thought of how far away that already feels.

No matter what the possibilities hold for the two of them, as Oliver makes his purchase and leaves the bookstore, he's already dreaming up the conventions where he's hanging out with Winter as the Swordsman to his Boy-King.

Fingers crossed that he won't have to write fan fiction about what it's like to kiss Winter.

Meet the Authors

ANNA-MARIE McLEMORE writes magical realism and fairy tales from the Latinx and LGBTQ+ communities she calls home. Her work has been longlisted for the National Book Award for Young People's Literature, a finalist for the William C. Morris Award, and named a Stonewall Honor Book. Find her online at annamariemclemore.com or on Twitter @LaAnnaMarie.

Previous work: *The Weight of Feathers* (2015); *When the Moon Was Ours* (2016); *Wild Beauty* (2017); *Blanca & Roja* (2018); contributor to multiple anthologies.

DANIELLE PAIGE writes *New York Times* bestselling young adult books and works in the television industry, where she's received a Writers Guild of America Award and was nominated for several Daytime Emmys. She is a graduate of Columbia University and currently lives in New York City. You can find her @daniellempaige on Twitter and Instagram.

Previous work: *Dorothy Must Die* (2014); *The Wicked Will Rise* (2015); *Yellow Brick War* (2016); *Stealing Snow* (2016); *The End of Oz* (2017); and several *Dorothy Must Die* novellas.

LAUREN GIBALDI is a public librarian who's been, among other things, a magazine editor, high school English teacher, bookseller, and circus aerialist (seriously). She lives in Orlando, Florida, with her husband and daughters. Find her online at laurengibaldi.com or on Twitter @laurengibaldi.

Previous work: *The Night We Said Yes* (2015); *Autofocus*

(2016); *This Tiny Perfect World* (2018); contributor to multiple anthologies.

TARUN SHANKER and KELLY ZEKAS are the co-authors of the *These Vicious Masks* trilogy. Tarun is a mild-mannered assistant by day and a milder-mannered writer by night, while Kelly is an actor and writer. Tarun can be found online at tarunshanker.com and on Twitter @tkshanker. Kelly can be found on Twitter @KellyZekas.

Previous work: *These Vicious Masks* (2016); *These Ruthless Deeds* (2017); *These Vengeful Souls* (2018).

LEATRICE "ELLE" MCKINNEY, who writes as L.L. McKinney, is a poet and active member of the kidlit community. She's an advocate for equality and inclusion in publishing, and the creator of the hashtag #WhatWoCWritersHear. Her debut novel, *A Blade So Black*, was recently optioned for television. Find her online at llmckinney.com or on Twitter @ElleOnWords.

Previous work: *A Blade So Black* (2018); *A Dream So Dark* (2019).

LORI M. LEE is a writer who lives in Wisconsin with her husband, kids, and an excitable shih tzu. Find her online at lorimlee.com or on Twitter @LoriMLee.

Previous work: *Gates of Thread and Stone* (2014); *The Infinite* (2015); contributor to multiple anthologies.

SANGU MANDANNA has been writing fiction since she was four years old. She lives in Norwich, England, with her husband and three kids. Find her online at sangumandanna.com and on Twitter @SanguMandanna.

Previous work: *The Lost Girl* (2012); *A Spark of White*

Fire (2018); *A House of Rage and Sorrow* (2019); contributor to multiple anthologies.

SAMIRA AHMED was born in Bombay, India, and grew up in a small town in Illinois in a house that smelled like fried onions, cardamom, and potpourri. A graduate of the University of Chicago, she taught high school English, helped create dozens of small high schools, and fought to secure billions of additional dollars to fairly fund public schools. She's lived in Vermont, Chicago, New York City, and Kauai. Follow her on Twitter and Instagram @sam_aye_ahm.

Previous work: *Love, Hate & Other Filters* (2018); *Internment* (2019).

CAROLINE TUNG RICHMOND is an award-winning author of YA novels and short stories. She is also the program director of We Need Diverse Books. She lives in northern Virginia with her family. Find her online at carolinetrichmond.com or on Twitter @ctrichmond.

Previous work: *The Only Thing to Fear* (2014); *The Darkest Hour* (2016); *Live in Infamy* (2018); *Hungry Hearts*, co-edited with Elsie Chapman (2019); contributor to multiple anthologies.

TARA SIM is a writer of all things magical. She can often be found in the wilds of the Bay Area, California. Find her online at tarasim.com or on Twitter @EachStarAWorld.

Previous work: *Timekeeper* (2016); *Chainbreaker* (2018); *Firestarter* (2019).

KARUNA RIAZI is a born and raised New Yorker, with a loving, large extended family and the rather trying experience of being the eldest sibling in her particular clan. Besides pursuing a BA in English literature from Hofstra University, she is an online diversity advocate, blogger, and publishing intern. Karuna is fond of tea, baking, Korean dramas, and writing about tough girls forging their own paths toward their destinies.

Previous work: *The Gauntlet* (2017) and The Battle (2019).

MICHELLE RUIZ KEIL is a novelist and playwright with an eye for the enchanted. Find her online at michelleruizkeil.com or on Twitter @MichelleRKeil.

Previous work: *All of Us with Wings* (2019).

ELSIE CHAPMAN is a Canadian author who now lives in Tokyo with her family. She writes books for kids and teens, is the editor of multiple anthologies, and is also a We Need Diverse Books team member. Find her online at elsiechapman.com or on Twitter @elsiechapman.

Previous work: *Dualed* (2013); *Divided* (2014); *Along the Indigo* (2018); *A Thousand Beginnings and Endings*, co-edited with Ellen Oh (2018); *All the Ways Home* (2019); *Hungry Hearts*, co-edited with Caroline Tung Richmond (2019); contributor to multiple anthologies.

ERIC SMITH is an author and literary agent who has worked on *New York Times* bestselling and award-winning books, and sometimes tries to write his own. He lives with his wife and son in Philadelphia. Find him online at ericsmithrocks. com, on Twitter @ericsmithrocks, and pretty much anywhere people talk about books.

Previous work: *The Geek's Guide to Dating* (2013); *Inked* (2015); *Branded* (2016); *Welcome Home* (2017); *The Girl and the Grove* (2018); *Don't Read the Comments* (2020); contributor to multiple anthologies.

LYDIA KANG is the author of multiple books for adults and young adults. She is a practicing physician, believes in science and knocking on wood, and lives in Omaha with her husband and three children. Find her online at lydiakang.com or on Twitter @LydiaYKang.

Previous work: *Control* (2013); *Catalyst* (2015); *A Beautiful Poison* (2017); *Quackery: A Brief History of the Worst Ways to Cure Everything*, with Nate Pedersen (2017); *The November Girl* (2017); *The Impossible Girl* (2018); *Toxic* (2018); contributor to multiple anthologies.

ADAM SILVERA was born and raised in the Bronx. He has worked as a bookseller, as a consultant at a literary development company, and as a reviewer of children's and young adult novels. He now writes full-time in Los Angeles and is tall for no reason.

Previous work: *More Happy Than Not* (2015); *History Is All You Left Me* (2017); *They Both Die at the End* (2017); *What If It's Us*, with Becky Albertalli (2018).